FAMILY BUSINESS

Previously published Worldwide Mystery titles by
S. J. ROZAN

PAPER SON

FAMILY BUSINESS

S. J. ROZAN

W**O**RLDWIDE

TORONTO • NEW YORK • LONDON
AMSTERDAM • PARIS • SYDNEY • HAMBURG
STOCKHOLM • ATHENS • TOKYO • MILAN
MADRID • WARSAW • BUDAPEST • AUCKLAND

WORLDWIDE™

Recycling programs
for this product may
not exist in your area.

ISBN-13: 978-1-335-58949-1

Family Business

First published in 2021 by Pegasus Crime,
an imprint of Pegasus Books, Ltd.
This edition published in 2023 with revised text.

Copyright © 2021 by S. J. Rozan
Copyright © 2023 by S. J. Rozan, revised text edition

For questions and comments about the quality of this book,
please contact us at CustomerService@Harlequin.com.

Harlequin Enterprises ULC
22 Adelaide St. West, 41st Floor
Toronto, Ontario M5H 4E3, Canada
www.ReaderService.com

Printed in U.S.A.

ONE

THE NEWS SWEPT back and forth through Chinatown all afternoon: Big Brother Choi was dead.

I heard it early, though not in Chinatown. Mary Kee and I were sitting in Washington Square Park in the late-day fall sunshine, drinking mango tea and watching a magic show by the fountain. To the music of a nearby string band a red-rouged young Black man pulled coins from the ears of giggling children. When Mary's phone sang "I Fought the Law," she sighed.

I said, "Don't answer."

"Girlfriend, you don't mean that. That's Chris's ring." She slipped the phone out.

"Oh! Answer."

Chris Chiang is a detective third grade at the Fifth Precinct, in the center of Chinatown. Mary's a detective second grade. Since Chris made detective, they'd been partnered. Cops' days off aren't sacrosanct to top brass, but they are to other cops. If Chris was calling Mary on her day off, something big must have happened.

Mary leaned forward, curling around the phone to make a sound shield. "Hi… Yeah… No problem. What's up?… Wow. When? How?… Okay, well, that's good… Yeah, it still could be for sure… Okay, thanks, Chris."

"So?" I said as she clicked off. The magician gave a little girl a marker so she could write her name on a ping-pong ball.

"No immediate crisis."

The magician put the ping-pong ball in a hat, turned the hat over, and shook. When nothing fell out he mugged a big puzzled look at the crowd.

"But a later-on crisis?"

"Chris was just giving me a heads-up. Big Brother Choi died."

"Wow. What happened?"

"Massive heart attack. Not to worry, there."

I hadn't really been worried. It wasn't likely Big Brother Choi had been rubbed out by a rival tong leader and a Chinatown tong war was about to start. Those ham-handed days were largely gone.

But Mary's "there" implied something else, and I knew what it was, the reason Chris Chiang had called. A seismic shudder was about to move through the streets we'd grown up on.

Our high school physics prof had told us that nature abhors a vacuum.

So does power.

The magician, who'd been rubbing his chin in thought, brightened. He tiptoed over to a boy in a baseball cap, pointed to get the crowd staring that way, and lifted the cap. The ping-pong ball with the girl's name on it was perched on the boy's head.

DOING ERRANDS IN Chinatown in the late afternoon, I heard the news again and again. Older merchants looked over their shoulders and whispered it to customers; middle-aged ladies in the park set their lips and nodded knowingly; young punks pulled on their cigarettes and sneered that it was about time.

My mother, when I got home, asked me if I'd heard the news.

I was tempted to yawn and say, "Oh, you mean about Big Brother Choi? Yeah, hours ago," just to mess with her, but she was clearly bursting, so I said, "What news?"

"Your brother has been promoted."

Oh. Clutch-stomping gear change.

"Which brother?" I asked automatically. I have four older brothers. When my mother speaks of one of her children to another, she rarely says who she means. We're just supposed to know. I've always thought that was a little unfair because when she's talking about me to them, they don't have to think very hard. This time, though, my question was just a reflex. I'd already worked it out.

Of my brothers, one—Andrew—is a freelance photographer, so if it was him, he'd promoted himself. The other three are an organic chemistry professor, an ER doctor, and a lawyer. Ted's full professorship is a tenured, endowed chair, so there's not very far up for him to go. Elliott loves working the ER so much that I don't think he'd leave it even if they offered to make him head of the hospital. And Tim is my mother's favorite. So I had a suspicion, but I asked anyway.

"Tien-Hua, of course."

Right. Tim.

"He made partner? Ma, that's wonderful!"

Tim and I haven't always gotten along. Until I was born he was the baby, so there's an understandable resentment there; also, he's a stodgy judgmental know-it-all wet blanket and has been since we were kids.

Still, he was young to make partner at his white-shoe law firm, and Asian, and this was something he'd wanted badly. At giant corporate firms like Harriman McGill it's up or out. Tim was in mergers and acquisitions, and he liked the work, probably because it was as boring as he was. A new job in another top firm would be hard to come by if he was passed over for promotion at Harriman. No wonder Ma was beaming.

"I'll call him," I said. "After I put the groceries away."

"Yes, I'm sure he'll be happy to hear your congratulations. Also, in case you don't know this yet, Big Brother Choi is dead."

TWO

"So WHO IS this guy?" Bill Smith, my partner, brought me a mug of jasmine green from the tea stash I keep at his place. I'd had dinner with my mother—chicken chow fun—and headed out to Bill's Tribeca apartment. I'd said I had to work late. That was the "don't tell" part. My mother did the "don't ask." I'm positive she knows about the change in my relationship with Bill, but I don't think she's quite ready to hear it out loud. In some situations, timing is everything.

"Who?" I asked. "My brother Tim?" I mean, I had to mess with *someone*.

"No, funny person, the other brother, Big Brother Choi. I know which one Tim is. He's the one who dislikes me most."

"He's actually the only one who still dislikes you at all. Ted and Elliott have moved on to 'you know, he's okay,' and Andrew thinks you're great."

"A wondrous family is Chin. I think Gertrude Stein wrote that. I like Andrew, too. Now. Big Brother Choi?"

"Chinatown OG. Sent here from Hong Kong in the late eighties specifically to take over the New York branch of the Li Min Jin tong. Li Min Jin, 'Upright People Will Advance.' What's so funny?"

"I'm picturing the opposite. An army of lounging soldiers."

I'd have snorted, but that's my mother's signature

response, and I'm trying to avoid it. "The Li Min Jin was a mess when he got here. The Hong Kong leadership sent him because the New York leader was weak and the members were all double-crossing and backstabbing each other."

"Literally?"

I shrugged. "It's a tong. In Choi's day he was a terror. He whipped the tong into shape and got to work. The Li Min Jin was smaller than some of the other tongs, but Choi was big on encroaching on other guys' territories, which really isn't done. There was always pushback, which meant violence. It's kind of surprising no one bumped him off back then. They might've, except in the nineties he made some kind of alliance with one of the other small tongs, which also isn't done. The Ma Tou—the Horsehead tong."

"Why isn't it done?"

"Because tongs are sworn brotherhoods. Like family. You may not be crazy about your family"—Bill isn't, about his—"but you don't have two at once."

"Unless you get married. That's the traditional way powerful families make alliances."

"True. But the tongs generally don't allow women soldiers, so there's no one to marry."

"Missing a good bet. If I had an army, I'd have you in it."

"I'd have to see the perks before I enlisted."

"They're numerous and varied. So if it isn't done, why did they do it?"

"Why Choi did it is obvious—it gave him power. Almost doubled his territory. Within a year or so the head of the Ma Tou—a guy named Long Lo—released his soldiers from their oaths and faded away. The soldiers who wanted to joined the Li Min Jin. The real question was always what was in it for Long Lo."

"Maybe he just wanted to retire."

"He was still relatively young. I guess he might've seen the writing on the wall. Over time the tongs have lost a lot of power, and the gangs they ran. Gang kids grow up. They go straight or to prison. Not that Chinatown doesn't still have corruption, self-dealing, and general evil. But now it's more like everywhere else."

"Meaning?"

"Small-time crime's still all over the place—illegal gambling, people getting mugged, merchants cheating customers—but the big-ticket stuff has gotten more… abstract. Cerebral. White collar. And more integrated with the rest of the city. Your corruption is now our corruption."

"The melting pot, a beautiful thing."

I sipped my tea. "Though to give him his due, speaking of integrated corruption, Big Brother Choi popped up on the right side of an issue a few months ago. You know the proposal for the corner of Bayard and Mott? Phoenix Towers? Twenty stories, mixed middle-income and luxury housing, which by the time it's built I guarantee you will have morphed into all luxury? 'Unanticipated construction costs, Mr. Mayor. We need this variance to make our investment back, and New York really better think about keeping us developers happy or we'll take our construction jobs and by the way our campaign contributions elsewhere.' With community facilities on the ground floor as the lipstick on the pig?"

Bill grinned. "I do declare, your speech has gotten more colorful since we went down south."

"Oh, shut up," I suggested, though I suspected he

was right. "Anyway, the holdout property for Phoenix Towers is the Li Min Jin building. Second one in on Bayard, with the curved roof eaves? They actually imported the tiles for those from China, in the late 1800s. Phoenix Towers can't proceed without that property. It's smack in the middle of the parcel the developer's trying to put together. He's got commitments on the rest, but each one's contingent on his getting all the others, or the deals are off. Tim says that's fairly common in real estate."

"You talked to Tim about this project?"

"He just made partner, so I called to congratulate him. While we were on the phone we talked about Big Brother Choi, like everyone else in Chinatown is doing. Tim's treasurer of the Chinatown Heritage Society, so he's been following the Phoenix Towers project pretty closely. I asked what he thought would happen with it now."

"Holy cow, you asked Tim a question? You must have really wanted to know."

"I had my mansplaining filters set to industrial strength. But yeah, I did want to know. He said it probably depends on who rises to the top of the tong. It was Big Brother Choi who was absolutely refusing to sell. Apparently, though, there's another faction."

"It was Choi's decision to make? The tong's building?"

"Probably not, in a legal sense, but no one went up against him."

"And now they might."

"If they do, they'd better do it soon. Tim's very put out at the timing of Choi's death."

"So's Choi, I bet. What's Tim's problem?"

"Where do you want me to start? But about this, he says there's some kind of deadline on all the commitments at the end of this month. Owners can pull out, and a couple of them already said they would if the developer hasn't put the parcel together, because they don't want their real estate tied up forever in a pipe dream."

"Are we thinking then that Choi may have been helped along that lonesome road?"

"I'm sure a lot of people are, but Mary says no. On the contrary, the pathologist at the autopsy apparently wondered how anyone with arteries like that lived as long as he did. So the developer may get a chance to buy the building after all. Which Tim is taking very personally."

"Poor Tim. But listen, I have to ask. Keeping that development from happening is the good guy side? Isn't the developer Chinese American?"

I lowered my tea. "This is you playing devil's advocate, right? That's obnoxious, you know. Of course it's the good guy side. Jackson Ting may have Chinese parents, but when did that ever stop anyone from being a greedy SOB? He climbed up on his charm and other people's money from his dad's half-dozen middle-class apartment buildings in Queens to much bigger projects in Manhattan. Now he's out to prove he can play with the big kids. If he has to trash Chinatown to prove it, well, you can't stop progress."

"That's what'll happen if Phoenix Towers gets built?"

"Come on. Twenty stories on the narrowest streets in New York? That whole gentrification thing? Hipsters and new Google hires moving in? Pardon my language, but, white people?" I resettled in my chair and glared at him. "Every time you do that, you raise my blood pressure."

"The realities of sociology and politics in Chinatown are not as clear to outsiders as to you. I rely upon you for guidance."

I sighed. "Sometimes you're such an ass."

"No argument. So, assuming everything you just said is correct—which obviously there's no question it is, since it's you—what was a Chinatown OG doing on the good guy side?"

I glared a little more, then relaxed. "No one's sure, actually. The cynics think he was just holding out for a better offer from Ting, squeezing him as the deadline got near. I don't think that's it, though. I think Choi was a crook, but he was Chinatown's crook. And a part of Chinatown was his. He saw Phoenix Towers as a threat to his domain, and he wasn't going to let it happen."

"And that's why his death is a big deal?"

"Part of why."

"What's the other part?"

I was about to explain about the protection rackets, the gambling dens, all the old-time criminal small businesses Big Brother Choi and the Li Min Jin had been running that might seem attractive now for a little strong-arm takeover action, plus, of course, the succession fight in the tong itself. But as I opened my mouth, my phone rang. I checked the screen. "I think we might be going to find out," I said. "It's Grandfather Gao."

THREE

THE NEXT MORNING promptly at eight Bill and I presented ourselves at Grandfather Gao's door.

"I'm sorry to bring you out so early." Grandfather Gao, who wasn't really my grandfather, admitted us to his herb shop, which to me was much more than an herb shop.

My father died when I was thirteen. I took it hard, boiling with rage I didn't know what to do with. My mother started sending me to the old herbalist to pick up this or that, many more remedies and tonics than we'd ever needed before. Although my fury at the world made me resent being my mother's errand girl, going to the herb shop was an errand I never minded. Before Grandfather Gao started to grind the required herbs with his mortar and pestle, he'd put the kettle on. Once he'd made the medicinal mixture and folded it in white paper tied with red string, we'd sit in the dim, incense-sweet shop and drink tea together as though I, the angry fatherless thirteen-year-old baby of my family, were an honored customer. He'd ask about school; he'd ask about my brothers; he'd ask what I thought of this or that. He himself often spoke in nature metaphors I didn't understand, but I knew he was wise, and he was interested in what I had to say, and that was enough.

Grandfather Gao had also been then, and was still, a

senior advisor to the San Ge Xiongdi—the Three Brothers—tong.

"It's not that early, Grandfather," I said. For me that was true. Bill had grumbled all through his coffee, something about civilized hours. I'd ignored him.

"I'm so happy to see you, Chin Ling Wan-Ju," said Grandfather Gao. "Also you, Mr. Smith."

"Always an honor, Mr. Gao."

Grandfather Gao, who had seemed old to me when I was thirteen, was ancient now, but still unstooped and agile. He locked the door behind us—the shop opened at ten, the reason he'd asked us to come early—and led us past the counters with their jars and bowls, the cabinets behind them stacked high with drawers full of flowers and leaves and stems. The aromas of the wares blended with the sweet smoke of the incense on the shelf in front of the figure of Guan Yu, guardian of commerce. In the sitting area, the teapot was already in the center of the low lion-footed table. A woman sat in one of the elaborately carved rosewood chairs.

"Please," said Grandfather Gao. "Honor me by joining us." He spoke in English, I assumed for Bill's benefit. "Chin Ling Wan-Ju, Mr. Bill Smith, allow me to present Wu Mao-Li."

The woman gave a smile and a brief nod of the head. She looked a little older than I, maybe mid-thirties. Even though she was sitting, I could tell she was tall. She had high cheekbones and an elegant oval face. Her glossy black hair was styled in a trendy but short low-maintenance cut. She wore brown slacks, a pale brown sweater, flat ankle boots, and a confident air. Around her neck a jade circle, a bi, hung from a gold chain. I wear one myself, though mine's smaller. So do all my brothers. It's a common baby gift among Chinese people. Jade's said to offer protection. My father started saving up for mine when they realized my mother was pregnant. It took him until my second birthday, so the family story goes, to pay it off.

Grandfather Gao, with a smile, offered me a pillow to put behind me on the rosewood chair, as he had when I was young and the chair much too big for me. I accepted it; the chair was still big. He poured tea.

"I trust your family is well?" Grandfather Gao said to me. He knew better than to ask after Bill's family.

"Yes, thank you, Grandfather. Everyone's fine." I sipped my tea; a scented green, very subtle. "Tien-Hua has just been made a partner in his firm."

"I'm happy to hear that. Please send him my congratulations."

"I will. Your children and grandchildren are also well?"

"Yes, they are. Thank you for asking."

I asked specifically about Grandfather Gao's youngest grandson, who'd been a classmate of mine at PS 124. Grandfather Gao asked about my nieces and nephews. Once everyone had been reported on, the requirements of courtesy were fulfilled, and we could move on to why we were here.

"I'm sure you've heard about the passing of Choi Meng," Grandfather Gao began. "Meng" is Chinese for "elder brother," but it occurred to me it might also have been Big Brother Choi's actual name.

"Yes, we have."

"He was the uncle of Wu Mao-Li." Grandfather Gao nodded to the woman sitting beside him.

"Please," she said to me and Bill, "call me Mel." Her

voice was smooth, authoritative, and perfectly pitched for the space, neither too loud nor too soft. The voice you'd use chairing a board meeting or running a seminar. "Though I can see you're surprised at my name," she said to me with an amused smile.

My cheeks grew warm. "In that pronunciation—"

"It's a masculine name, yes. Uncle Meng was my mother's older brother, so she invited him to choose the names of her children. He picked boy's names so when jealous spirits heard our parents talk about us they'd go looking for sons to steal and ignore daughters. Also, in the human realm, he wanted the same thing—for people not to dismiss us before they met us because we were women. My English name is Melanie, but I've always been called Mel. My younger sister is Natalie. Nat."

"You're saying Big Brother Choi was a feminist? I didn't know that," I said.

"In a lot of areas he held traditional views, but in others, he could be fairly progressive."

"You knew your uncle well?"

"My mother brought us here often when we were children. Nat and I loved coming to Chinatown. But we were raised in Scarsdale. My Chinese is pretty rudimentary." She glanced at Grandfather Gao. He nodded again, apparently a signal for her to continue. "Uncle Meng introduced me to Mr. Gao back then. I understood they were rivals, but Uncle Meng said if I ever needed anything and he wasn't around, I should come here. To Mr. Gao."

"Choi Meng," said Grandfather Gao, "in many of his dealings, was not the most honorable of men." He looked steadily at Mel Wu as he said that, and she returned his look. "But," he continued, "he loved his family sincerely. If he thought I could be of help to his sister's daughter, it is my honor to try."

"I guess us being here means you think we can help, too," I said. "What kind of help do you need, Mel? And call me Lydia."

"Uncle Meng has left the Bayard Street building to me."

FOUR

I LOOKED AT the three other people sitting around the low table in the shadows of Grandfather Gao's herb shop: Bill, Grandfather Gao himself, and a woman who had just inherited a hornet's nest. "Wait," I said. "The Li Min Jin building? Big Brother Choi actually owned it?"

"He leased it to the Li Min Jin for a dollar a year," Mel Wu said. "It's all legal, the paperwork's correct." She smiled. "The Li Min Jin is a 501(c)(3) nonprofit."

"A nonprofit? Seriously?"

"They sponsor martial arts clubs, bands, sports teams, school trips. Plantings in the park. A widows and orphans fund."

Uh-huh. And they make widows and orphans. Either growing up in Scarsdale makes you so naïve that Mel Wu really didn't know what the Li Min Jin was, or she wasn't fazed by the whole tong thing. I was putting my money on the second.

"I called Uncle Meng's lawyer yesterday," she said, "to tell him Uncle Meng was gone. He called me back an hour later, once he'd found and reread the will. The estate"—she gave a small smile—"the part in legit bank accounts and so on, anyway, goes to Nat and me evenly, outside of small trusts for her kids. But the surprise is the building. It turns out yes, he did own it. The lawyer told me that when Uncle Meng came here from Hong Kong in the eighties and took over the Li Min Jin, they were renting that building, as they always had. The landlord was a minor tong member who'd inherited it from his tong member father, et cetera. But the tong had never bothered to buy it. After the merger with the other tong, Uncle Meng did. He said he wanted his family to always have a home. Then about five years ago, it seems, he filed a new deed making both of us, himself and me, what's called joint tenants with right of survivorship. He never told me, but there's no reason he would have had to. Aside from avoiding my jaw dropping when I found out."

My jaw was mentally dropping, too. "What about the Li Min Jin? Do they know the building isn't coming to them?"

"They know he owned it, obviously. Whether they know he left it to me and not them, I don't know."

"But *you* know what kind of position you're in now?"

"If you mean, am I aware of how badly half the Li Min Jin wants to keep the building and the other half wants to sell it for the fortune they think they'd make, yes. Though since it's mine, if I do sell it, there'd be nothing in it for them. Legally."

"Legally," Bill said, speaking for the first time, as Grandfather Gao leaned forward to refill my cup. "But they might come around for a piece of the action anyway."

"I'm sure they would." Nope, not fazed. "But as it happens, I'm inclined not to sell. It's obvious Uncle Meng wanted the Phoenix Towers project stopped. That's fine with me."

"You're against the project?" Bill asked.

"From what I've seen the community doesn't want it. The Chinatown Heritage Society doesn't want it. Uncle

Meng didn't want it. That might be enough for me, but also, taking the larger urban-planning view, it might be a mistake on the part of the city to sacrifice the character of Chinatown and the tourist dollars it attracts for the transient value of two years' worth of construction jobs. Not to mention the value in human terms of residents not being gentrified out of their homes."

Oh my God, Mel Wu talked like Tim. She must have caught the look on my face because she smiled. "I'm a real estate attorney. Tenants' rights, housing justice, environmental justice, that sort of thing." Her smile wasn't actually confrontational, though I did get the feeling that words like "bleeding heart" would be better left unsaid. "I'm not anti-development across the board. Sometimes it's a necessary evil, and other times it can be an actual good. Between us, I think Jackson Ting's a jerk, but that wouldn't stop me from supporting a project of his I believed in. Not this one, though. I think Phoenix Towers is a mistake."

"You think he's a jerk—you mean you know him? I guess that makes sense, both of you being real estate people."

"That's true, and our paths do sometimes cross professionally, but I've known Jackson since middle school."

"But you're from Scarsdale, isn't that what you said? I thought he was from some fancy part of Queens."

"Forest Hills. But he went to Winter Prep, in Valhalla, with me and my sister. He was in my class."

"Long commute."

"It's a boarding school," Bill said, with a tiny smile. Wise guy. He really does know the strangest things.

I asked Mel Wu, "Does Ting know you're against his project?"

"We haven't had any reason to discuss it, though he knows what I do for a living, so he might have guessed. So far I've just been watching as an outsider. Now I have a chance to step in. Nat, her kids, and I are Uncle Meng's only living relatives, and I'd like to do as he wanted. Though that creates its own problems."

"Like what?"

"I'm an attorney, an officer of the court. I can't be landlady to a tong, nonprofit or not." That nailed shut the naïveté question. "If I keep the building, I'll have to evict the Li Min Jin. Evictions in New York are difficult by design. The building is what New York City law classifies as a clubhouse, meaning essentially short-term stays, though Uncle Meng did live there. In theory, it would be an easier eviction than other residential types, but it would still carry a whole host of difficulties."

Difficulties. I thought about what might happen if Mel Wu from Scarsdale tried to evict the Li Min Jin.

"I suppose," she said, "I could serve them papers and then call the sheriff when they don't leave, but it's not much of a stretch from there to imagine an armed standoff on Bayard Street. I don't want to be responsible for that."

"But what will you do?"

"I don't know yet. I could try to buy them out, though what Uncle Meng left me doesn't come close to what Jackson's offering for the building."

"But his money wouldn't come to them if you took the offer, anyway."

"As your partner pointed out"—Mel Wu nodded at Bill—"legally, it wouldn't, but they'd want a share. A deal-sweetener, to facilitate their peacefully vacating as the law requires." She grinned wryly. "Or I could hand the whole building over to the Chinatown Heritage Society and make it their problem."

That made me grin, too. "My brother's society treasurer. The one I just told Grandfather Gao made partner at his law firm. I'd kind of love to see him in that position."

"What firm?"

"Harriman McGill."

"That's impressive. Is he in the real estate department?"

"No, M and A."

"Well, you might get the chance. I'll have to decide soon."

The room fell silent. "Mel," I said, "it seems like you have all this thought out and you know what you're doing. I mean, I'm happy to meet you, but why are we here?"

Grandfather Gao refilled the teacups again. Mel said, "As I said, Uncle Meng lived in the building. The whole top floor was his apartment. He was classified as the super."

"Well, in a way I guess he was."

"In a way. I need to go up there. In addition to inheriting the building, I'm also the executor of the estate. I need to know what else is in the apartment, other papers, valuables. I'd also like to generally check out the building. And I've gotten a call from Mr. Chang. Chang Yao-Zu. He's Uncle Meng's chief lieutenant."

"So he's currently the tong leader?"

"Yes, I suppose so, but that's not why he called. He says there are things Uncle Meng wanted me to know. Things Uncle Meng didn't want to write down but that may bear on my handling of the building's future. So I called Mr. Gao to ask whether he thought it would be all right if I went to the building alone. I'm used to inspecting property, but this seemed an exceptional situation."

"Very prudent," Grandfather Gao said. "My answer was, it would be improper." By which he might have also meant dangerous, but he didn't say that. "Clearly I can't accompany Mao-Li myself. I suggested perhaps you would be willing to go. As you speak Chinese." He smiled at Bill. "You also, Mr. Smith."

"As I am so large," Bill said.

"Precisely."

"We'd be glad to," I said to Mel Wu. I glanced at Bill, who nodded. If truth be told I was dying to have a look inside the Li Min Jin building, and at Big Brother Choi's apartment. "When were you thinking of going?"

"Mr. Chang asked if we could delay our meeting until after the funeral. I think what he was really saying, in case I needed a hint, was that it would be in aggressively bad taste for me to go to the building before then. He suggested Wednesday morning."

"You're not worried something might…disappear from the apartment in that time?"

"Why, just because everyone in the building is a bunch of gangsters?"

"That's kind of what I meant, yes."

"Mr. Chang was intensely loyal to Uncle Meng. He'll have people protecting Uncle Meng's door until it's clear who has the right to enter. He'd also protect me if I needed it, but I don't want to put him in that position."

"Very thoughtful."

"I have no reason to make his life harder. I think he might have trouble holding the tong together as it is. He's a rather cold, formal man, but I've known him all my life. He used to slip us candies when we went to visit Uncle Meng. I'm happy to respect his wishes. Can you meet me at the building Wednesday?"

"Absolutely," I said.

Grandfather Gao spoke. "When you go, please do not go armed. The Li Min Jin might consider that a deliberate provocation."

"Of course," I said, looking at Bill to make sure he agreed.

"And will you come to the funeral, too?" Mel Wu said. "And to the cemetery afterward, if you have the time? I'd like to establish your presence."

"Yes, of course, if you like." Translation: Try to keep me away.

Mel Wu looked at Grandfather Gao, who nodded. "Wah Wing Sang," Mel said. "Tuesday, ten o'clock."

FIVE

BILL AND I walked past the line of shiny black cars draped with white and yellow flowers, the hearse at the front holding a large black-framed photo of Big Brother Choi on its roof, and entered Wah Wing Sang Funeral Home at 9:45 Tuesday morning.

The establishment was using its largest room for the Choi funeral, and even so the place was so crowded with mourners, so thick with incense smoke, and so choked with bouquets and wreaths you could hardly move. Striking in a severely simple black suit, Mel Wu stood near the coffin on its flower-draped altar. Beside her was a young woman also in a black suit, but one with more cutting-edge flair. She looked so much like Mel she could only be her younger sister, Natalie. Next to Natalie a bear-sized white man held the hand of a small boy and carried a baby in his arms.

At the altar's head hovered a thin-haired, long-faced older man. At its foot three more people stood. The one closest to the coffin, surprisingly, was a woman. Her hair was cut short, and she had tattoos on the backs of her hands. Like the men in the room, she wore a black suit and tie. Straight-backed and sharp-faced, her age around fifty, she was younger than the guy at the altar's head but no more friendly-looking. To her left, a tall young man with an athlete's bearing had a don't-mess-with-me squint in his eyes, although who'd mess with anyone at a funeral I wasn't sure. I had a feeling I knew him, but his name didn't pop up. Beside him scowled a bony stoop-shouldered man around the same age as the guy at the head. If these were the top soldiers of the Li Min Jin, as the honor guard locations implied, the office Christmas party must be a blast.

A steady stream of people were stepping up to the Wu sisters to offer condolences. Bill and I joined the line.

"Ah. Lydia, Bill, thank you for coming," said Mel when we reached her. "This is Natalie Wu Harris, my sister, and her husband, Paul." Natalie shared Mel's high cheekbones and glossy black hair, though Natalie's was long and pinned into a classy chignon. The calm poise, though, was missing, replaced by a coiled impatience. I got the sense that standing around greeting people at a gangster's funeral was not her idea of a good time, although I thought it was less the gangster's funeral and more the standing around that seemed to be the problem. I got another sense, too: that each Wu sister was used to getting her way, though likely by different means.

Natalie and I shook hands. "Good to meet you. Mel's told me about you," she said. Laying a hand on the shoulder of the boy beside her, she said, "This is Matthew. Matty, say hello to Lydia and Bill."

The boy, somewhere around four and wearing a navy-blue suit, craned his neck to look up at me, stuck out an obedient hand, and said, "Hello."

"Hello, Matthew," I said, as did Bill when his turn came.

Mel said, "Matty, tell Lydia and Bill who that is." She pointed to the wide-eyed toddler in Paul Harris's huge arms.

"My sister, Emily," the boy said promptly. He reached a hand up and held the baby's foot in a proprietary move.

"She's lucky to have you," I said. Matthew gave a solemn nod.

Mel stepped back to include the older man and spoke again. "Lydia Chin, Bill Smith, this is Chang Yao-Zu. He was a close friend of Uncle Meng's." The man at his post at the head of the casket gave us a nod. We offered our pleased-to-meet-yous, expressed condolences, and moved across the room out of the way.

"So that's Chang, now the boss man," Bill said.

"And *who* is that woman at the other end of the coffin?"

"The exception that proves the rule? You said the tongs generally don't have women soldiers, but you didn't say never."

"She's got to be. And those are the honor guard spots, at the head and foot. She must not only be a soldier, she must have rank. How about that? I guess Big Brother Choi really was a feminist."

"And the young guy next to her?"

"I think I know him but I can't—oh, wait! Ironman! Ironman Ma. He was in Ted's class at school. He was a weightlifter, always working out, that's why they called him that. I didn't know he'd joined the tong. He must be somebody, too, to be standing at the coffin."

"Maybe besides being a feminist, Big Brother Choi was a sports fan," Bill said. "What about the other one? The one who looks like Scrooge?"

"I have no idea who that is. A fun-looking bunch, huh?"

"A scream. So what happens now?"

"Just do what I do." I walked to the coffin and bowed in respect. Bill did the same.

Big Brother Choi, in suit and tie, was laid out in a
casket lined in white satin. The embalmer had no doubt
done the best job he could—this was Big Brother Choi,
after all—but as usual at an open-casket funeral, I was
creeped out by the makeup, the careful positioning of
the hands, the attempt to make this empty shell seem
to still contain life.

As we moved back from the coffin, a somber-faced
gent from the funeral home offered me three sticks of
incense. After a tiny pause he offered three to Bill, too.
We lit them off the flames in an urn and, again bowing, stuck them in the sand in another, larger urn, where
many sticks of incense lit by earlier arrivals already
smoldered. I'd brought a stack of hell money. I gave
half to Bill, and we returned to the first, fiery urn and
threw the bills into the flames. They curled, blackened,
and spiraled into the air as smoke, so Big Brother Choi
wouldn't go needy into the next world.

Bill and I took seats on padded folding chairs. I saw
Mary Kee and Chris Chiang, both in black trousers,
polished black crepe-soled shoes, and leather jackets,
standing against the rear wall with a Black man who
was also dressed as they were. I had to smile at the
sight of them. Undercover cops can disappear inside
their disguises, but plainclothes cops can be spotted a
mile away. The comings and goings at the funeral of a
major gangster of any ethnic group are irresistible to
the NYPD. I wondered who the Black man was.

The chairs were starting to fill when a stir in the
crowd made me turn to the door. Grandfather Gao, erect
and elegant in a beautifully tailored black suit and open
overcoat, had just come in, accompanied by two other
senior members of the Three Brothers tong. Some of the
faces of the men in the crowd hardened; these must have

been Li Min Jin members. But this was their leader's funeral. They disliked the Three Brothers representatives out of loyalty and custom, but the insult if they hadn't come would have been much worse.

I looked around to see if I could spot soldiers from the other tongs. A chubby older man with his hands folded over his belly looked familiar. So did a bald fellow whose sharp, darting glances were emphasized by his wire-rimmed glasses. A tall man, a little younger than those two, making him not yet sixty, was seated near the front. He didn't look familiar, but the aura of barely concealed threat emanating from him was the same as theirs. One or two more also caught my eye. I wondered if I was being observant, or just paranoid.

Grandfather Gao and his companions greeted the Wu sisters, bowed to Big Brother Choi, lit and placed their incense, burned their hell notes, and sat.

The receiving line continued. I looked around again, this time to see who of the Chinatown who's-who was here.

"Uh-oh," Bill muttered to me. "The jig is up."

I turned to see the Wu sisters' hands being pressed by a dignified middle-aged woman in a dark business suit and a pillbox hat. Beside her was my brother Tim.

"How did you know?" I said. "That's exactly how I always feel when I see him where I don't expect him. Like he caught me up to something. Probably because he was always tattling on me when we were kids."

"Probably because you were always up to something. So what's he doing here?"

At that moment Tim, reaching for incense from the undertaker, caught my eye. I smiled. He frowned. What else was new? He and his companion walked to the urns.

"The woman he's with," I said to Bill. "Adele Fong.

From an old Chinatown family. Executive director of the Chinatown Heritage Society. Tim's the treasurer. I guess resisting development makes strange bedfellows."

"Tim and Adele Fong?"

"Tim, Adele Fong, and Big Brother Choi."

Luckily all the chairs near us were taken. Adele Fong and Tim found seats a few rows ahead and across the aisle. Tim gave me another frown, I gave him another smile, and he turned and faced forward.

While the Buddhist monks were beginning to line up around the coffin to start the ceremony, the door opened again. Jackson Ting slipped in and took a seat in the back.

Faces hardened at Ting's entrance, too, more than just those of the Li Min Jin men. He and his Phoenix Towers project weren't popular around here. Ting calmly crossed his legs, set his handsome face in an attitude of respectful reverence, and sat waiting for the ceremony to begin. He seemed completely relaxed; in fact he radiated the kind of unperturbed composure that read as confidence but not arrogance. It was a smart move, I thought, to show up here. Paying respects at the funeral of an elder, a powerful community leader, crook or not, adversary or not, showed an appreciation of protocol and correctness that might soften some hearts.

The next hour was filled with chanting and gongs, prayers and eulogies, bowing and incense. Finally everyone stood. The coffin was closed. Eight hard-faced men hefted it onto their shoulders, slow-walked it from the chapel, and slid it into the waiting hearse. As the funeral band tuned up, the mourners filed out to the sidewalk. Mary, Chris, and the Black cop slipped out first, to stand across the street by the park. Chris used a small camera to snap photos of the action, sometimes directed by the Black guy.

People once again lined up to press the hands of the Wu sisters and receive from one or the other of them a small red envelope containing coins. The generosity of a red-envelope gift from the family would cancel out any ill luck accruing to the mourners from proximity to the dead. Bill and I went up also, shook hands, murmured condolences, and accepted our red envelopes. We moved down the sidewalk and watched people pay their respects. Among them were my brother Tim and Adele Fong. Adele spoke to Nat while Tim took Mel's hand in both of his and spoke earnestly, which was his only mode besides sarcastically.

"Check out your brother," Bill said. "If I didn't know better, I'd swear he was hitting on Mel Wu."

"Say what?" I watched the two speak. "No, he's probably just trying to figure out if the same law book wrote their dialogue."

Tim finally dropped Mel's hand, turned, and then, speaking of ill luck, came striding toward us, pocketing his red envelope. He closed in and demanded, "What are you doing here?" Without waiting for my answer, he rounded on Bill. "Are these gangsters clients of yours?"

"Big Brother Choi was an important member of the Chinatown community," I said before the absurdity of that question got Bill into a whole "who me?" thing with Tim. "I'm running a community-based business. I thought it was only right to pay my respects."

"'Community-based business.' You're ambulance chasing, you mean. Really, Lyd, it's not a good look for you to be trolling for clients among the bottom-feeders."

I said, "Nice metaphor, bro. Also, you're here. Is

hanging with the bottom-feeders a good look for new partners at Harriman McGill?"

He huffed. He actually huffed. "I'm here representing the Chinatown Heritage Society. The partners at Harriman recognize and applaud my community involvement. They appreciate the value of maintaining historic communities and the architectural resources that sustain them."

Not for the first time, I wondered how my practical mother and my easygoing father had produced this stiff.

"I'm here," he said importantly, "because the Society, and in fact all of Chinatown, owe a debt to Choi Meng."

I lifted one eyebrow. Bill thinks it's funny when I do that. "Big Brother Choi was a CHS donor?"

"No. Not money. But whatever his reason, our goals aligned when he refused to sell the Li Min Jin building to Jackson Ting."

Our goals aligned. Honestly. "He's here, by the way."

"Ting? He is?" Tim looked around, spotted Jackson Ting farther up the sidewalk talking to some businessmen, and might have muttered "ass-kisser," or maybe my own thought just spoke itself. He faced me again, turning his back as though Ting would notice. Or care. "Adele wanted to attend to pay the Society's respects and asked me to come with her. I was busy, but of course I agreed. I didn't want her to have to come alone."

"You're a fine fellow, Tim Chin. Hello, Mrs. Fong. Good to see you."

"Good morning, Lydia." Adele Fong had finished her sidewalk conversation with the Wu sisters and located her funeral date. She smiled. "And you must be Mr. Smith, Lydia's business partner. Tim's told me about you."

"Only the good things, I hope," Bill replied, though he and I both knew the chances of that were small. "I'm pleased to meet you. I understand your Society does a lot of good work in the community."

"Oh, it's hardly my Society," Adele Fong said graciously. "We're fortunate to have a hard-working board"—she nodded at Tim—"and many enthusiastic volunteers. Excuse me, but Tim, I need to get back. If you're planning to go along to the cemetery I can—"

"No, no, I have to get to the office. I'll drop you on the way. Lydia, Bill." Tim nodded and took Adele Fong's elbow, and they turned and walked away.

I grinned as I watched them. "I think you get points for saying nice things to someone Tim obviously likes to impress."

"Enough to move the needle on his opinion of me?" Bill asked.

"Don't get greedy."

"I suppose," Bill said, "that this wouldn't have been the appropriate time for Mel to drop the bombshell to Tim and Mrs. Fong that the Society might find itself owning the Li Min Jin building."

"No, it wouldn't have, and besides that, if she'd told him, you can be sure he'd have told me he had a big secret that he couldn't tell me."

Bill lit a cigarette. Some of the mourners began to enter the waiting cars. The rest remained on the sidewalk, talking and smoking. I saw Jackson Ting go up to Mel Wu, take her hand, offer his condolences. Crossing paths again. Natalie and her family, meanwhile, ignored Ting and climbed into the limo behind the hearse. Ting glanced at them, then walked away. Mel joined them in the car.

She'd arranged a Wah Wing Sang car for me and Bill. Behind the five funeral home cars, a line of private cars waited around the corner. Engines revved, the funeral band struck up, and the procession took off.

We wound slowly through the streets of Chinatown, the band walking ahead, its loud music scaring away any evil spirits that skulked at the border between the world of the living and the world of the dead. Though if some of the stories about Big Brother Choi's younger days were true, there weren't a lot of evil spirits that would have the nerve to threaten his ghost or his mourners. People on the sidewalks stopped and watched the procession inch past. Pedestrians jaywalking—a Chinatown sport—scurried out of the way.

Once Big Brother Choi had been reminded of what the neighborhood looked like, so that he'd be able to find it when he returned on those days of the year when the dead visit the living, the funeral procession headed over the Manhattan Bridge, but not before one final pass by the Li Min Jin building.

"Look," said Bill as we turned onto Bayard. I followed his pointing finger.

Jackson Ting stood on the corner where Phoenix Towers would go, hands in pockets, watching the procession roll by.

SIX

THE DRIVE TO the Cypress Hills Cemetery on the border of Brooklyn and Queens took half an hour at funeral procession pace. As we rolled along the BQE Bill looked over at me. "Are you all right?"

"Yes, I'm okay. I guess I haven't been in a funeral procession since my father died. It's kind of weird."

"Is he in one of the cemeteries out this way?"

"No, in New Jersey. We all go out there on Qing Ming and sweep his grave."

Bill took my hand and squeezed it but didn't say anything else. We sat like that for the rest of the ride.

A stout middle-aged White woman in sensible shoes waited at the main building just inside the Cypress Hills gates. The procession stopped for her to climb into the hearse to guide the driver to Choi Meng's final resting place.

"It's huge," I said to Bill as we wound through the wooded grounds. Midday sun lit up the colors of the autumn leaves. "This cemetery."

"One of New York's oldest. Jackie Robinson's here. And Mae West."

"No kidding? Well, so are all of Chinatown's premier tong soldiers."

"Really?"

"I looked it up. See where we're going, up on the hill?

All Chinese headstones. Not all tong-related, of course, but each of the tongs has a section."

"And all the stones face the same way, a few degrees off the grid. Feng shui?"

"You better believe it. No one wants to spend eternity looking in the wrong direction."

The hearse wound up a steep hill and stopped. The line of cars behind it halted too. Bill and I got out and made our way with everyone else to an open gravesite near the hilltop.

"Your people really pack 'em in," Bill said, looking around.

"We don't need as much space to spread out as you do. A lot of times we unbury the body after a few years, clean the bones, and rebury them in an urn. That's what we did for my dad. We can fit more of us into a plot that way. You can spend eternity with your family."

"To each his own. Though Big Brother Choi seems to have a little extra space."

"He was the boss."

"But not the first boss. This tong's been around for a century or so, no? Where are the other bosses?"

"The boss before Choi Meng—that's probably him, there, also at the top. But it used to be if you died abroad your relatives would ship you back to China, if they could afford it," I told him. "To the ancestral village. That pretty much ended after the revolution, but before that everyone with money did it. The other bosses must have gone home."

We reached Choi Meng's gravesite. Mr. Chang, Ironman, Scrooge, and the sharp-faced woman were there already, having traveled in the funeral home car behind the Wu family. As the cars parked and emptied, an impressive crowd of formidable men gathered, some with their wives, a few with their adolescent or grown sons. No daughters. Grandfather Gao, I saw, hadn't come, and the men I'd fingered as from other tongs had stayed away, too. Apparently the funeral rites were one thing, the burial rites another.

Choi Meng's spot was certainly primo, high up with a spectacular view over the cemetery's rolling hills and the rooftops of Brooklyn. I was surprised to find a double gravestone of gray granite, carved with Chinese characters. Having just died, Choi Meng had a traditional wooden plaque stuck into the ground at the head of his grave; the carving on his half of the stone would be done later. But on the other half of the stone I read that this was the final resting place of Ni Mei-Mei, beloved wife of Choi Meng. Her dates were 1954 to 1990. A small enamel plaque with her photo was mounted on the stone.

"I didn't know he'd ever been married," I said to Bill. "Look how young she was."

"She's been gone a long time."

"And he stayed single."

The head pallbearer opened the back of the hearse. "Turn around," I said. "It's bad luck to view the body while it's being put in the ground."

With everyone else, we waited with our backs to the grave until the undertaker announced that Choi Meng was at rest. We turned again. The Buddhist priest chanted some prayers; the Wu sisters, along with Natalie's husband, Paul, and their son, Matthew, threw handfuls of dirt into the grave; there was another prayer; and it was done.

Mourners stepped up to the grave to tell Choi Meng silently whatever they wanted him to know on his final journey. The crowd thinned as people got into their cars, some to head back to Chinatown for the reception, some to go home. Once everyone but those in the funeral home cars had gone, Mel Wu walked to the limo she'd come in and retrieved a bouquet of white carnations. I thought she'd put them by her uncle's grave, but she went on past it, to a set of graves around the other side of the hill. Mr. Chang, as though he'd expected this, walked with her. So did the woman soldier, Ironman, and Scrooge. I glanced at Bill, and we went also.

Near the top of the hill on that side stood another double headstone. Staying back a discreet distance, I read the names and dates. "Long Lo," I told Bill. "And his wife. He was head of the Ma Tou."

"The Horsehead tong, that the Li Min Jin absorbed?"

"This must be their section."

Mel Wu set her flowers in a bronze vase fastened to the headstone. She and the others bowed three times. They stood quietly side by side. A breeze stirred the leaves.

"Thank you," Chang said in English. "For remembering."

"We always brought flowers here when we came with Uncle Meng to visit Aunt Mei-Mei's grave. I wouldn't have felt right being here and not doing this. They must have been great friends."

"They were important to each other."

Mel smiled at me and Bill as she turned to walk back to the limo. Chang gave us the once-over, but his expression didn't change. The woman soldier openly assessed us. Scrooge and Ironman both pointedly ignored us. We reached the cars, where Natalie and her family waited, baby Emily asleep on her father's shoulder. I gave a final glance at Choi Meng's grave as we got in the cars and headed back to Chinatown.

SEVEN

When my phone rang Wednesday morning Bill and I were ready, sitting in the cool, yellow-leafed sunshine in Columbus Park. Bill was drinking coffee, I was drinking milk tea, and we were both watching the men play xiangqi and the women play gin. Why the games in Chinatown parks break along gender lines is a question no one has ever been able to answer to my satisfaction, but it's undeniably true. My personal theory is that the women are way more cutthroat than the men, and card games move faster than board games.

The call was the one we'd been waiting for, from Mel Wu. "I just left the lawyer's office. I should be there in fifteen minutes."

"We'll be waiting."

We gave it another ten minutes, sorted our recycling, and went to stand on the corner by the park. Mel appeared not two minutes after we got there, stepping out of a town car. She wore a dark green pantsuit that looked like cashmere to me, an ivory silk shirt, and green-and-white wingtips. "A woman who doesn't wear heels," I said as I greeted her. "Warms my heart."

"I was a gymnast in high school. Ruined my feet for anything but flats."

We walked along Bayard and stopped at the door of the Li Min Jin building. Mel knocked politely on it, although she'd told us the leather portfolio in her shoulder bag held copies of the will and the deed and a set of keys to the apartment, all provided to her by Big Brother Choi's attorney.

The door was opened by a broad, beefy guy. Behind him, the woman who had stood at the foot of Big Brother Choi's coffin eyed us, then told him in Cantonese everything was fine. Beefy stepped back. The woman, today dressed in a gray pantsuit and white shirt, gave Mel a chilly nod. Mel returned one exactly the same. I got the sense she was fine-tuning her friendliness level to what she received, and I wondered if that was a lawyer thing. Tim didn't do it; he was just pompous to everyone.

"Good morning," Mel said to the woman. "Tan Lu-Lien, this is Lydia Chin and Bill Smith. Lydia, Bill, Tan Lu-Lien."

"I'm happy to meet you," I said in Chinese. "Chin Ling Wan-Ju. Have you eaten yet?" This is a standard greeting. No one who asks it really wants the answer; it's the Chinese equivalent of "How are you?" The answer to the English question is "Fine, thank you," and to the Chinese, "Yes, thank you," and in neither case does it matter whether the answer's true.

Tan Lu-Lien offered an affirmative, grunted reply.

"Is Mr. Chang here?" Mel asked. "He's expecting me."

"Chang Yao-Zu is upstairs. I'll take you up." Tan Lu-Lien looked us over. Two women and a White man: not the usual thing in the headquarters of a Chinatown tong. With poorly hidden distaste on her sharp face, she stepped aside to let us in, leaving Beefy to shut the door. She turned and led the way through the wide lobby to the staircase in the back. I considered pointing out that she wasn't the usual thing, either, but that seemed like a bad way to begin a relationship.

The building's interior was well kept, if workaday. Vinyl floors, exposed pipes on walls that had been painted and repainted for over a hundred years. Fluorescent light fixtures hanging from an acoustic-tile ceiling, which I assumed was as much for fireproofing as it was for noise, the fire codes having changed more than once since the building's construction. A staircase, vinyl treads with metal nosings, ran up the center of the building in the back. Doors opened off the hallways of the U-shaped floors above. Nestled into the tight turns of the stairwell was an open-cage elevator.

I didn't think open cages were legal anymore in New York, and I didn't think I wanted to ride in this one, but Tan Lu-Lien pulled back the gate, Mel and Bill stepped inside, and if I didn't get in too, I'd have to race them to the top floor. So I entered, Tan stepped in behind me and slid the gate shut, and we rose so shakily and slowly that I was convinced my instincts had been correct, and besides, I could have beaten them without running.

We slid up past floors of more vinyl tile and fluorescent lights. The air smelled of cigarette smoke and chicken broth. Through open doors on the second and third floors we could see groups of men drinking tea, reading newspapers, and playing cards, mah-jongg, or xiangqi. Some looked up to watch us rise; some just continued their games. Higher up, most doors were shut; these were probably the bedrooms where the tong put up visiting overseas members or new immigrants who hadn't yet found places of their own.

The elevator rattled up to the top landing and settled to a wobbly stop. "I'm seasick," I whispered to Bill once we got out. He snickered, but low—laughing in the house of the dead is in poor taste in every culture.

Opposite the elevator stood the floor's single door. Unlike the other doors we'd risen by, this one was wide, made from solid-looking red-painted wood, with an elaborately carved frame and a gold-lettered black plaque above. The doorframe rested uneasily in the aging plaster wall surrounding it. Beside it sat a folding chair, no doubt for the tong soldier guarding the place. The soldier, however, wasn't there. Bill looked from the plaque to me. "Upright People Will Advance," I said.

"The Li Min Jin motto," said Bill.

"Also," said Mel, "it's a warning. About who gets to enter the boss's lair."

Tan, meanwhile, was looking around in impatience. "Chang Yao-Zu told me to bring you up here," she said, as though that fact alone should be enough to cause Chang Yao-Zu to appear. But he didn't. "He was here." Tan pointed to the chair. She called out, "Yao-Zu!"

Chang Yao-Zu still did not appear.

Frowning, Tan hesitated, then, with a look back at Mel, knocked on the red door.

No answer.

She frowned more deeply and knocked again. Again, nothing.

"It's all right. He's probably busy," Mel said.

Or he's avoiding his new landlady, I thought. *Be interesting to know why.* Tan tried the knob, but the door was locked.

Mel reached into her shoulder bag, withdrew the portfolio, and extracted a set of keys. Tan's eyes narrowed. She reached out to prevent Mel from violating the sanctum but the look Mel flashed as she stepped to the lock was friendly, warm, and full of warning. It stopped the tong soldier cold. It was the difference, I thought, between Mel's smiling lips and her stony eyes. Would it be hard to learn to do that? Maybe she'd teach me.

The door had two heavy locks and Mel turned each with a different key, though the upper one seemed to have been unlocked because she had to turn it back again before the door swung open.

In total contrast to the utilitarian drabness of the lower floors, the room we entered might have been a classical scholar's study. Curved rosewood chairs, a low writing desk, a feng shui mirror on the wall opposite the door to reflect evil spirits back out again. Brushes in a brush holder, scroll paintings on the walls, carpets on the floor, latticework over the open window.

It was not the normal scholar's study state of affairs, however, for a bleeding body to be sprawled across the tea table.

EIGHT

THE BODY WAS that of Chang Yao-Zu, top tong lieutenant, the man Tan Lu-Lien had expected to find sitting
outside the door. The man Mel Wu had arranged to
meet, because he had a message for her from her uncle.

The NYPD detective who ran up the six floors to
the crime scene and arrived not even winded was Mary
Kee.

Chris Chiang was behind her, but not by much. I
was pleased, though, to see he was panting just a little.
Mary's a big old jock, hard to keep up with.

Mary and Chris weren't the first cops on the scene.
A couple of uniformed officers had raced over from
the Fifth Precinct on Elizabeth Street in answer to my
911 call. They had a little trouble getting in the building until Tan Lu-Lien shouted down the stairwell to
Beefy blocking the door and the other men milling behind him. I watched as Beefy looked up at Tan, nodded,
and escorted the two officers to the elevator, leaned in
to press the button, and sent them up.

Tan had already shouted in Cantonese that no one
was to leave the building until she said so. A certain
amount of grumbling had risen, but Beefy had walked
over, stood with his back to the door, and crossed his
arms. No one had challenged him. By now heads were
poking out of doorways and men were in the halls on
every floor. Tan didn't answer the shouts, in Cantonese,

of "What happened?" and "What's going on?" but she also didn't insult anyone by saying "Nothing."

The cops in the elevator eventually made it to the top floor. They took one look around and called for a detective, the ME, and a Crime Scene team. I'd gently herded Mel Wu and Tan Lu-Lien out into the hall, and Bill had remained just inside the open door on the off chance that whoever killed Chang was still in the apartment and might make a run for the fire escape. Since the lattice was swinging free and the fire escape window was open, it was likely that run had already been made, but fortune favors the prepared mind. Now that the cops were here, one of them shooed Bill into the hall and took his place. The other stayed with us, throwing around suspicious glares until Mary and Chris arrived, when at Mary's instructions he went back down to help Beefy guard the door. That would not be the beginning of a beautiful friendship, I suspected.

Mary threw around a few suspicious glares herself. As she and Chris stepped into the apartment, she said she'd be speaking to each of us and not to leave. Mel and Bill and I stood near the door, Mel presumably because she didn't know quite what to do and was taking her lead from us, Bill and I in case there was anything to see or overhear. Tan started to pace the U-shaped hallway.

When Tan had made it to the hallway's farthest reaches I whispered to Mel, "Who *is* she?"

"Lu-Lien? She's—the traditional title for the position she holds in the tong is White Paper Fan. The person who gives financial and business advice to the tong leader."

"She's the tong CFO?"

"I guess you'd say that. When he first came to New

York and took over, Uncle Meng handled the money himself. I think that was the reason he let her in in the first place, even though she was a woman. He couldn't keep doing everything, but he didn't know which of the tong soldiers he could trust with the money."

"Sounds like he was watching his back all the time," Bill said.

"I don't think it was that bad. Certainly not after a few years. But when Tan came—she's also from Hong Kong, though she wasn't with the Li Min Jin there— Uncle Meng was hugely relieved to have the help. I think he also liked the idea of someone who'd owe her entire position to him."

"How did the tong members feel about that?" I asked.

"I imagine there was a lot of resentment, until they all started making money. Apparently she's quite a financial whiz. She straightened out whatever residual messes remained and began investing. It was her idea to incorporate the Li Min Jin as a nonprofit. For years now she's been Uncle Meng's third in command. Now with him and Mr. Chang gone…" Mel trailed off, maybe thinking again about what we'd seen inside the door. Her silence was just as well. Tan's pacing had swung her around near us. She passed us with a scowl and kept on going. I wondered if the scowl was for a reason or was just her resting face.

A ruckus downstairs made us all peer over the railing. Ironman Ma was at the door, causing a standoff between the cop and Beefy about whether he could come in. "Let him in!" Tan called in Cantonese, but the cop suddenly didn't speak the language—or English either, when she tried that. As things got heated, I suggested to the cop in the hall with us that Mary would want to handle this. He hesitated, then opened the door.

"Mary?" I said. "Ironman Ma's downstairs. He wants in, but the cop won't let him."

Mary straightened up from where she'd been bending over the body, gave me a look, came out, and yelled down the stairwell to the cop to let Ironman in and bring him up. She gave me the same look again as she went back in.

"What?" I muttered, but not loud enough for her to hear. Mary's work focus is like her athletic focus. She doesn't take disruption well.

Ironman Ma didn't go near the elevator but came charging up the stairs, leaving his cop escort in the dust. The cop at Big Brother Choi's door stepped in front of him to stop him from entering the apartment. "Ma!" called Tan Lu-Lien, waving him over. Passing Bill and me without a glance, he stalked over to her at the end of the hallway. They spoke together in urgent, whispered Cantonese.

Two Asian officers I didn't know appeared at the front door downstairs. I assumed Mary had called for them. Chris Chiang came out of the apartment, winked at me, and trotted down. I peered over the railing to see him and the officers set about canvassing the men in the building. Chris started with Beefy himself.

With Tan and Ironman at the end of the hall, I took the opportunity to ask Mel, "How are you doing?" She was pale, but calm.

"All right, I guess." She shook her head. "Except for funerals, I've never seen anyone dead before. Especially not…"

"I know. Sit down. Don't think about it."

She gave a shaky smile and remained standing. "I'm not sure what else to think about."

"Well, think about this. Was the room—except for the body—more or less as you expected?"

The elevator rattled up again, disgorging a Tyvek-suited trio: the ME and two techs carrying crime scene gear. It creaked back down to pick up some more. Wise of them not to all try to ride up at once.

Mel nodded. "The best light is in that room, so it was Uncle Meng's study. Those paintings on the wall, he did them. My sister and I used to watch him paint. We'd sit and have tea and sweets at that low table—" She put her hand to her mouth. Not the distraction I'd been going for.

Bill picked up the ball. "How about the rest of the room? Did you see anything obviously wrong, anything out of place or missing?"

"Well, isn't that interesting," came another voice. "I was about to ask that myself." Mary stood at the open red door. "Ms. Wu, if you'll come with me, please." Looking down the hall, she raised her voice. "Ms. Tan, you'll be next. And then you, Mr. Ma. You two"—she pointed at me and Bill—"don't leave."

As if. Mary stepped aside so Mel could enter Big Brother Choi's living quarters. She closed the door behind them.

Ironman Ma remained at the end of the hall, leaning over the stairwell, hands gripping the railing. Tan Lu-Lien resumed her pacing. When she swung around near us I asked in Cantonese, "Big Sister Tan, are you all right?" Under other circumstances, because she was older than I, the proper respectful title might have been "Auntie," but that seemed a little weird here.

Tan wasn't crazy about "Big Sister," either, or maybe she just wasn't crazy about me. She snapped a hard look and paced on.

Under the beady eye of the uniformed cop, Bill and I stayed silent. After maybe ten minutes, Mary opened the door, let Mel out, and gestured Tan in. For some reason that got me another evil look from Tan before she vanished inside.

"That must have been hard," I said to Mel after the door had closed. "Are you okay?"

She nodded. "The detective wanted to know why we were here. She seemed surprised when I told her I own the building now."

"Everyone in Chinatown is going to be surprised. Not everyone is going to be happy."

She smiled wanly. "Some people outside Chinatown may not be so happy, either."

"Jackson Ting."

"For one. God, I wish I knew what Mr. Chang had wanted to tell me."

"Did you tell the detective he'd called you?"

"Yes. She was very interested. She asked the obvious question, whether I thought that had anything to do with his death. Could he have been killed to keep him from telling me whatever it was. But I have no way of knowing. She said if anything occurred to me or I find out anything, to let her know." Mel took a deep breath. "Listen, they said I could leave, and I think I will. I took a quick look around because the detective asked me to, and she asked if I'd come back and look more thoroughly after the forensics people are done, but that might be a while and…" She trailed off, then started again. "I'm sorry I got you two into this."

"It's certainly not your fault. Call me later, okay?"

"Yes, I will." Mel turned, squared her shoulders, and started down the stairs. As she made her way along each hall to the next flight, her unhurried steps and her calm look projected a composure I was sure she didn't feel.

After another minute or so Mary opened the apartment door. Scowling still, Tan Lu-Lien brushed past us and headed downstairs.

"Mr. Ma!" Mary called. Ironman straightened, set his jaw, and strode over. When he reached us, though, he stopped.

With tilted head he said, "Lydia? Lydia Chin? Is that you? What are you doing here?" He grinned an endearing lopsided grin. I found myself smiling back.

"Hi, Ironman. Yes, it's me. This is my partner, Bill Smith. We came up here with Choi Meng's niece."

"Choi Meng's niece? I thought I saw her. Did she leave? Poor kid, this must be hard on her. Bill, pleased to meet you. Edison Ma, but everyone calls me Ironman." He turned up his palms as though embarrassed at the nickname. I was willing to bet he was anything but. He said, "Lydia, you look great. How long has it been?"

Mary, still standing in the open doorway, snapped, "Mr. Ma? Can you and Lydia have this reunion later? I have a dead man here."

Ironman's face hardened in a flash. He stepped forward and followed Mary in.

NINE

A FEW MINUTES later the door opened and Ironman Ma came out. Before he could say anything Mary said, "Okay, you two. Inside."

Ironman gave me a glance and mouthed *I'll call you.* I nodded and walked in past Mary, followed by Bill.

"You're not going to interview us individually to see if our stories match?" I said.

"If you haven't gotten them straight by now you're not the gumshoes I thought you were. Come through here. Don't touch anything. Crime Scene hasn't done the bedroom yet."

"What killed him?" I asked as she led us past the body, now covered, the ME packing up his tools, and the techs dusting, measuring, and photographing. We entered the bedroom on the left.

"A kitchen knife," she said.

The bedroom was large, taking up the whole wing of the floor on the west side. It was furnished with a carved-screen platform bed, some handsome wardrobes and cabinets, and a thick carpet figured with clouds and dragons. Poems in calligraphy and scroll paintings of herons and frogs, pine trees, and paths through misty mountains hung on the red walls. At the room's far end Big Brother Choi had set up his family altar with candles, incense, ancestor tablets, a bowl of oranges, and a small Buddha statue.

A table beside the bed held three silver-framed photos. In one, a young man stood formally beside a seated young woman, both of them looking serious in Qing robes. A marriage photo? Another photo showed the same couple in the 1950s. Their pose was similar but more relaxed, and in front of the woman stood two small children. Everyone was now dressed in the latest fifties fashions. The remaining photo was of a different young woman, beautiful and smiling.

"Who are these?" I asked Mary.

Mary smirked. "There are advantages to being an actual cop. I get to ask the questions first. Mel Wu told me." She pointed. "Big Brother Choi's parents. Them again, with Choi and his sister—Mel Wu's mother. This one here is Choi's wife."

I looked at that photo. It looked like it had been taken around the same time as the one on her grave.

"Mel Wu told me he was devoted to her," Mary said. "Why are you two here?"

"Didn't Mel Wu tell you that, too?"

"Don't start."

"We were supposed to be a cross between moral support and bodyguards," Bill said, stepping in.

"Go on."

"She'd asked Mr. Gao if he thought it would be okay for her to come up here alone, and he said it would be better if she didn't."

"Grandfather Gao?" Mary asked.

I nodded. "Big Brother Choi told her years ago she could trust him."

"Quite the endorsement, considering the source. Why did she want to come up here?"

"She owns the building now, plus she's executor of the estate. And Chang had something he wanted to tell her, something he said Big Brother Choi wanted her to know. Come on, I know she told you all that."

"And I know *you* know I'm trying to make sure she told you and me the same things and also that you'll tell me the truth about what she told you so stop screwing around. Bill, what are you grinning at?"

"Female bonding," Bill said. "Like everything female—deadlier than the male."

Mary and I exchanged an eye roll.

"Listen," I said. "Of course we'd tell you anything we knew—you know that, too. Everything seemed fine until we got up here. Tan was surprised not to find Chang in the hall, and more surprised that Mel had the keys. We backed out again as soon as we saw the body."

"You believe Tan?"

"Believe what? That she was surprised? I guess it's possible she knew Chang was up here dead and wanted witnesses to finding the body. She made a great little strangled noise, but you can fake that. But I really don't think she knew Mel had keys. Her face—she really looked surprised, and also angry. Like Mel had no right."

"Bill?"

"I have to agree. She may have known Chang was dead, but if she didn't know Mel had keys, how was she intending to get in so we could all find the body together?"

"Unless she had keys of her own, and Mel just didn't give her a chance to take them out," I said.

"I asked her," said Mary. "She says she doesn't. Chang was the only one who did."

"I don't suppose Tan was willing to turn out her pockets for you, without a warrant."

"Actually, she did. Which, if you ask me, for a tong

member is even more suspicious than if she'd refused. You didn't see her take anything from her pocket and hide it under a potted plant in the hall or anything, did you?"

"Nope."

She looked at Bill, who shook his head.

"But seriously," I said, "there's an elephant in the room here. Tan's a woman. Mel says she's number three in the tong. Did you know about her?"

"Like I said. There are advantages to being an actual cop."

"Why didn't you ever tell me? Wait, I know—I never asked. Really? For Pete's sake!"

Mary relented. "I haven't known very long. Chris and I asked one of the Organized Crime guys to come to the funeral to identify people for us. I was surprised about her, too."

"That's the guy you were with?"

"Jon Cobb. He knows all the tong players, and he's fluent in the Romanian and Russian mobs, too. So besides the body, did you two notice anything else you feel like withholding but you're going to tell me?"

Bill said, "Only one of the locks was locked."

"Sorry?"

"Not that I was going to withhold it. But I just went over it in my head while you guys were arguing. Mel had to turn the top lock back again. So it must have been open when she put the key in it."

Mary looked at me. "Should we tell him we weren't arguing?"

"I kind of was."

Ignoring me, she said to Bill, "That's interesting. The top's a deadbolt, but the bottom has both a deadbolt and a latch."

"If it was only latched," Bill said, "and the top was unlocked, that means maybe the killer left the apartment through the door, not necessarily through the fire escape window. The door would have latched behind him."

"I wonder if Mel Wu remembers about the bottom lock, whether it was on the bolt?" Mary took out her phone and made a voice memo to ask. "You guys, did anything seem strange to you when you first came in the building? Out of place?"

I said, "Besides that we were walking into Li Min Jin HQ? *We* were seriously out of place. No one came sneaking furtively down the staircase or went slinking through the halls, if that's what you mean. Tan didn't like us. That might not be strange, though. Is she in charge now?"

"It seems so, temporarily. There'll be a selection process for a new leader."

"Votes?" Bill asked. "Or knives and guns?"

"Our dead guy here was a heavy favorite," Mary said. "So maybe that answers that question."

"Did Big Brother Choi anoint him?" I asked.

"Choi never named a successor. But Chang was his top lieutenant."

"He was a heavy favorite, but it wasn't unanimous? So there's another faction? Who's the underdog? Is it Tan? That would give her a lovely motive."

"I don't know which side Tan's on. As number three, she may have been loyal to number two—Chang—or she may have reported directly to Choi. Or God knows what. It's a tong. I need to sit down with Organized Crime again."

"Speaking of them, who was the third guy at the end of the coffin at the funeral? The Scroogey one?"

"Loo Hu-Li. Started with the Black Shadows as a

kid, moved up into the tong, has been a member all his life. Longer, actually, than anyone else, even Choi Meng. He was here when Choi got here. Chang there"—she thumbed at the body in the other room—"he'd been a Ma Tou soldier and came in after the merger. As Chang rose he eventually pushed Loo back in the line, and then when Tan turned out to be so valuable, Loo got pushed back again. That can't leave too good a taste in your mouth."

"So he's been grinding his teeth all this time," I said, continuing the dental metaphor. "And now with Choi gone, he sees a chance to take over the tong? So he does Chang in? Does that mean Tan's in danger?"

"I don't know what it means. Though in a cage match between Loo and Tan, the smart money would be on her."

"But you're considering him a suspect?"

"Be serious. Every member of this tong, plus everyone in this building, plus everyone who might have wanted to lift something from this apartment and happened to find Chang here, plus everyone in Chinatown and his mother, and probably even *your* mother, are suspects."

"My mother never would have left such a mess on the good furniture."

Mary laughed. "Okay, you guys can go. If you think of anything else—"

"You'll be the first."

"O'Neill," Mary said to a uniformed cop as we walked back through the apartment, "take these two down in the elevator."

"I don't think so, thanks," I said. "We'll walk."

Mary shut the apartment door behind us. As Bill

and I headed to the staircase, he said, "You don't trust that elevator?"

"I bet it hasn't been inspected since the day it was installed. Besides, we can snoop better this way."

We did snoop, but it didn't pay off much. The doors to a couple of the bedrooms were open. They were clean, small—probably illegally subdivided from earlier illegal subdivisions—and looked like what you'd find in a hostel: vinyl floors, single beds, a few shelves, bedside tables. Some seemed occupied, some not. On one end of the U-shaped hall was a communal bathroom. The two lower floors held common rooms with the remains of interrupted card and mah-jongg games on the tables. Small groups of men sat smoking and talking, while Chris Chiang and the two Asian uniforms could be seen in a room interviewing them one by one. No one was whiling away the hours playing games right now. Chang Yao-Zu, the heir apparent, had been murdered.

TEN

"WHERE TO?" Bill asked when we hit the crowded midday street.

"I want to go home and change. Not that I'm steeped in Chang's blood, but I feel...not quite clean. Then I might as well go do paperwork. I'll let you know when Mel calls, but I have a feeling now that she's been there and they all know who she is—and she's going to go back again with Mary—that nothing that happens in the Li Min Jin building might need us anymore."

"Too bad, right?"

"Why, you nosy guy. But yeah," I agreed. "Too bad."

We kissed goodbye on the corner. Bill headed home and I did too. As I walked through Columbus Park, I saw the tall gangster I'd seen at the funeral, the one I didn't know, sitting on a bench sipping coffee. His eyes seemed fixed on the Li Min Jin building. *Wondering what's going to happen with that prime piece of property, pal?* I thought. *Welcome to the party.*

When I got home my mother was out playing mahjongg, which was just as well. She would have asked how my morning had gone, and I would've had to either tell her or lie. Neither was an appealing prospect. I showered and put on a sweatshirt and jeans. Leaving the apartment, I dropped off the clothes I'd been wearing at the dry cleaner. I popped into the bakery, bought half a dozen egg tarts, and headed along Canal to my office, where I found out the feeling I'd told Bill about was wrong.

My office is a room-plus-bathroom I sublet across the hall from a street-front travel agency. Chinese people don't like to ask for help, so going to a private investigator is hard enough. Having to do it in a way where anyone—say, your mother-in-law, who happens to be strolling down the sidewalk—can see that you can't handle your own problems is a nonstarter.

So my name's on the bell as "Lydia Chin" without the "Investigations." When you come in, the first door in the hallway is Golden Adventure, and anyone on the street who sees you will think you're considering a trip to the homeland. The women at Golden Adventure will direct you to me. If I'm not in, they'll let you sit and wait for me. If you don't have my phone number, they'll give it to you. For these services, besides the monthly rent, I bring them sweets. Today it was egg tarts.

"Hi, guys," I said, sticking my head in the door. I lifted the box. "Fay Da's best."

"Thanks," said Gina, at the closest desk. She nodded at the guest chairs. I turned to see Natalie Wu Harris, Mel's sister, tapping her phone screen. When she saw me, she put the phone away and stood.

"I hope it's okay," she said, running a hand through her glossy hair, worn loose. "That I'm here."

"Of course it is." I probably didn't quite hide my surprise. "Is everything all right? Did Mel tell you what happened?"

"Yes. Can we talk?"

"Come with me." I gave Gina the bakery box, took Natalie across the hall, unlocked my office door, and ushered her in.

My office doesn't have the street-window cheer of Golden Adventure. Its one window opens on the air shaft, and if I weren't renting the place from them, they'd probably use it for a storeroom. I do try to keep it well lighted and welcoming—potted plants, colorful framed prints—but I could see Natalie's face fall as she entered. Well, she should talk to Bill. He's never had an office, and when we're working separate cases, he operates out of a bar.

"Would you like tea?" I asked, reaching for the kettle.

"No thanks." She sat in my brightly upholstered guest chair and crossed one leg over the other. She wore tapered black slacks, a rust-colored sweater, and a jacket with an interesting asymmetrical cut—some new designer I didn't recognize. And beautiful spectator brogues.

I left the kettle and sat behind my desk. Natalie just looked at me and didn't speak. I figured maybe I should prime the pump.

"Your family has the best footwear," I said.

"I broke my foot in a bike accident when I was fifteen. Wearing heels was agony after that."

Nothing more, just a stare that was almost challenging. I tried again. "I wasn't expecting anyone. I went home and changed."

She softened a little. "I'd have thrown my clothes away."

"Mel told you what happened?"

"She said there was a lot of blood."

"He'd been stabbed."

She looked away and nodded. "He was a nice man. I know he was a gangster, but I didn't know it when we were children, and he was always nice to us."

"I'm sorry." I waited.

After a few moments she said, "I was going to come see you anyway. Before Mel called me about Mr. Chang. This may not be a great time, and I don't know if Mr. Chang's death is going to make this harder or easier. But I need you to persuade Mel to sell the building to Jackson Ting."

ELEVEN

"YOU DON'T SEEM SURPRISED," Natalie Wu said.

"That you think differently from your sister about your uncle's bequest? I'm not. That happens a lot in families. But I'm not sure why you've come to me."

"I don't know anyone else who knows much about Chinatown. Mel likes you. I want you to convince her it would be a good thing for her to sell." Now her look turned challenging again.

"I don't think it would be a good thing," I said. "For Chinatown. I have a feeling you don't particularly, either. Why do you want me to do this? I know there's a lot of money involved—"

"It's not the money."

"Then what?"

She bit her lip. It could have been reluctance to tell her story. Or irritation at my asking for it. I stood and plugged the kettle in after all.

"Jackson Ting came to see me," she said. "He really wants that building."

I looked over from where I was spooning tea into the pot, but I didn't say anything.

"We went to school together. Jackson and I. Mel, too. Prep school. In Valhalla."

"Mel told me." I wondered how much longer Natalie intended to beat around the bush. Since my planned afternoon activity had been paperwork, though, I was disposed to listen for a while. "If it's about the building," I asked, "why didn't he go to Mel?"

"They don't like each other. She wouldn't care about what he wants."

"But you do?"

She clammed up again. It took until the kettle boiled, the tea—Iron Buddha; I thought it might help—was finished steeping, and I'd poured it into my best porcelain guest mugs and handed her one before she spoke.

"I guess you'd call it blackmail, what he's doing." She said that with a nonchalance that I was pretty sure she wasn't feeling.

"Jackson Ting is blackmailing you?"

She sipped her tea. "To get the building. For the Phoenix Towers project."

"I see. And…?"

"And nothing. That's all."

"No, of course it's not all." I put my mug down. "You're going to have to tell me what he has on you if you want me to be able to help you."

"He doesn't have anything. And all the help I want is for you to get Mel to sell him the building."

"It's hard to blackmail somebody over nothing."

"Not if you lie."

"Ting is lying? What about?"

She took a sip of tea, then another. "He's going to say Matty is his son."

Thank you, Iron Buddha. "Is he?"

"No!"

"Are you completely sure?"

"Come on. You think I had an affair with Jackson?"

"It's usually what's behind that sort of claim."

"I—" Another sip. "Okay, look, Jackson and I did date for a while. In high school, and then a little after.

It gave Mel fits. She couldn't stand him. But that was over long before I started seeing Paul. Jackson's lying."

"Then what's the problem?"

"Are you serious? He's going to do it publicly, he says so. His PR person will call the media, send out goddamn press releases. He'll say his son's being raised in a tong family. For God's sake! Paul's parents hate the idea that he married a Chinese girl, and they don't even know anything about Uncle Meng. Wait until they find that out."

"So the problem isn't that Jackson really is Matty's dad?"

"I told you, no! The problem is it'll be all over the news! Stuff like this makes great clickbait. Jackson says he's going to get a court order to make Matty take a DNA test."

"But the results—"

"Forget the results! Paul's parents will still think Jackson's making the claim because we were screwing around. With one of my own, you see. They've always thought I was only ever after Paul's money. Jesus. I didn't even know he *had* money until we were engaged!" She drank more tea. If it had cooled, she could have warmed it with the steam coming out of her ears. "And will Paul believe me, do you think? He'll have to believe the DNA, but that Jackson and I were over long ago? Yes, he'll believe that—ninety-nine point nine percent. But he'll always have that tiny doubt. It'll grow. It'll get in the way of everything. There's no way I can ever prove it's not true."

She gave me a hard stare as though I'd contradicted her. Or as though it were my fault. Or as though even if it weren't my fault to begin with, if I didn't fix it that would make it my fault now.

I said, "And this is unless Mel sells him the Li Min Jin building?"

"If she does he'll leave me alone."

"Have you talked to her about it?"

"Are you insane? She'd march right into his office and shoot him."

"Literally?"

"No. No, obviously not literally! But she'd be furious. She's always trying to protect me."

"Whether you need it or not, huh?"

"Damn right."

I sipped my own tea. Time to lower the temperature in here a little bit. "I have four older brothers," I said. "Put together they might not be a match for Mel, but from the day I was born they considered me their responsibility. By the time I started dating, my father had died, so every guy I went out with had to pass a four-brother smell test."

She looked up. "Did they?"

"Not a single one. That's how I developed the next-level sneaking-around skills so useful in my current career."

That got me a small smile. "I should come work for you. I have those skills, too. Plus I used to work security at House of Yes."

"You were a bouncer?"

"I was the hard-ass dame in the office the bouncers brought the pickpockets and pushers to, to cool off while they waited for the cops. I smoked Virginia Slims and covered 'em so the bouncers could get back to the floor."

"Covered them?"

"With my little silver revolver. Plus," she said, "they were handcuffed to the chair. Not that I don't know how to use the gun. Believe me, I can take care of myself."

Was that a threat to use the gun on Jackson if I didn't come through? "I'm sure you can," I said. "Those sneaking-around skills—that's what you used back when you were dating Jackson? To hide your relationship?"

"God, no. That was half the point."

"What was?"

She looked me right in the eyes. "Mel was beautiful and smart and athletic. She knew what she wanted, went after it, and got it. I was the other Wu girl. It felt like everywhere I went, Mel was there first, like everything in my life was secondhand. Do you know why she wears flats?"

The switch in subject perplexed me. "She said she has gymnast feet and she can't wear heels."

"Half true. I told you I broke my foot. When the cast came off I tried to go back to heels—it's what the Winter Prep girls wore—but I couldn't. Mel suddenly decided her feet hurt from gymnastics and she had to wear flats. If Mel Wu did it, it was cool, and the next thing you know all the girls are wearing them. So there I was, cool again, but it had nothing to do with me.

"Then out of nowhere Jackson asked me out. He was in her class, and he asked me, not her. He was a spoiled little shit, but he was hot and rich, and every girl in school was jealous."

"Even Mel?"

"No, like I said, she didn't like him. She didn't like me dating him. That was almost as good."

Families. I thought about my brother Tim, and Bill.

"Does she like Paul?" I asked.

Natalie shrugged. "Paul, sure. But when his family tried to talk him out of marrying me, that pissed her off. She said I should think about whether I wanted to be stuck with them forever."

"Why were they against it?"

"A Chinese chick with a rep?"

"You had a rep?"

"I was never exactly Miss Priss. After high school I went to FIT. We all dyed our hair pink. Smoked dope, went clubbing, that kind of stuff. You know."

I did know, but I wasn't sure I was happy with Natalie assuming I knew. "And Paul?"

"We met at CBGB when I was working and he was out with friends. He came with them to the club on a dare, for God's sake. Not his kind of place, you can imagine. So you can guess. He fell hard for me even though he said my kind of life, my world, made him nervous. Me, I'd dated other guys before him who couldn't keep up. It was amusing, but it never lasted long. With Paul it was different. I suddenly wanted to stop. Leave the craziness. I wanted to live in *his* world. Get married, have a family, be a soccer mom. SUV, house in the suburbs, someone to cook for. Someone who needed me, for a change."

"But his folks were against it."

"Yeah, them. He had to put his foot down." She smiled. "I don't know if you noticed when you were looking at footwear, but he has pretty big feet."

"So after he did that, it was okay?"

She drank more tea before she answered. "It's never been okay. After we were married, we had a hard time getting pregnant, and they were leaning on him that whole time."

"Leaning on him?"

"To ditch me. 'Don't worry, everyone makes mistakes, you can still find yourself a nice blond girl who'll give us White grandchildren.'"

"They said that?"

"I don't know what they said. He wouldn't tell me, and he told them to bug off, but they kept at it. Until we finally gave them a grandson. Matty's only half White, but they're deigning to put up with it."

"And a granddaughter."

"Poor Emily. She's Cinderella as far as they're concerned. Honestly, they're not nice people. They wouldn't mind even now if Paul and I split and he married the nice blond girl. I would, though. I would mind." Her eyes hardened. "I finally found what I want, and I'm not going to let Jackson Ting take it away from me."

I believed her. "And you can't tell Mel?"

"If Mel blows up at Jackson, it'll only make him madder. That would make *her* madder. It'll turn into a war between the two of them. He might go public just to piss her off. It won't be about me or even the building anymore." Natalie took a breath. "It won't help anything if she knows. No one can know. He said not to tell anyone. He can't even know I told you." She stared at me until I nodded. "All my life Mel has been saving my ass. I just need her to do it one more time. I just need her to sell Jackson the goddamn building."

I said nothing. Natalie must have taken my silence for reluctance, which it was, because she said, "Look, I know it wasn't what Uncle Meng wanted, but really, a run-down building full of gangsters—why would Mel

S.J. ROZAN   73

even want to be stuck with that? And where someone was just murdered? Why would she want that?"

It wasn't a real question, so I didn't quote Mel's character-of-Chinatown reasoning or her anti-gentrification analysis to Natalie. I also didn't tell her that this neighborhood was my home, and Mel being willing to be stuck with that building was the key to its survival.

"And it has to be soon," Natalie said.

"Why?"

"There's some kind of deadline at the end of this month. The other site owners can pull out. If he gets the building after that, he'd have to corral them all again, and even if he can, it would cost a fortune."

"More money than he has?"

"This is real estate. The money's not his. He says it would be more money than his investors are willing to pay. So. Can you get my sister to sell?" Natalie asked. "Can you do that?"

TWELVE

I SAT THINKING for a while after Natalie left. Then I called Bill, waved goodbye to my paperwork, and made my way to Shorty's Bar. Going to Shorty's was pretty much the same as going to Bill's. He lives two floors above it.

The bright sunshine didn't hide the chill in the air. The trees, what few there were between Laight Street and my office, glowed in red, rust, and gold. When I pushed through Shorty's door I slid my sunglasses up into my hair, looked around, and spotted Bill at the bar.

"Hey," he said. "Long time. Want lunch?"

"How about just some guacamole?"

"You got it, Lydia," Shorty said from behind the bar. "You want a beer?"

"In yer dreams."

I've been coming here since Bill and I met. Shorty knows I hardly ever drink. Can't fault him for trying, though. It's a bar.

Bill swung down off his barstool, and we took a booth against the wall, under black-and-white photos of New York baseball heroes through the years. The bar's two TVs were both tuned to the same sports channel, and the midday guys—mostly cops unwinding from the graveyard shift or on their day off—drank beer and watched three men in suits debating the meaning of charts full of stats. Every now and then the screen would switch to a shot of the Yankee Stadium grounds crew readying the emerald grass for a playoff game. Then would come a car commercial.

"When does the game start?" I asked Bill.

He checked his watch. "A little less than an hour."

"I promise I'll be gone by then."

"You don't have to leave. I'll just ignore you."

Ella, the cabaret singer who moonlighted as Shorty's daytime waitress—maybe that's sunlighted—brought over chips, guacamole, and a seltzer I hadn't ordered but Shorty knew I wanted. "Your burger's coming right up, hon," she said to Bill.

We both thanked her and got down to business. I told Bill what Natalie had said, and what she wanted.

"You think it's true?" he asked.

"Which part?"

"Let's start with, Ting says the kid's his. They looked mixed-race to me, those kids."

"Natalie says the kids are Paul's and the DNA would prove it. But she also says that's not the point. People will talk. Natalie's afraid of her in-laws. She says they hate her. Jackson's going to play the rescuing-my-innocent-son-from-a-tong-family card. Oh, he's not my son? Well, given how you and I were carrying on, he could've been. And by the way, it's still a tong family."

Ella came back with Bill's burger. "You want another?" She pointed a jewel-studded crimson nail at his half-finished beer.

"Soon, but not yet."

"Okay, hon. You just let me know." Ella flashed a smile and sashayed away, dreads swinging.

Bill turned to me. "Is she flirting with me?"

"She's being your wing woman." I scooped a chip

through the guacamole. "She's trying to help you out by making it seem to me like you're desirable to other women, so I'll step up my game."

"Is it working?"

"No."

"Okay," Bill said, doctoring his burger. "What about the part that says if Ting gets the building, he'll go away?"

"That's a bigger problem. When do blackmailers ever go away? What if he needs more financing for some other project, or something? I don't know what else he might want from the Wu sisters, but if there ever is anything and this works this time, he'll know how to get it."

Bill put the top bun back on his burger and took a bite.

"Also," he eventually said, "and I say this at the risk of having a bowl of chips dumped on my head, you have a personal stake in this. What some might even see as a conflict of interest."

"You mean, it would be completely hypocritical of me to persuade client A to do something client B wanted if client A didn't want to do it in the first place and if furthermore I believed that thing could actually destroy an entire neighborhood which just happens to be my hometown?"

"That's it in a nutshell, yes."

"You're right, and there's no way I'll do it. In fact, if Mel were leaning toward selling the building, I'd try to persuade her the other way. But poor Natalie. Jackson Ting could seriously mess up her life."

I munched on chips and guacamole, thinking, while Bill ate his burger and, I hoped, thought too. The TV sets showed the stadium stands starting to fill. The camera split-screened to the bullpens, where the pitchers were warming up. I turned back to Bill when he said, "At the root of every great fortune is a great crime."

"Sorry?"

"Balzac." He wiped his hands on a napkin. "The original quote is longer, something like, 'The secret of a great success for which you can't account is a crime that's never been discovered.'"

"Cynical, but probably correct."

"Definitely correct. Life is full of little moments every day when you decide whether to do something you know is wrong. Do you leave the car at a hydrant for a few minutes? You weigh the pros and cons. Pro, you can do your business fast. Con, your car could get towed. Plus you could interfere with firefighters. How important is your business? How likely is the risk? You weigh all that and decide whether to go ahead."

"What are you saying?"

"Those are little moments. People aiming higher than their dry cleaning have the same moments, but bigger. Do I risk insider trading on the info I just got? Do I keep two sets of books? Bribe a congressman? Blackmail someone?"

I finished my seltzer. "You're suggesting we find out what's behind Jackson Ting's fortune."

"Blackmailers don't go away. But it can be possible to play them to a stalemate."

"You're a genius." I stood to leave. "We'll talk tonight. Enjoy the game."

Ella winked as I walked out the door.

THIRTEEN

I WENT BACK to Chinatown and sat on a bench in Columbus Park, near where the old men and women were singing folk songs to the accompaniment of an erhu, a bamboo flute, an accordion, and a banjo. Adaptable, the Chinese people. I took out my phone and made a call.

"Hey, cousin! What's buzzin'?" From the echo, I could tell Linus Wong had me on speakerphone.

"Hi, Linus. Everything is finus," I answered.

"Seriously?"

"I've been saving that one up."

"Throw it back. Hey, I hear Uncle Tim made partner, the old stiff. Your mom called my mom." Tim, of course, was Linus's cousin, as I was, not his uncle. "Uncle" had more to do with "the old stiff" than with their actual relationship.

"She called everyone in Chinatown, so she had to start on the outer boroughs."

"Well, tell him congrats for me."

"Thanks, I will."

A woman's voice asked, "Hey, is that Lydia?"

"Yes. Hi, Trella," I said to Linus's girlfriend and partner. "How are you?"

"Everything's good. Hey, Woof, it's Lydia."

I heard the thump of a tail. I could picture the big yellow dog curled up on the rug in the converted garage behind Linus's parents' house in Queens. That garage was the home of the business Linus and Trella ran:

Wong Security, a cyber-defense firm whose slogan was 'Protecting People Like You from People Like Us.'

I said, "Hi, Woof. Arf arf arf. Listen, you have time for a job?"

"You asking Woof?" said Linus.

"Is he in charge of scheduling now?"

"Only walks and biscuits. What do you need? And is it illegal?"

"No."

"Oh. Well, let's do it anyway, what do you say, Trell?"

"Maybe the illegal part will come later," Trella said hopefully.

"Not if I can help it," I told them. "I just need to know some things about a guy named Jackson Ting."

"Jackson Ting?" Linus asked. "Who's that?"

"He's a real estate developer, right?" Trella said. Trella's a little more closely tied to the real world than my brainy but batty cousin.

"Right. He wants to put a twenty-story tower at the corner of Bayard and Mott."

"Oh, wow," said Linus. "Bet that gets Auntie Yong-Yun's cheongsam in a twist."

His Auntie Yong-Yun, of course, is my mother. "A lot of people are unhappy about it."

"And so you want to see if this guy—Ting?—has skeletons in his closet. So you can blackmail him and stop him."

"Skeletons, yes. Blackmail, no."

"Right," Linus agreed promptly. "Because that would be illegal."

"Exactly."

"Uh-huh. All right then. Trell, let's get out the shovels and start digging."

"*All* I want from you"—I emphasized the "all"—"is

to locate his bank accounts and that sort of thing. Not rifle through them, just find them. You have my password to the databases." PI's have access to databases not available to civilians, and Linus and Trella have access to skills not available to me. I could do this, but it would be much faster and probably more complete if they did. "And you will only do what's legal, do we understand each other? Because for one thing, I don't want you guys to end up behind bars, and for another thing, the passwords are mine, so I'd end up there with you."

"What if we accidentally find something juicy? Porn, drugs, arms deals, you know?"

"Follow it until just before you start breaking the law. *Before*. Okay?"

"You're no fun."

"And while you're doing that, run the same checks on my clients. Melanie Wu, Chinese name Wu Mao-Li, and her sister Natalie Wu, married name Harris, Chinese name I have no idea. And Natalie's husband, Paul Harris." I gave them Mel's and Nat's addresses.

"Your clients?" said Linus. "Isn't that, I don't know, disloyal or something?"

"You don't run checks on your clients?" Actually, I'd already run a cursory search on Mel when she'd hired me, but Linus can dig deeper and I wanted Natalie checked out, so he might as well do them both.

"Sure we do," he said, "but we're sort of in the double-cross business. We never want to find out we got hired to hide stuff from people who had a legit right to see it."

"For a guy who's disappointed when I say don't do anything illegal, you have an interesting moral code."

"Legal and legit are totally different concepts. Isn't that right, Trella?"

Trella said, "I just work here."

"Okay, guys. Thanks, and let me know when you have something. Give my love to your folks, Linus. Bye, Woof. Talk later."

Next I dropped into the dojo. No classes were scheduled, but I needed a workout to clear my head. The place was empty when I arrived except for one of the other senior students whose cleaning day it was. He was sweeping the floor when I came in. After I suited up and helped him wash down the mats, we did form together for a while, worked the heavy bags, and finished up with some low-contact sparring. Low-contact is actually harder than full-contact, because you have to gauge the exact distance and power of each move. When we were done, we were both sweating and breathing hard, and we'd had a great time. We bowed to each other, locked the place up, and left.

At home I took another shower, but not before my mother called from the kitchen, "Your brother's coming for dinner."

I ran through the possibilities. Ted and Elliott each have wives and two kids. When they come, they swoop in here like flocks of pigeons, and my mother starts preparing days in advance. Andrew comes over pretty often because my mother's teaching his fiancé, Tony, to cook Chinese food, but he usually lets me know when they're coming because we enjoy hanging out together. That left one probable brother. I went to the stove to give my mother a kiss and take a sniff from the stewpot. "Smells great."

"I'm making ngau lam mein."

Noodles with braised brisket. One of Tim's favorites. That clinched it.

"Great. After I shower I'll set the table."

"You'll be staying home for dinner?" she said with extravagantly wide eyes. "It's a good thing I made enough beef."

"Ma. You always make enough for an army."

She grunted and turned back to her wok, pretending my attendance at dinner—and therefore on my brother—didn't matter either way.

After my shower I did set the table, then settled at my desk to do my own online investigation of Jackson Ting. Linus and Trella would be looking for the "skeletons in the closet" section on his resume. For myself, I was hoping to get a feel for the man, or at least his public persona.

From Winter Prep, where he'd met the Wu sisters, Ting had gone on to major in business at Adelphi and then to Fordham for his MBA. Both were top forty schools; neither was top ten, but both were near home and would let him keep working in his father's firm while he was at school. That had been his whole early career: working with his dad, whose firm managed, owned, and occasionally built mid-sized apartment buildings in Queens. About eight years ago, the elder Ting had retired and Jackson took over. The father died two years later, and Jackson made the jump across the river and into bigger Manhattan projects.

At some point in there he'd married a nice Chinese American girl. At least, I assumed she was nice; she sure was pretty and expensively groomed. They now had a toddler and a baby. I searched the *New York Times* archives and found their wedding in the "Vows" section.

The article gave the date they'd met: a little over three years ago. Apparently a whirlwind romance. Natalie's son, Matthew, was four. So Ting making public his claim on Matthew probably wouldn't throw a wrench into his marriage. Too bad. At least on that front there was no bluff to call.

I did a little more googling of Ting's firm and projects and of the architects and contractors whose names came up. I had a feeling, based on the scarcity of awards and what I saw of their other buildings, that the architects were B list like Ting's education. I'd ask Bill; those are the kinds of things he knows. It made sense, though. Star architects are less likely to do what the client tells them, and developers generally like "good enough," which tends to be cheaper than "great." The contractors weren't firms I'd heard of, but how many building contractors would be? Bill would know about them, too.

I keep a kettle and a stash of tea in my room at home so when I'm working here, I won't disturb my mother every time I want a cup—and, okay, so she won't distract me. I decided I needed some bracing Assam. While it was steeping, Mel Wu called.

"How are you?" I asked.

"Recovering. I'm having a little trouble getting Mr. Chang out of my mind and focusing on other things. I've known him all my life. Not well, just the way you know adults when you're a child. He was always there when we went to see Uncle Meng."

"So he must have joined the tong as a young man." The best thing to do when someone's grieving, my mother always says, is to let them talk about the person they've lost. Also, I was interested.

"He was with the other tong. The Ma Tou, one that

merged with the Li Min Jin. Long Lo—you saw his grave—he was their head. When he released his soldiers from their oaths, Uncle Meng said they were all welcome in the Li Min Jin if they wanted to join. A lot of them did. Mr. Chang had been some sort of rising star in the Ma Tou, and he became Uncle Meng's second in command a few years later." She paused. "Oh, listen to me! I guess it's strange to talk about gangsters as rising stars. You have to remember that when we were children, Nat and I, we didn't know anything about Uncle Meng's life, really."

"No, of course. Tell me about Tan Lu-Lien. Was she a tong member then?" I took the tea strainer from my mug and placed it on a saucer.

"I remember her, yes. I didn't know when I was young how strange it was that she was there."

"Your uncle seems to have been a liberal-minded man. Accepting a woman soldier, and letting a guy from another tong rise so high. Instead of favoring his own men, I mean."

"I guess," Mel said. "I always thought of Uncle Meng as old-fashioned, I suppose because whenever we saw him there'd be a lot of incense and prayers and things. And sweets, and Chinese games. He taught me Chinese chess. Xiangqi, I think? But Mom tried to protect us from knowing who he really was. She loved him, and we were his only family, so once he came to New York, he wanted to stay close, but she didn't want us involved in the tong's business. I was in high school before I even knew what a tong was. When I did find out, I tried to keep it from Natalie as long as I could."

"You've always protected her, haven't you?"

"I guess that's what comes with being the older sister.

I was the responsible one. Nat was wild. She'd sprain her ankle skateboarding with the boys down the court-house steps, I'd tape it up and swear to whatever lie she told our parents. The only thing was, I told her I'd draw the line at drugs—if she got in trouble for that, she was on her own."

"Did she?"

"No. She knew I meant it."

"I get the feeling you don't back down."

"The opposite. I dig in even deeper when I'm pushed. Not necessarily a good quality, but a useful one for a lawyer."

"Is Natalie still wild?"

"No, no. She calmed down when she met Paul. He's been really good for her. Do you have sisters? Or broth-ers?"

"Four older brothers. Two were constantly trying to protect me, one was my pal, and one was always ready to throw me under a bus."

"I'm sure that last isn't true."

"Only metaphorically. Oh, but you've met him. Tim. He was at the funeral."

"With the woman from the Chinatown Heritage So-ciety?"

"He's on the board."

"He seemed lovely."

"That's a trick he has. Mel, I have another question, if you don't think it's too personal. Why do you sup-pose Big Brother Choi never remarried? Especially if family was so important to him."

I could hear the smile in her voice. "I asked him that once, when I was about ten. It's such a sad roman-tic story. He said he loved Auntie Mei-Mei very, very much. They tried and tried to have a baby. They finally did, but the baby was small and weak and he only lived a few days. That broke Auntie Mei-Mei's heart. She rarely left the apartment after that, and she died a year later. *That* broke Uncle Meng's heart. He said he was staying single in this world so he could be with her in the next world. He said then they'd be a family forever."

"Oh, that *is* sad." *He was still a gangster, Lydia,* I told myself. *You don't need to get all sympathetic.*

"Uncle Meng, and now Mr. Chang…" Mel trailed off. "Thanks for letting me ramble on. Talking about the past, it does seem to help."

"I'm glad."

I could practically hear her square her shoulders. "I actually called for a reason, though. I'm meeting that detective at the apartment in the morning to look around. Will you come with me?"

Back to the Choi apartment? Really? Try to stop me. "I—yes, of course. But I think I should tell you that that detective, Mary Kee, is a friend of mine. We grew up together. She might get a little annoyed to see me back at her crime scene."

"Will it cause a problem between you?"

"Nothing worse than a few squinty glares. It might be pushing the envelope to bring Bill, too, though."

"That's all right if it's okay with you. I don't think I need to make any points with the tong men the way I did the first time. This is different."

"Different in what way? I mean, of course I'll be glad to go. I'm just wondering."

"The detective asked me to come back to look over the apartment more thoroughly. I'm happy to help, but she's only interested in solving the murder. As she should be, of course. But—well, maybe it's silly. It's just, until we know why Mr. Chang was killed, I can't help thinking it might have something to do with the building. Do you think I'm off base?"

"Not at all. Though it could just be an internal tong thing, for the leadership."

"It could. But he had something to tell me, from Uncle Meng. Just me, not me and Nat. That says to me it was probably about the building, which is my problem, not hers."

I glanced at the Phoenix Towers brochure open on my laptop screen. *Not Nat's problem? If you only knew.*

"Also," Mel said, "on a purely emotional level, I admit I don't relish the thought of walking into that apartment alone."

"Mary—Detective Kee—will be with you." *What are you doing, Lydia, trying to talk her out of it?* "But that's not the same, I get it."

"So you'll come?"

"Of course. Tell me what time and I'll meet you."

After we hung up I sipped at my tea, checked the sports news online, and called Bill. "Game still on?"

"Would I be answering the phone?"

"Would I be calling?"

"So why'd you ask?"

"Seemed polite. Good guys win?"

"You mean the Yankees?"

"I mean whoever you were rooting for. I don't care about baseball, but I'm always on your side."

"Your loyalty is the stuff of legends. Yes, they creamed 'em. What's up?"

"Two things. One, Mel's meeting Mary at Big Brother Choi's apartment tomorrow and she invited me along."

"You mean you twisted her arm to let you go."

"I would've if I had to, but it was actually her idea. She's kind of skittish about going back there. You know, because of the body and the blood and stuff. But I think it would be pushing it with Mary to have you along, too."

"Always the bridesmaid. All right, I'll await your report. I have a few more calls to make, anyway. What's thing two?"

"I'm staying home for dinner. Just thought I'd let you know."

"Two rejections in the same phone call, and not even a record for you. Heartbreaking, but I'll live with it. You're feeling the need to bask in your mother's sunny presence?"

"Better. Tim's coming over."

"Now I'm confused. Isn't that usually a reason to run for the hills?"

"In general, yes. But I've spent the afternoon online trying to look under Jackson Ting's rocks, and I can't even find his rocks."

"I love it when you talk dirty."

"You're the more experienced investigator in this partnership, and I'm always trying to learn from you. Anyway, the great crime you prophesied is nowhere in sight. Tim has a dog in this fight, so I thought I'd see what he knows."

"And being Tim, he'll be only too happy to tell you, and in endless detail. Careful, though. If he does you a favor, you'll owe him one back. That kind of thing can escalate. And by the way, the metaphors are getting out of hand."

"It was that trip to the South, like you said."

"Well, have a good night, y'all. And if you need me to call with an emergency so you can jump up and run off, send up a flare."

"What kind of emergency?"

"I don't know. Something to do with my rocks."

I deserved that, but I hung up on him anyway.

FOURTEEN

TIM ARRIVED RIGHT on time, his usual handsome (if you like pudgy), well-dressed (if you like stodgy), pleasant (if you like patronizing) self. He took off his shoes, gave Ma a kiss, and said, "Lyd? You're home for dinner? Couldn't get a date?" He handed me the bag of oranges he'd brought.

"Oh, I canceled a hot one for you, bro."

"Who, Smith? You're getting pretty desperate if you think he's hot."

"You don't seem to have a date yourself, I see." I took the oranges to the kitchen and arranged them in a big blue bowl.

"Speak Chinese," Ma commanded in Chinese. "Also, say nice things to each other."

"Smells great in here, Ma," said Tim, switching languages. "I guess Ling Wan-Ju didn't help with the cooking."

"She wouldn't let me," I said. "She was afraid I might poison you."

"You two never change." Ma shooed us out of the kitchen and poured sesame oil in the wok to stir-fry the bok choy.

"Why does she keep thinking we'll change?" Tim went back to English as we took seats in the living room. "You'd have to turn into a nice normal sister."

"By normal you mean one whose profession doesn't

embarrass a stuffed shirt like you. Good luck with that. But hey, I'm nice. I called to congratulate you on making partner."

"Because Ma made you."

"She didn't. But she was the one who told me about it. I bet you called Ted, Elliot, and Andrew. You could've called me."

"Come on, you wouldn't have cared."

"Try me."

Ma, bustling from the kitchen with a platter of sizzling jiaozi, interrupted our glaring session. I fetched the bok choy, Tim carried the casserole dish between two big kitchen mitts, and we sat down to dinner. Over the dumplings, conversation centered on our other brothers, their families, their kids. When we hit the ngau lam mein and the bok choy, we moved on to Tim and his new position in the firm.

After a not totally unbearable period of him humble-bragging, Tim turned to me. "So. You pick up any clients at Choi Meng's funeral last week?"

Ma squinted from one of us to the other, the change in subject putting her on the alert for hostilities, but she didn't say anything.

"Mel Wu," I said. "The niece." Mel was already my client by the time I got to the funeral, but why does Tim need to know everything?

Tim's eyes widened and he gave me an acknowledging nod. "Nice catch. What does she want?"

"Help. You know I can't say more than that."

"Your relationship's not privileged unless you're working for an attorney."

"She is an attorney. Also, privileged isn't the same as

private. Information I'm required to reveal in court I don't have to tell my brother over the dinner table."

"Ooh," he said. "Feel the burn."

"I do want to ask you something, though."

"Oh, you tell me to butt out, then you want to ask me something? Why should I tell you anything?"

"Because she's your sister!" Ma dug the serving chopsticks into the casserole dish and dumped a mound of noodles onto Tim's plate, following them up with some choice chunks of long-simmered beef. "Will you two please stop fighting? You'll ruin dinner."

"Nothing can ruin your ngau lam mein, Ma," said Tim. "Not even her. Okay, Lyd, go ahead, ask. What can I do for you?"

"Oh, forget it. You probably don't know anyway."

Ma shot me a dirty look.

"Yes, all right," I said quickly. "I'm interested in Jackson Ting."

Tim laughed. "You're not serious? One, he's married. Two, he's out of your league."

Ma's dirty look swung to Tim. "'Out of your league,' this means this man is too good for her?"

"Well…"

"No one is too good for any of my children. Although," she said thoughtfully, "many people are not good enough. But Ling Wan-Ju." She turned back to me with an odd expression: a mixture of hope and worry. "Is he really married, this man you're interested in?"

I got it. The hope was that my interest in another man might mean I was losing interest in Bill. The worry was that the man might be unavailable. "Sorry, Ma," I said. "This is a purely professional interest. Jackson

Ting is a real estate developer. I'm working on a case that involves him."

"The one for Mel Wu?" Tim asked as my mother's face fell.

"Go fish. But I'm thinking that because of the Heritage Society you might have already dug up dirt on Ting."

"Mel Wu," he said thoughtfully. "She's a real estate lawyer. Her uncle was head of the tong that won't sell their building to Ting. Lyd, if you're working for the tong, directly or indirectly, I will kill you."

Ma's eyes widened. Whether at the idea of me working for the tong or at the picture of Tim standing over me with a bloody cleaver, I couldn't tell.

"If I thought you were worried about my safety I'd be appreciative," I said. "As it is, you're a jerk. You scared Ma because you're afraid something I do will tarnish your glow at Harriman McGill. No, I'm not working for the tong. No, I won't tell you what I'm doing for Mel Wu. No, she didn't ask me to look into Jackson Ting. Thanks anyway." I squeezed a piece of meat between my chopsticks and stuck it in my mouth.

Tim looked away, reddening. Ma looked at him, frowning. I looked at my dinner. After a brief, uncomfortable silence, Tim relented. "The Society did do some digging into Jackson Ting. To see if there was anything dicey about the Phoenix Towers project. We couldn't find anything."

"The Phoenix Towers project?" Ma said. "On Bayard Street? The ugly big building for rich people?"

"Basically, yes, Ma," Tim said.

"'Dicey,' do you mean that you think it's going to be a gambling house?"

"No," said Tim as I hid a smile. "'Dicey' means bad."

"Bad." She nodded, digesting this new slang. Tim had translated the English word literally into Chinese, so I didn't think using it among her pals was going to get her very far, but I said nothing. "So you mean, you were looking for bad things about that project? Many people will have to move from their homes for it to get built. Isn't that a bad thing?"

"Yes, but it's legal," Tim said.

"It should not be."

Tim shrugged. "Maybe, but it is."

Ma looked at me. "You're looking for bad things about this project, too?"

"About Jackson Ting in general. This project, other projects, whatever."

"Can you stop this dicey building for rich people from being built if you find them?"

Tim shook his head. "Don't know, Ma." He gave me a long, appraising look. "Of course," he said slowly, "I'm an attorney. The Heritage Society is a nonprofit. We can only apply legitimate research methods."

"What are you saying?" I demanded.

"Oh, come on, Lyd. Don't deny you've contravened the law before. Disregarded it. Skirted it. Went around—"

"I know what 'contravene' means. It's what you hate about my profession."

He shrugged. "One of a number of things. But if Jackson Ting is up to anything shady…"

"Shady?" Ma asked.

"Like dicey," I said, and to Tim, "so suddenly my embarrassing profession might be valuable to you?"

"One uses the tools one has."

"Oh! Oh! Tools? Uses? Why you—" I stopped myself. I felt like a cartoon character with a light bulb over my head. "Hire me."

"What?"

"I'm going to be looking anyway. If you want to be able to use what I find, hire me. So the information's privileged."

Tim stared. Ma, probably wondering if chunks of beef were about to go flying across the table, narrowed her eyes.

"You know," said Tim, looking hard at me, "amazingly, that's not a bad idea. You're hired. I hope you don't expect to get paid, though."

"It's not a contract if there's no payment. Oh, you're surprised I know that? I am in business, you know. It doesn't have to be money. It's called a consideration. But since consideration isn't your strong point, how about money?"

"A dollar."

"Cheapskate." But hell, I already had two clients. "I accept. I'll draw up a contract after dinner."

Our mother beamed. "My children are working together on an important case. This makes me quite happy." She put down her chopsticks and smiled from one of us to the other. "I'll help too."

FIFTEEN

"AND THEN HE blamed me!" I was on the phone with Bill later that night, after Tim left and my mother and I cleaned up. "He got me alone and absolutely hissed, 'Good job, sis, now Ma thinks she's a detective. You'd better not let anything happen to her.' Who does he think he is?"

"The real question is who does he think *she* is? She can take care of herself, if I'm remembering right."

"In general, yes, you'd better believe it. But Bill, these are gangsters. Tong guys! Not Jackson Ting himself, as far as I know, but everyone else crawling all over the Bayard Street building. Ting wants it, Mel owns it, half the Li Min Jin's on one side and half on the other—"

"Hey. For one thing, I bet your mother knows better than to get tangled up with the Li Min Jin. And all she's going to be doing anyway is looking for info on Jackson Ting. That should keep her a few steps away from them."

"I'm not convinced. Is there another thing?"

"I bet the Li Min Jin knows better than to tangle with your mother. Not only does she have that formidable Ma Chin thing going for her, she has Grandfather Gao in her corner."

"Ah. Now there you might be onto something."

"I'm not just a pretty face, you know. In fact I'm not any kind of a pretty face."

"Fishing for compliments never works."

"It does when you do it."

"Because I deserve them. Okay, talk to you in the morning, after I go to the building with Mel." I added, "Pretty boy," and hung up.

MARY WAS WAITING outside the Bayard Street building the next morning when I walked up.

"Mel Wu's my client," I said before she could scowl at me. "She asked me to come."

"I know, she called me. It's all right. You're just going to come and go, yes?"

"Whatever Mel wants me to do."

"That's what she's going to want you to do."

"Okay then."

That little thrust-and-parry was interrupted by Mel Wu. "Good morning," she said as she stepped up to us. "I hope I haven't kept you waiting, Detective Kee. Lydia, thank you for coming."

"No problem," Mary and I said at the same time, but we didn't jinx-you-owe-me-a-Coke because this was a professional meeting.

Mary knocked on the Li Min Jin door. It was opened immediately by a uniformed Asian NYPD officer. A few paces back in the hallway stood Beefy, arms crossed. "Sung." Mary nodded to the cop. "Anything exciting?"

"I've only been on an hour. Place is quiet. Guys going out, guys coming in, guys staying put." He grinned and lowered his voice. "They don't seem to like us."

"They don't like us. After we're through upstairs, unless I need Forensics to come back I'll release the crime scene and you can go. Who's up there?"

"Wagman."

"Oh, I bet they love that." Mary turned to Mel. "Elevator?"

Mel looked at me and I shook my head, so we all took the stairs. Yesterday's workout notwithstanding, I was still third when we got to the sixth floor. Mel might not be a nearly championship-level gymnast anymore, but she was still plenty fit. Mary, of course, played hockey, soccer, softball, and pretty much everything else.

Another uniformed cop, a White guy, stood from the folding chair outside Big Brother Choi's apartment when we reached the sixth floor. He flexed his hands.

"Hey, Wagman," Mary said. "Anything?"

"Not even dirty looks. No one came up here."

"What about the graveyard shift?"

"Narváez said the same. No one."

"Okay. I think after we're done here you and Sung can probably go." She pulled down the crime scene tape and opened the door.

Mel hesitated, then set her shoulders and walked in. I followed. Except for the dusting powder on the windowsills and doorframes, the now-dried blood on the low table and the floor, and the lack of body, the place seemed pretty much the same.

"Just look around," Mary said to Mel. "Take as long as you need. Is this how you'd expect it to look, say if you were coming to visit your uncle? Everything here, in the right place, that sort of thing?"

Stepping around the blood, Mel wandered through the study, ending at the latticed window, which was now closed and locked. She looked out for a few moments, then turned and walked into the room on the right, where I hadn't been before. A dining table took up the center, with more scroll paintings on the walls around it. Beyond it was a kitchen, with that scrubbed but forlorn look of a useful space no one uses. Mel smiled as she looked around it. "Uncle Meng didn't cook. A restaurant would send meals or someone would pick them up. Or he'd go out. My mother generally made Western food, but when she cooked Cantonese she'd make extra and freeze it so we could bring him some next time we came."

We walked back through the dining room and study. Mary asked, "Is there a safe, a hidey-hole, someplace he stored valuables?"

"I don't know. I never saw one, but that doesn't mean there isn't. You must have done things like tap the walls to see if they're hollow."

Mary nodded. "Did he have a gun?"

Mel turned her head sharply. "He was the head of the Li Min Jin. He wouldn't have let us see him with a gun, but I'm sure he had one."

"We didn't find one."

"Then it's either hidden or it's gone."

Reaching the bedroom, Mel looked slowly around. She walked over to stand in front of the family altar.

After a length of time Mary said, "What are you seeing?"

"Something's missing," Mel said. "Or at least, something's different." She bit her lip. "I'm trying to reconstruct it in my mind. I've seen this altar so many times... It changed now and then. Uncle Meng would use a new bowl for the oranges or put on a different cloth. But basically the same things were on it... Now it's different, but dammit, I can't quite say how." She turned to Mary. "May I take a photo?"

"Go ahead."

Mel took out her phone and took a few shots of the altar. I snapped some, too. She said, "There may be photos in one of my mother's albums. Nat has those. I'll look through them. Though I may be wrong, and even if I'm right, it may mean nothing."

"Still," Mary said. "If you would."

We took another turn through the apartment. I took photos in every room, for no particular reason except I didn't know when I'd get back in again. Finally we were done.

"I'm sorry I couldn't be more help," Mel said.

"Don't worry," Mary said. "I appreciate your coming." We all left, Mary locking up behind us. "I'm going to release the crime scene when I get back to the station," she said to us and to Wagman at the door. As we started down the stairs she told Mel, "You can come in whenever you want. It's yours now. But let me know if anything happens, if you think of anything, okay?"

We went down three flights without incident. It might have been a joke: a cop, a PI, and the owner, all women, walk through a tong building. Except I didn't know the punch line.

When we hit the third floor, a door opened. I got the sense that it had been ajar, and the room's inhabitant had been listening for us. Tan Lu-Lien stood in the doorway, wearing gray slacks, a crisp white shirt, and a navy V-neck sweater. "Wu Mao-Li," she said to Mel, and continued in English, "I wonder if you'll have tea with me?"

At Mel's hesitation Tan looked at me and added, "Chin Ling Wan-Ju, also, of course." That rather pointedly left out Mary, but there are disadvantages to being an actual cop. Mary gave me a look and I gave her one back, meaning *You'll tell me all about it?* and *Of course.*

SIXTEEN

THE DOOR LED into a large room in the same location as Big Brother Choi's study, the center of the U in the rear of the building. The light here, halfway down the building, didn't come pouring in as it did above, but it wasn't a dark tunnel, either. A computer-topped steel office desk sat by the window, and a gold dragon on a blue rug warmed up the vinyl tile floor in front of it. Framed brush paintings of bamboo and pine hung on the walls, along with two photographs. In one, ferries passed each other on glittering water; in the other, lights glowed on seven peaks. I knew them: The boats were the Star Ferries crossing Hong Kong Harbor, and the lights were Hong Kong's night skyline. According to Mel, Hong Kong was Tan's home. How long had it been since she'd seen those sights?

Tan nodded us to armchairs around a low table. She clicked the kettle on, waited until the water began to simmer and turned it off just before it boiled. Stopping the water before it quite boils is the correct technique for green tea, though it's a detail most people don't bother with. Tan poured the water into a gourd-shaped Yixing pot and swished it gently around.

Small handleless teacups painted with vines shared the tabletop with a plate of lou gong beng—flaky pastry filled with red bean curd, peanuts, and star anise. I love this stuff, and it's not that easy to find, even at the best Chinatown bakeries. When Tan brought the teapot to the table, I asked where she'd gotten them.

She smiled slightly, pausing before she spoke. "I made them. My cooking is passable, though my abilities in the kitchen aren't common knowledge." Her English was crisp and British, with a slight trace of Chinese rhythms. To Mel she said, "Choi Meng enjoyed my cooking. I made him many dinners."

"In his kitchen? It seems so unused."

"Of course not. I brought his favorite dishes from home. The men thought I'd stopped at a restaurant on my way here. Any display of skill at women's work would be dangerous for me. You understand."

She sat and poured tea, first for Mel, then me, then herself.

"I do understand," Mel said. "I imagine you always must have been on guard. Even with my uncle on your side."

"Your uncle recognized skill and devotion." Tan settled back in her chair.

Mel sipped. "This is delicious," she said, as was proper: Compliment the food before talking about anything else.

"Thank you. It's a longjing from Ten Ren Company." Interesting. The correct Chinese response to a compliment, especially about food, is to disparage what's being praised so you don't appear boastful. Tan didn't indulge in that artifice, but she didn't take credit for anything beyond choosing the tea, either.

I took a lou gong beng and bit into it. "Oh my god," I said. "Tan Lu-Lien, your cooking is way beyond passable. This is fantastic."

"I'm glad you like it." Tan picked up her cup and

sipped. We all sat drinking tea while Mel and I waited to hear why we'd been invited in. My money was heavily on the idea this wasn't just a be-nice-to-the-new-land-lady party.

Finally Tan said, "Mao-Li, I was surprised, as I probably shouldn't have been, to find your uncle had left this building to you and not to the Li Min Jin."

"Surprised why? And why shouldn't you have been?"

"The tong was Choi Meng's family. One reason he bought this building, he said, was so the Li Min Jin would always have a home. For that reason I expected he would leave it to the Li Min Jin. But of course, you're also family. Blood family. Why wouldn't he leave his valuable property to you? I'm embarrassed by my foolish assumption. So now, Mao-Li, I need to know your intentions for the building."

"My intentions?" Mel repeated. "Do you mean, will I allow the Li Min Jin to stay?"

"Or will you keep the building for other uses? Or will you sell it and allow Jackson Ting to tear it down?"

Mel's eyebrows knit together. "I haven't thought that far," she hedged. "I'm surprised you have. My uncle's death, and Mr. Chang's, are about all I can deal with right now."

"I appreciate that. They're both powerful blows. But I must think about the future."

"As far as the building's concerned, I'm afraid you'll have to wait."

"I'm sorry, but it would be best if I knew your plans sooner rather than later."

"Best why? Best for whom?"

"Mao-Li." Tan spoke in measured tones. "With the death of Chang Yao-Zu, I am temporarily the leader of the Li Min Jin." I watched the tattoos move on the backs of Tan's hands. On the right, the character for power; on the left, a dragon.

"Only temporarily?" Mel asked.

"Until Chang Yao-Zu's funeral, which it's my duty to arrange. Immediately after that, whether or not an arrest has been made and knowing full well that his killer might be a member of this tong, there will be a selection process for the new leader. I won't survive it."

Mel's eyes widened, and I felt mine do the same. Tan gave a hint of a smile. "Within the tong, I mean. The process is no longer carried out by assassination. If I were a man, I could expect to be chosen, but I won't be. My skills and experience are nothing beside my gender. My rank has been hard enough for some to swallow these past years, but no one dared speak up against me. It won't be like that now.

"If Chang Yao-Zu had lived, my position wouldn't have changed. He'd have been the leader, with no serious challenger. I'd have been one of his lieutenants, as I've been Choi Meng's. But Chang's death thrusts me into the leader's role. If I can't maintain that position—and I know I can't—there'll be no place for me here. I won't be able to stay."

Wow, I thought. Up or out. Just like Tim's law firm.

"Who are the men in contention now?" I asked.

Tan looked at me with distaste. This was clearly not what she'd asked Mel here to discuss. "Ironman Ma and Loo Hu-Li," she said, in a voice that hinted she saw answering me as quicker and more efficient than kicking me out or beating me to a pulp, but she was prepared to do either if I didn't shut up.

Mel seemed to pick up on Tan's attitude, because

she changed the subject. "Tan Lu-Lien," she said, "one of the reasons I came here yesterday was that Chang Yao-Zu had something to tell me. A message, he said, from Uncle Meng. Something not written down but important. I don't know what it was about, but it's possible knowing it would influence my thinking about this building. Do you have any idea what it was?"

"A message for you from Choi Meng? No, I don't." Tan gazed across the room. "I was here when Chang Yao-Zu came to the Li Min Jin, once the two tongs combined. He'd had high rank in the Ma Tou, and your uncle began to raise him up through the ranks here fairly quickly."

"Were you jealous?" Mel asked.

Tan laughed. "I was twenty-three, and a woman. That I was in the tong at all was a miracle. I kept to my duties and watched. It was interesting to see."

"To see what? How the other men reacted?"

Tan didn't answer.

"How about Loo Hu-Li?" I ventured. "He couldn't have been happy."

"Loo Hu-Li hasn't been happy for an hour altogether since I've known him," Tan said. So he was Scrooge, after all. "If you're asking me whether he finally took this opportunity to kill Chang Yao-Zu, hoping to assume the leadership, I don't know."

You just said you guys don't do this by assassination anymore, I thought, but her matter-of-fact tone suggested I not mention that. Instead I asked her, "Don't you feel like you might be in danger, too?"

She fixed me with her steely gaze. "Chin Ling Wan-Ju, it's a bit insulting to know you either haven't heard or haven't believed what I've said. I'm in no danger because I'm no threat. The men in this tong will make their decision and I'll leave. It's that simple."

"They'll just let you go? With everything you know?"

"And the alternative? To lock me in the basement and force me to continue my work?" Her contempt for my thinking couldn't have been more clear. "That would imply I'm irreplaceable. And that, held against my will, my work could still be trusted." It would also be kidnapping and, essentially, slavery, but those things didn't seem to be the deal breakers.

Mel asked, "Are you not irreplaceable to the Li Min Jin?"

Tan regarded her. "My knowledge is arcane to all these men, but they won't admit that. I won't keep it secret. I'll sit with the new leader and explain the financial workings of the Li Min Jin. Our investments, businesses, real estate holdings, all our assets. The leader will understand whatever he can and tell me he understands it all. We'll change the signatures on the various accounts, I'll give him a list of the passwords, and I'll leave him with the paperwork." She paused. "Our resources may be gathered in unorthodox ways, but the disposition of them is quite conventional."

Unorthodox ways. Uh-huh. I determined this might be a good time to say the nothing she clearly wanted from me.

Tan eyed us and put down her cup. "They'll make mistakes," she went on. "They'll almost certainly lose nonprofit status. None of them understand what that requires. The tong will go back to operating in the shadows of what they'll call a social club, but that's how tongs and triads have worked for two hundred years. They can survive without me."

Mel asked, "What will you do?"

"I'll go back to Hong Kong."

"Back home."

Tan looked at the photo on the wall for a long silent moment. Sitting back in her armchair, she said, "I was born in Hong Kong. We were poor. Very early I saw who had power—not the schoolgirls in their blue skirts and blouses, walking home in cringing groups to protect themselves from the leering men. And from the gang boys, who roamed the streets. At fourteen I joined the Black Shadows. I fought my way in. At first Johnny Gee, the leader, was amused. He was sure I'd lose a fight, fail an initiation task. I never did. So he decided to take me to his bed, as he did with the girls who hung around hoping to attract a gang boy's attention. I refused. I liked Johnny, and eventually, after my place in the tong was secure, we did become lovers. But to do it then, on those terms, would have doomed my chances of becoming an equal member.

"As I thought he might, Johnny sent someone—his lieutenant, Cho—to teach me a lesson. We fought. I won. I could have killed Cho, but I judged that would be a mistake. I left him lying where we'd fought and walked back to the teahouse where the Black Shadows gathered. I told them where he was. I stood, wearing his blood and my own, while Johnny sent a boy to see. The boy came back, reporting that he'd found Cho injured. He'd called an ambulance and watched from across the street as they took him to hospital.

"I didn't know what to expect next. Johnny might have killed me. I stayed where I was. Johnny and the others stared. Then he began to laugh. He jumped up, slapped me on the back, and welcomed me to the Black

Shadows. After that no one challenged me. Not even Cho, once he recovered. I moved quickly through the ranks and became a Red Pole, an enforcer. It was one of my duties to deal with disobedient members. I enjoyed it." She picked up her tea again and sipped, seeming to be waiting for a response.

Mel said nothing. I supposed being raised in Scarsdale might make this kind of story a little unsettling.

It might also leave holes in your local knowledge. "The Black Shadows are the gang affiliated with the Li Min Jin," I said.

Tan's small smile seemed directed at "affiliated," but she nodded. "In Hong Kong, and here," she said. "When I came to New York I brought my *affiliation* with me. I was too old for a street gang. Coercing payments from merchants and mugging tourists provides fewer thrills as you age, and stabbing members of other gangs in fights over territory might make a boy feel like a man, but for myself, I was no longer interested in that sort of crude exercise of power. I had relatives in New York and decided to start again, here, where no one knew me.

"I'd stayed in school during my gang years, and as it turned out I had a talent for numbers. Early on Johnny Gee put me in charge of the Black Shadows' financial affairs."

"From Red Pole to White Paper Fan?" *Boy, Lydia, you sound like an expert.*

Tan gave me the look you'd give a show-off child. "To use the traditional titles, yes. Few of the gangs and tongs do anymore. The Black Shadows weren't as formal as that."

"The Li Min Jin is, though," said Mel. "Isn't it?"

"Your uncle was traditional in many ways. That was one."

"Forgive us the interruptions," Mel said. "Please continue."

Tan nodded. "As Johnny Gee and the other boys grew into men, they found that what I'd done, my investments, my purchases of land and businesses, had made the Black Shadows not wealthy, but well enough off. Those who wanted to put their pasts behind them and become respectable were able to do so. I understand that some of them, in the years since I left, have done well. Of course I had a share also, which I liquidated and brought with me when I came to America." She smiled. "I'd never been out of Hong Kong. As the plane rose into the clouds I looked out and saw the Dragon Boat festivities in the harbor. Then Hong Kong was gone. The flight was interminable. When the pilot announced we were descending, I looked out the window once again, to see my new home. We were flying over what I now know was Flushing Meadow Park. I saw banners, kites, and Dragon Boats. I laughed. How much luckier a sign could I hope for? My cousin and her husband were waiting for me at the airport, as they said they'd be. Not long after, I offered my services to Choi Meng for the Li Min Jin."

"I see," said Mel.

Tan gave Mel a long, steady look. "I'm not sure you do. I told you the story of my past so you'll understand I'm resolute about achieving my goals. I determined to join the Black Shadows and I did. I chose my time to leave Hong Kong and come to New York. I found a way into the Li Min Jin. Now, before I leave New York and the Li Min Jin, there are things I must do, and to do them I need to know what will become of this building."

"I can't tell you yet. I have a lot of factors to weigh."

"I suggest you weigh them, then. And let me know your decision. Sooner, Wu Mao-Li, rather than later."

SEVENTEEN

MEL AND I got nothing more from Tan Lu-Lien, nor she from us. I had nothing to give, of course. Mel wouldn't be pushed into a decision on the building—or into revealing the lines of her thinking—and Tan refused to elaborate further. When I put down my cup, Tan didn't move to refill it. That was the end of the tea party.

"Boy," I said to Mel when we were back out on Bayard Street. "That woman is more intimidating drinking tea than any other tong member I've ever met swinging his fists."

"Agreed." Mel stared back at the building. "Was she threatening me? I mean, I've known her all my life!"

"Should auld acquaintance be forgot. I think this was the stage before that. She was saying she *will* threaten you unless you deliver. And that if she threatens you, you can count on her to carry through. Equal rights aside, the Li Min Jin is losing out by not making her the new leader."

"They certainly are."

"Though," I went on, "one man's ceiling is another man's floor. A weakening of any tong is good for Chinatown."

"Except," Mel said thoughtfully, "for people who're glad the Li Min Jin has been holding out on Jackson Ting and stopping Phoenix Towers. People who don't know the building's mine now and think the tong owns it—those people might want to keep the tong powerful, at least for a while."

"And who would those people be?"

Mel looked off down the street, where shoppers were going in and out of the fruit store and the stationery store, and tourists with three-scoop cones were leaving the Chinatown Ice Cream Factory.

"For one thing," I said, answering my own question, "they'd include people like my brother and the Chinatown Heritage Society."

"Your brother would support strengthening the tong?"

"Oh, no, no, no. Mr. Straight Arrow?" I didn't tell her about the cow Tim had had over dinner the previous night when he thought I might be working for the Li Min Jin. "But at the funeral he was mumbling about goals aligning. He might not be unhappy if the tong stayed strong long enough to face down Jackson Ting."

Mel nodded, and then she gestured to the buildings set to be demolished if Phoenix Towers were allowed to proceed. "Also, anyone living there."

"And let's not forget tong members who don't want to lose their building. Members who haven't heard about you, or at least hadn't yesterday morning, and thought it was the Li Min Jin's decision. They'd want a leader who didn't want to sell."

"And so you're thinking"—Mel brought her gaze back to me—"if people thought Mr. Chang *did* want to sell, he might have been killed by someone in the opposition. Someone inside or outside the tong. It might have nothing to do with Uncle Meng's message to me."

"If Tan Lu-Lien's right, Chang would have crushed any challenger. If he wouldn't have lost a vote, or whatever it is they do, and someone wanted him gone, he'd have needed to be removed another way."

"God," Mel said, shaking her head. "I wish I knew what it was he was going to tell me."

"Do you suppose there's anyone else who'd know? Though if Tan, in her position, didn't even know he *had* a message for you from your uncle... Still, how about Loo Hu-Li? Would it be worth asking him? Or Ironman Ma?"

"I hardly know Ironman Ma at all. I don't know if my uncle, or Mr. Chang, would have confided in him. But Mr. Loo, he was here when Uncle Meng came from Hong Kong. He's the last remaining member from those days." Mel smiled. "What Tan said about him—that's my memory, too. He always looked as though he had a toothache. But I guess we could ask him. Although if Mr. Chang wasn't a shoo-in and did have a challenger, it would have been Mr. Loo."

"Which means Loo might be Chang's killer. Yes. I think we need to talk to him anyway," I said. "Because he also might not be. If he can tell us something, great. If he can't, or won't, we won't know any less than we do now."

"Except we will have alerted Mr. Loo that there's something to know. But then we can watch and see what he does about it."

I grinned. "Shaking trees. You think like a detective."

"I'm going to take that as a compliment."

"As intended. But you know, thinking like one doesn't mean you have to act like one. If the fact that he might be the killer makes you nervous about speaking to him, I can try him without you."

"No, no, I'll come. Mr. Loo might feel some obligation to me as Uncle Meng's family. If you think it's worth it, let's do it."

It might have been worth it, but we couldn't do it. We went back and knocked at the Li Min Jin's door only to discover Mr. Loo was not in. While Beefy was telling us that, the cop at the door got a call on his cell. The cop upstairs did, too, and came galloping down the five flights. The crime scene had been released. With unseemly glee they both trotted past us and off down the street, leaving Beefy to close the door in our faces.

MEL WENT TO her office, glad, she said, to have work to focus on. I called Bill.

"Have a good time with the gangsters?" he asked.

"My head is spinning. How about if I walk over and pick you up and we stroll to the river?"

"I never say no when a beautiful woman offers to pick me up. I'll meet you downstairs. I'll be the one who looks excited. You'll be the one who looks like the Exorcist."

He was waiting outside Shorty's when I got there. He ground out his cigarette, and we walked the couple of blocks down Laight Street to the park by the Hudson. The midday sun cast weaving shadows from the half-bare branches as we sat at a table under the trees. "So it was a profitable morning?" Bill asked.

"I don't really know." I recounted for him our trek through Big Brother Choi's apartment, where the only outstanding fact wasn't even a fact: Mel's sense that something was amiss at the family altar. Then I told him about Tan Lu-Lien, who she was and what she'd wanted.

"Sounds like my kind of gal."

"You'd have hit it off big time. You could've compared tattoos and arm wrestled and who knows what all. I bet she even smokes." I watched ducks paddling around by the pier and sun glittering off the water. "I don't know what she's really getting at," I said. "She says she doesn't care what Mel decides, she just needs to know, but that doesn't make sense to me. Although she's definitely a plan A, plan B, plans C through double Z type. Maybe she's just arranging her exit in different ways based on Mel's decision."

"Will Mel tell her, once she decides?"

"I'm not sure, though I don't see why she wouldn't. She didn't seem to quite believe Tan was threatening her, but her decision on the building will be public soon enough. I'm hoping Loo can shed light on Big Brother Choi's last message. But whether he can or not, Mel's going to have to decide something. And in case her inclination is not in the direction of Jackson Ting, did you come up with anything useful in our chess game with him?"

"Mostly background. Interesting, but I'm not sure how useful it is."

I shifted to face him. "Please proceed."

"I called some suppliers and contractors I know. Some had done work for Ting and others hadn't, but they all knew who he was and no one sang his praises. He wants fast and cheap. He likes glitz, but he doesn't care about quality. He makes rash decisions and then refuses to rethink them. And he kisses up to people he considers important."

"And his bad points?"

"Hah. They also say he argues about every bill that crosses his bookkeeper's desk, but he attends all the five-thousand-dollar-a-plate dinners he can get to. They did admit, reluctantly, that once he's agreed on a price he pays promptly. Sounded to me like that's about the only reason they keep bidding on his work. You don't get a fair price, but you can keep your cash flow going."

"Is that how the construction business works?"

"Isn't it how every business works? The guys at the top squeeze the guys at the bottom?"

"Probably," I said glumly. "Did anyone have any suggestions about where to find the skeletons in his closet?"

"Sorry. For what it's worth, they're all sure he has them. Though they don't necessarily want them found."

"What do you mean? Why not?"

"Some of these guys are eyeing the Phoenix Towers project with lust in their hearts."

"Self-interest rears its ugly head again. Well, I put Linus and Trella on the trail of Jackson Ting's finances. Haven't heard back, but they haven't been at it long."

As I said that my phone burst out with "Two Out of Three Ain't Bad."

"Linus making a dramatic entrance?" Bill said.

"That's not his ring. That's the client ring." I tapped the phone on. "Lydia Chin."

"Hey, Lyd! It's Ironman. What's happening?"

I raised my eyebrows at Bill while I said, "Well, hey. Not much, Ironman. What about you?"

Bill raised his eyebrows back. He leaned in to listen, but I swatted him away.

"You looked so gorgeous yesterday," Ironman said, "that I wondered why we ever lost touch. Can I buy you a drink?"

"You don't have to lay it on so thick. I'd be happy to have a drink with you. When were you thinking?"

"That wasn't laying it on thick," he protested. "Just telling it like it is. So how about now? Make up for lost time, you know?"

"You mean now, right now? Okay, but it's a little early for a drink. I'd go for tea."

"Tea it is. Miansai?"

"Twenty minutes?"

"Too long to wait."

"I'll see if I can make it in nineteen." I clicked off.

"Ironman Ma?" Bill said as I put the phone away. "Gangsters have your phone number?"

"Many have yours," I pointed out. "He's taking me out for a cup of tea. Because I'm gorgeous."

"Although you are, in fact, gorgeous, do we really think that's his reason?"

"Are you kidding? I've been this same gorgeous for the last ten years and I haven't heard a peep from him. Well, gotta go. Told him twenty minutes and we're meeting at a hoity-toity tea place on the Lower East Side."

"Not in Chinatown?"

"Interesting, no?"

I stood and so did Bill. "You don't mind if I come with you."

"I do."

"Not as a bodyguard. Heaven forfend. But the implication of your meeting place is he doesn't want to be seen with you. Not a sentiment I'd ever feel, by the way."

"I should hope not."

"I'm just wondering who it might be by whom he doesn't want to be seen."

"Did you really say that?"

"I can say it again."

"Don't bother. Let's go."

EIGHTEEN

BILL AND I zipped through Soho to the tea shop. As we approached it, Bill crossed to the other side of the street. Right before I pulled open Miansai's door I saw him take up his post, slouching into a doorway and looking for all the world like just another New York bum. He does that so well.

Miansai is a place I don't like. It's a tea shop within a retail store, and the bags, belts, and bracelets are their focus. Their teas tend toward mocha pumpkin spice chai latte and that kind of nonsense. The indoor tea bar was empty, so I walked through to the patio at the back. Ironman wasn't waiting for me. Strike one. I chose a table in the sun and had just ordered a pot of Kenyan organic first-flush BOP—the simplest thing on the tea menu—when Ironman breezed out from the shop. He spoke to the waitress as he blew by her and landed at my table like he was stealing second.

"God, was I right or was I right? You look delicious." He grinned. "Why have we not seen each other in all this time?"

Noting the bulge of a holster under his classy sport coat, I said, "Could it be because I'm a private investigator and you're a gangster?"

"Oh, come on, Lyd! I'm a tong member. We're not all gangsters."

Lyd. My brothers, yes; arrogant smarmy criminals,

no. Strike two. My teeth grated, but I smiled. "Oh really? What is it you people do, then?"

"We're a nonprofit. Me, I run our youth programs."

"Oh, you're the liaison with the Black Shadows? Or do you do on-playground recruitment?"

"Hey! Basketball! Nine-man! Ping-pong! We sponsor a track team and a Little League team. Lion dancers and drummers. We have a guy who teaches martial arts to little kids, kindergarteners. You should see them throwing their cute little kicks. Wholesome shit like that, baby, that's what I do."

"Wow. Who wrote that speech? Besides, I'd have bet anything you were a Red Pole. An enforcer."

He shook his head, grinning, as though I'd said something adorable. The waitress came out and brought our tea—my Kenyan black and something pale and spicy-smelling in a heavy mug for Ironman. Mocha pumpkin spice chai latte, no doubt. She also put down a plate of tiny iced cookies and a dish of dates.

"So," Ironman said, popping a date in his mouth. "You really are a private eye, huh? How'd you get into that?"

"I was hoping to be able to help the cops run in guys like you." I poured myself a cup of tea.

"And your cute friend Mary—I remember you guys hung out in high school. She's some scary detective now, huh?"

"I'll tell her you said so."

"What about that big White guy, he's your partner? Your business partner, or your personal partner?"

"You seem to know a lot about me, Ironman."

"I'm interested. Like I said, making up for lost time."

"You haven't asked about my brothers."

"Ted's a professor at Queens College." He ticked

off on his fingers. "Elliot's a doctor. They both have kids. Andrew's a photographer. He's gay. Tim's a lawyer. He's straight but he's still single and if he hasn't changed since high school I can guess why that is. They're all good. And your mom's fine, too. She looks good, the old lady. I saw her just this morning, out on Canal Street buying fish." He smiled, showing gleaming teeth, while I thought, *Damn. Talk about things that sound like threats.* Strike three.

"I'm touched that you recognized her, Ironman. I always liked your mom, too. She's still behind the counter at Bright Star Bakery, I see. I guess she must enjoy the job because I know a filial son like you must have offered to support her if she wanted to retire. Or if you didn't, your sister, who was always nicer than you anyway, would have. Or your sister's husband. Even though they have three kids to think about, out there in Montclair." I had done my homework, too, as soon as I'd ID'd him at the funeral. "So how about"—I leaned forward—"we drop the vague intimidation, which, I have to tell you, is pissing me the hell off, which is not language I use lightly."

I sat back and sipped. The tea, at least, was good.

Ironman's face briefly darkened, but he got himself under control fast. He broke into a grin. "Check it out! They teach you that at PI school?"

I shrugged. "I was an A student."

"You always were a Goody Two-shoes." This was seriously not true, but because he clearly needed to shore up his wounded male pride, I didn't argue.

"So, okay," he said. "Let's forget about everyone else. Who cares? Let's talk about you. So, tell me something. Because I'm interested. Why were you at our building yesterday, and this morning? That hotness you were with—that's Old Choi's niece. I've known her since she and her sister were just bug-eyed rich kids coming down to Chinatown to gawk. In fact, I tried to date her once, but Old Choi shut me down. Is she your private eye client or something?"

I smiled. "Ah. Now we come to the subject of this meeting."

"This isn't a meeting, pretty one, it's a date. On a date you need something to talk about while you're looking each other over."

"If that's it, we can talk about how you're in contention to head the Li Min Jin now that Chang Yao-Zu's been killed."

"Whoa, Ms. Private Eye! Where'd you hear that?"

"It's all over Chinatown, Mr. Youth Programs."

"You shouldn't listen to gossip."

"You shouldn't be a tong member. Thanks for the tea." I got up to go.

"No, wait." He grabbed my hand. "Come on, sit down. We're just getting started."

"Doing what?"

"Getting to know each other again."

"Ironman, you're handsome and charming, and I don't want to know you."

"Sit down." His grip barely tightened and his voice barely hardened, and now I saw the man I'd seen yesterday and at Choi Meng's funeral. The man who might become the next head of the Li Min Jin.

I sat. "Okay, now what?"

He lifted his mug and looked at me as he sipped. Again, the grin. "We go on getting to know each other."

"How?"

"We tell each other things."

"What things?"

"You tell me why you were at our building yesterday."

"And what do you tell me?"

"Something interesting about it."

"About the building?"

"Yes, gorgeous, about the building."

I drank more tea. "Mel Wu is my client, you're right. She's executor of Big Brother Choi's estate. She wanted to go up and take a look around, and she didn't feel safe in your building without bodyguards."

"She'd have been fine."

"Sure. Anyway, her looking around was derailed by Chang's body bleeding all over her uncle's living room. Did you kill him?"

"Are you serious?"

"Someone did."

"Well, it wasn't me." Ironman smiled and delicately traced a finger down the back of my hand. "Believe me, it wasn't."

I moved my hand away. "Since you didn't kill him, maybe you can tell me what the message was he had for Mel."

"Message?"

"From Choi Meng. Something he'd wanted her to know."

"Really? About what?"

"Unfortunately, Mr. Chang got himself killed before he could deliver it. So how about you tell me and I'll tell her?"

He gave a slow smug smile. He picked up a cookie, assessed it, and bit into it. "I don't know what it was, darling, but I bet I know what it was about."

"Go ahead."

He leaned across the table as though we were co-conspirators.

"The charm isn't working, Ironman. You owe me, and I want my trade."

He gave me puppy eyes. "You're a hard nut to crack, Lydia Chin."

"So I've heard. Do I get my trade or do I leave?"

He took another cookie, peered at it. I was contemplating upending the rest of them into his lap when he finally spoke. "I don't know what the message was. But whatever it was, it probably has something to do with whatever's buried in the building."

"Buried in the building? What does that mean?"

He shrugged. "Nobody knows exactly what it means. They say there's something valuable, buried in the building."

"Who are 'they'?"

"The people who say. They've said for years. And they also say Tan Lu-Lien's books don't balance." Again, the amused smile. "She's the tong's White Paper Fan, you know. That means—"

"She's the CFO. You guys really think your secret codes and all that stupid stuff are so secret? I knew that was her position, and I want to know who says her books don't balance."

"You want to know? Aha, I found something that interests you! Well, for your information, pretty much everyone says that."

"I doubt that, or she'd have been dealt with long ago, however you respectable citizens in your nonprofit deal with people these days." I poured myself more tea, though it had faded to lukewarm. "But if I understand your irritating wink-wink beating around the bush here, you're saying *some* of you think she's been skimming and burying her gains in the building somewhere in the form of hard cash."

"Or something else, something more easily trans-portable," he said reasonably. "Diamonds, you know, things like that."

"Why not just use a safe deposit box?"

"A White Paper Fan opening a safe deposit box might have been noticed."

"In another borough? Another state? Oh," I said, see-ing his eyes. "You have people watching her. Just you? Or you and Chang and what's his name, Loo?"

"Not Chang. He was Big Brother Choi's man and Tan is—was—Big Brother's woman."

"But you and Loo, huh?"

"Loo's a senile idiot. Why would I work with him?"

"You won't work with Loo and you're spying on Tan. So much for a sworn brotherhood." Besides, I thought, Tan's a sister.

"It's the responsibility of power to keep power in check."

"Now I *know* you didn't write that."

He shrugged. "We all have our obligations. Everyone knew Big Brother Choi would never sell. That makes the building a very safe hiding place. Or, it did."

"Not anymore?"

"Don't bat your eyes at me all innocent. Mel isn't just Big Brother's executor. The old bastard left her the building. Everything's changed."

"I suppose it has." I sipped at my tea. "Why," I mused, as though to myself, "would he not sell?"

Ironman took the bait, though not in words. He gave me a long, expectant look, like a teacher waiting on a pupil. After a moment I caught his meaning.

"You're not serious," I said. "You think they were in it together? You're telling me Choi was holding on to a multimillion-dollar piece of New York City real estate so he and Tan could use it as a piggy bank and stuff things in the walls?"

"Not entirely. He was a sentimental son of a bitch. He truly loved the old dump. But having a fortune hidden in it could make it a lot easier to turn down the fortune Ting was offering for it. At least until he got Ting up to a price he liked."

"For Pete's sake, Ironman. You're a tong member. He was your Big Brother."

"Oh, yes, and siblings always treat each other well, don't they? Yours always have?"

That stopped me. "I do see your point. But really, you think Choi was stealing from his own tong?"

"It wasn't his tong," Ironman snapped. His fist clenched. I wondered if he was aware of it. "He was the leader, but the power and the profit-sharing are supposed to be organized along very specific lines."

"Profit-sharing?" I tried to keep the squeak of derision out of my voice. "So, what, you didn't get your Christmas bonus?"

He relaxed. "Something like that." He tapped the back of my hand. *That's what you get for leaving your hands on the table, Lydia.* I pulled them into my lap again. "Another thing that's supposed to work on definite lines," he said, "is contact between us and the home-office Li Min Jin boys back in Hong Kong. Those lines are, there isn't any contact, except between the head here and the head there. Oh, you didn't know that, did you, smarty-pants?"

"I thought one of the objects of having a building was so you could put up visiting tong members. Isn't that contact?"

"Oh, sure, if we go there or they come here, it's all kissy-kissy, welcome brother, how can we help? But business, day-to-day tong business, is strictly on the top level. So it's a little mystifying why Tan Lu-Lien has been calling one of the Hong Kong hotshots over the last couple of months."

There was no point in asking how he knew. I wondered if Tan knew, though, how closely she was being watched.

"Who?" I asked.

"Oh, like the guy's name would mean anything to you?"

"Try me."

"Johnny Gee."

"He was head of the Black Shadows when she was in the gang in Hong Kong."

"Hey, not bad," he said with exaggerated wonder. "You study up?"

"So he moved up into the tong," I said, ignoring that. "Wouldn't it be natural for her to keep in touch with an old gang pal?"

"Natural or not, he's with the Li Min Jin Hong Kong and she's with the Li Min Jin New York, so that would be a no."

"If they don't discuss business, just pass the time?" I asked.

"How do you know what they discuss?"

"Obviously I don't."

"Do you have a theory?"

"No."

"Well, I do. For one thing, this old friendship of theirs is new. She started calling him six months ago. Before that, nada. Here's what I think. I think these calls were authorized by Big Brother here and the head in Hong Kong."

His superior smile clearly wanted me to ask why. As much as I wanted to know, I almost shrugged and said fine, just to drive him nuts. Luckily my inner PI won out over my inner teenager. "Why would they do that?"

"Tan understands the money. Maybe that's Johnny Gee's position in Hong Kong." I thought of Tan saying Johnny Gee had put her in charge of the Black Shadows' finances. If he'd had the talent or training to do that kind of thing himself, why would he give her the job? No, it wasn't likely Johnny Gee was the Li Min Jin Hong Kong's White Paper Fan. But I didn't say so.

"I think," Ironman said, "the Hong Kong boys are getting ready to kick us to the curb. I think Tan and Big Brother bled off the profits, Big Brother was going to sell the building, they were going to split what they had with the Hong Kong boys, and the rest of us were going to be cut loose. Then Big Brother went and died, but I bet that doesn't matter. He and Tan made a deal with Hong Kong, and she's going to keep it. And you know what?"

"What?"

"As far as I'm concerned, that's fine. I haven't liked the way things have been run for a while now. It's time for new blood, new organization, new thinking."

"For your community-service nonprofit."

"Yeah, sweetie, that's right. But here's the problem. She thinks she's going to take our money with her when she goes."

NINETEEN

I LEANED BACK in my chair in the back garden of Mian-sai, moving my hands and the rest of me out of Ironman Ma's grabbing range. "Well," I said, "as fascinating as all this is, Ironman, is there some reason you're telling it to me? Besides getting to know each other again?"

"That's not enough?"

"Nope."

He drained his mug of spiced whatever. "You spent a lot of time this morning with Tan Lu-Lien."

"She and Mel Wu were getting to know each other again."

"How sweet. Did you and Tan get to know each other, too?"

"I was just a fly on the wall."

"And Tan Lu-Lien is a spider." He lifted his eyebrows meaningfully. I wondered how many ways he had of being nonverbally patronizing.

But I got it. "Are you telling me she's gay?"

"Oh, for God's sake, Lyd, look at her." Lyd, again. If he kept this up, next time he came up to bat he'd be out before he started. "Look at how she dresses. How she walks. Tattoos not someplace sexy, but on her hands, for God's sake."

"How do you know she doesn't have them some-place sexy?"

"Oh? Does she?"

"Listen to yourself, Ironman. You can't stand her,

and I bet most of the tong members feel the same. If she'd acted like your idea of a woman, it could've been fatal for her even with Big Brother Choi's protection." Listen to *me*, defending a gangster to another gangster. I'd have to check myself for fleas once I got up from these dogs. "She says that if she were a man, she'd be the next leader, but as it is, she's out after the vote or whatever it is you guys do."

"Bullshit. She never would've been leader. A bean counter? Even a man. She's out for sure, and good riddance, but she's not taking our money. Go back and talk to her."

"What?"

"I want you to go back and see if you can find where the money's hidden. No, don't see if you can. Just do it. Find that money."

"Find your own money, Ironman." I eyed him. "Unless you're afraid Mel's going to evict you all and sell to Jackson Ting before you do."

"She's not going to sell to him."

I shrugged. "As far as I know she's still deciding. And whether she sells or not, she can still evict you."

"She's not going to sell to him, and she's not going to evict us. She's going to sell to me."

"She's going to what?"

He laughed. "Gotcha! See, you don't know everything, do you? I want that building. I want what's buried in it and I want *it*."

"Why?"

"Come on, you're so smart." He sat back. I was working it out but I held my tongue. Ironman gave a big theatrical sigh. "The Li Min Jin has a lot of business interests. Ongoing projects. Investments. You know. But the organization's full of old men, stuck in the past."

Investments. Projects. The organization. I said nothing.

"We need new vision. We need to start to see past the small-time bullshit to the big wide world out there."

"Chinese crime—it's not just for Chinatown anymore. Is that your slogan?"

"You know, you can be a real pain."

"I've heard that. And Big Brother Choi had no vision?"

"Big Brother Choi was happy just puttering along with what we had. I've heard the stories about what he was like when he was young, but he sure wasn't young anymore."

"But you are."

"If—*if*—you were right about me having a shot at the top spot, it'd be the old men who'd want to stop me. They'd be behind old Loo because they're all senile idiots like he is. If any of this were happening—I mean, it's all theoretical, but if it were—the tong would be split just about fifty-fifty. Guys with vision versus senile idiots. But if one of the vision guys had the building, that might tip the scale."

"I don't believe it. You're serious. You really want Mel to sell you the building?"

"Damn right I do, sweetheart. Then we can stay in it, the way her uncle wanted. Wouldn't that warm her heart, to do what dear Uncle Meng wanted? If she sells it to Ting, she's going to have to empty it, like you said. You know how hard it is to evict people in New York? And you know how hard it would be to evict *us*? I promise you her life will be a lot easier if she just sells me the building."

"That sounds like a threat."

He smiled. "For someone in the criminal business,

you seem awfully jumpy about seeing threats everywhere."

Only when they're actually there. "How are you
going to pay for this real estate investment?"

"Well, I could say that's none of your business, except it is. It's exactly your business because you're going
to find me my purchase price."

"I'm what?"

"Oh, enough of this shit. Go talk to Tan. Find me
that money."

I stared at him. I started to ask, *Are you high?* but as
the words came out I had a better idea. "Are you hiring me?"

Ironman stared back. He laughed. "Yeah. Yeah, sure,
I'm hiring you. I'm a client hiring you to find the money
Tan stole from the Li Min Jin."

"The money you think she stole. Based on a rumor."

"Nobody ever trusted her."

"Except Big Brother Choi."

"Big Brother Choi," Ironman Ma pointed out, "is
dead."

TWENTY

UNLIKE WITH MY BROTHER, I didn't negotiate a fee with this new client. It might come in handy to have Ironman's authorization to snoop around the Li Min Jin building, which was why I let him think he was hiring me. But I never wanted to be in a position of holding privileged information about the tong. If it turned out there was anything behind Ironman's suspicions, or if I found anything else of interest, I wanted to be able to shout it from the rooftops, or tell Mary, whichever seemed like a better idea.

Ironman Ma didn't seem to miss the business dimension of the transaction. He dropped two twenties on the table—even at these prices, a massively show-offy tip—and we rolled out of Miansai together. I'd have preferred to roll out on my own, to be free of him faster, but if I had, I might have missed what happened next.

I almost missed it anyway. The rumble of a motor-cycle isn't such a big deal in New York that you'd notice it. Gunshots, though—no matter what the "New York is a war zone" non–New Yorkers say—generally are.

We'd taken half a dozen steps when a bike roared up beside us. Its black-helmeted rider stuck an arm straight out. At me? At Ironman? Who cared? I tackled Iron-man, and we both crashed onto the sidewalk. A bullet whined. Glass exploded out of Miansai's storefront and rained down around us. Something else clonked to the sidewalk by my ear.

Ironman, trying to wrestle free of me, smacked an elbow into my mouth. He yanked the pistol from his belt. I smashed his hand onto the pavement. "Are you nuts?" I screeched. "There are people around!"

He shoved me away and jumped up, gun out. By then the motorcyclist had rocketed through the traffic and was gone. Ironman spun to me. "Don't you ever, *ever—*"

"You're welcome." I clambered to my feet. "And you socked me in the jaw. That better have been an accident. You think they were shooting at you, or me?"

"You? Who'd shoot at you?"

I looked down. The thing that had nearly hit me in the head was a paper-wrapped rock. I took out a tissue and reached for it, but Ironman saw it before I got there. He snatched it, pulled the rubber bands off, and unfolded the paper. Scanning it, he cursed mightily, then shoved it in his pocket and slammed the rock to the sidewalk. He slipped the gun back into his holster and stalked away.

I rubbed my shoulder, sore from the dive, and waited for Bill to cross the street.

"You okay?" he said. "You didn't seem dead, so I thought I'd stay out of sight. Let you finish your business with Ironman."

"Gee, thanks."

"I got the bike's plate number."

"Oh. Oh, well, that's actually useful."

People had materialized to gawk, and Miansai's stylish staff were out on the street gaping from their shattered window to the glass that used to be in it. I took out my phone.

"Who're you calling?" Bill asked.

"What's my choice?"

The phone rang twice and then Mary asked in my ear, "Something quick? I'm on duty and there's been shots fired—"

"On Crosby Street. I'm there."

A brief silence. "You just happen to be? Or—"

"Or. I was with Ironman Ma. I think they were for him."

"Anyone hurt?"

"My shoulder's bruised."

"You deserve it. You were with Ironman Ma. What's wrong with you? Where's the shooter?"

"On a motorcycle somewhere uptown by now."

"You have the plate?"

"Bill does." I passed the phone to Bill. "Mary wants the plate."

Bill gave her the number and gave me back the phone before Mary could yell at him.

"There was a note, too," I said to Mary.

"A note?"

"Wrapped around a rock. I didn't get a chance to read it. Ironman grabbed it."

"Do you have the rock?"

"Of course."

"Be here in five minutes," she said to me.

"On our way."

"You and Ironman?"

"Me and Bill. Ironman ran off. After he tried to shoot the shooter on a crowded street. Which I prevented."

"You're a hero. Five or I put out a BOLO." Mary clicked off.

It's a ten-minute walk from Miansai to the Elizabeth Street police station, which Mary knows full well. So we hustled. Uniforms, on their way to the scene, ran past us.

The Fifth Precinct is one of those limestone station houses built in the 1880s at the beginning of the NYPD, around the same time as the rest of Chinatown, which wasn't Chinatown yet. I told the desk sergeant, a guy named John Nee who was my writing partner in sixth grade at PS 124, that Mary was expecting us. He told us to wait and called upstairs anyway. When he said we could go on up, I gave him an eye roll and he gave me a grin.

Mary was behind her beat-up steel desk, and Chris Chiang was perched on the edge of it, talking to her, when we came into the squad room. Mary jumped to her feet.

"Sit down and spill it, you two," she said. "What were you doing hanging out with Ironman Ma? Weren't you supposed to call me after you talked to Tan Lu-Lien? Who's shooting at Ironman in the middle of the day in the middle of the street? Or were they shooting at you?"

Action in the squad room paused as the other two detectives there, one typing and the other interviewing a witness to something or other, looked over. At a shrug from Chris Chiang they went back to work. Bill and I sat on the scarred wooden chairs facing Mary's desk.

"Um," I said. "Here's the rock." I took it from my pocket wrapped in Kleenex and put it on the desk. "What should I spill first?"

"Are you all right?" She looked from one of us to the other.

"Like I said. Also, Ironman punched me in the

mouth, but I don't think he meant it. He was trying to get up after I tackled him."

"Like *I* said. You deserve it."

"Black bike," Bill said. "A Ducati, I think. Rider tall and thin. Black helmet, black plexi face shield, black leather jacket with a red stripe down the sleeve, black jeans."

"What?"

"I'm spilling. That's the shooter and the bike. I already gave you the plate number."

"And we already ran it." Mary paused as if she weren't going to tell us, but I knew her, so I just waited. She went on, "That plate belongs to a Harley stolen a month ago. The rest of the Harley's probably in whatever chop shop the shooter got the plate from. But thanks anyway."

"The description might be useful, though," I said, trying to defend Bill's honor.

"Yeah, maybe. And we may be able to pull prints from the rock, though I doubt it. Why were you with Ironman?"

"He called and invited me for tea."

"Why?"

Bill said, "Because she's gorgeous."

Mary said, "Shut up."

I said, "And he thinks you're cute, by the way, but scary. He saw me at the Li Min Jin building and wanted some inside info."

"On what?"

"At first, on whatever I knew. I told him the truth, which is that I know nothing. Then he hired me."

"He did what?"

"He and some of the other Li Min Jin members think

Tan Lu-Lien, maybe in cahoots with Big Brother Choi, has been skimming funds and hiding money, or maybe diamonds, in the Li Min Jin building walls."

I hadn't had time, on our jog over, to tell this to Bill, so he joined Mary and Chris in staring at me.

I expected some kind of incredulous response from Mary, but she said, "Well, well," and turned to Chris.

"There's been a rumor," Chris said. "Going back years. That something valuable's buried in the building. When Jackson Ting started sniffing around, we were interested to see what would happen."

"I'm a little tired of that word. Ironman kept telling me how *interested* he was. Anyway, that's what he said, and he wants me to go back and find whatever it is."

"Why you?" said Mary.

"Because I'm gorgeous. He says Tan is gay."

Mary took a second. "He wants you to be a honey trap? Are you serious?"

"He is."

Chris Chiang laughed. "It would totally work on me."

Mary shot him a look. He shrugged, still grinning. "When you saw Tan," Mary said, "you and Mel Wu, what did you talk about?"

"She wanted to know Mel's plans for the building." I recounted for Mary and Chris the story I'd told Bill already, of the tea party in Tan's office. When I was done, the two detectives exchanged glances.

"That does shore up the idea there's something there," Mary said. "Without Choi, Tan suddenly has less access to it. I wonder if that means it's in his apartment."

"It could mean that," I said, "but I have a feeling, nominal leader or not, that she doesn't get to wander around freely these days. So it could be anywhere. They can't wait to get rid of her, and they certainly don't trust her. Ironman implied they're watching her 24/7 and they have been for a while. She must know that. She might even be the one responsible for the shot at him."

"While she's being watched 24/7?" Mary said.

"There have to be an infinite number of punks in Chinatown who'd be happy to do a favor for a high-up member of the Li Min Jin."

"But why?" Bill asked reasonably. "No matter whom she eliminates, she's not going to inherit the leadership of the tong."

"Eliminating Ironman might make the removal of her fortune from the building easier?"

"Well, but if Mel sells to Jackson Ting, it'll take time to finalize the deal and clear the building," he said. "And evicting the tong if she doesn't sell will take even longer. Either way, all Tan has to do is sit back and wait until the building's emptied and then go in and grab whatever it is."

I said, "Ironman wants the building."

"He does?" said Mary.

"He thinks the Li Min Jin New York is about to be dissolved by the Li Min Jin Hong Kong. He wants to buy the building from Mel and set up a new, forward-looking—to use his word—'organization.' After, of course, they jettison Loo's faction. The 'senile old men.'"

"Who'll go quietly, sure. Would she sell to him, do you think?"

"I doubt it. Though he pointed out that she's going to have a hard time evicting the tong if she doesn't sell, and that selling to him would satisfy her uncle's wish that the tong not lose the building."

"Except it would be a different organization."

"In name only."

"And minus half the current members. What's Iron-man planning to use for money?"

"Whatever's buried in the building."

"Seriously?"

"I told you. I'm supposed to go back and find it for him. He thinks he hired me."

Mary blew out a big breath. "Okay, well, that's one thing you're definitely not going to do. If you go back to that building, I'll hurt you."

"If you hurt Lydia, I'll hurt you," Bill told her.

"And if you hurt Mary, I'll hurt you," Chris said, grinning and spreading his hands. "So, Lydia, stay away from that place and save us all a world of hurt, okay?"

TWENTY-ONE

"You get the feeling we barely escaped with our lives?"
I asked Bill once we'd issued out of the precinct doors
and back onto Elizabeth Street.

"I'll buy you lunch to celebrate."

I checked my watch. It was three o'clock by now.
No wonder I was starving. "Dumplings? Nom Wah?"

"Why not?"

As we threaded past fruit stalls and souvenir shops
over to Doyers, I called Mel. "Did you know Ironman
Ma wants you to sell the building to him?"

"Yes, he called me earlier."

"Did he actually make you an offer? Why didn't you
tell me?"

"He said he'd give me a good price, all cash, but he
didn't name a figure, and I didn't tell you because I
didn't take him seriously. Buyers who don't give a number are usually just gauging interest. I told him no. With
that kind of buyer, that's usually the end of it."

"Mel, you need to start thinking of this differently
from other real estate transactions. Ironman's a top tong
member. When he says 'cash,' he means illegally made
profits. When he says he wants the building, he wants
the building."

Mel was silent for a moment. Then, "Understood.
I'm still not going to do it."

"He thinks you might, because you'd be selling it

back to the tong and they wouldn't have to move. The way your uncle wanted."

"I hate to disappoint the ghost of Uncle Meng, but making a profit off the tong would be as bad as being their landlord. Ironman's out of luck."

"Okay then. Also, someone shot at him."

"Shot *at* him? Or shot him?"

Once a lawyer, always a lawyer. "At him. And threw a rock with a note on it. I don't think the shot was supposed to hit him, just to get his attention."

"What did the note say?"

"I don't know. I'm thinking it's all about the tong succession, but that seems to be mixed up with the building. Just be careful, okay?"

"You think someone's going to shoot at me?" She sounded not scared, but incredulous.

"Personally, I wouldn't dare. But someone might want to intimidate you into deciding one way or the other."

"Then they wouldn't really be shooting at me. Just near me. And throwing notes to tell me why. I'm starting to get fed up with these clowns."

"They're not clowns, Mel. They kill people."

"I know. But enough is enough."

"Just be careful," I repeated.

"I will. Thanks for the warning."

I hung up and Bill asked, "How is she?"

"More angry than scared."

"Good for her."

"I don't know. She might go stomping into the building and read the tong the riot act."

"You think?"

"Probably not, once she cools down, but still."

We reached Nom Wah and slid into a booth. I waved to Wilson Tang, the owner. He was yet another person I'd gone to grade school with. PS 124 was representing.

"I have an idea," I said to Bill.

"Please share."

"I'm getting interested in Tan Lu-Lien."

Bill gaped. "You're gay? How did I not know that?"

"You miss so much. Anyway, something about her doesn't add up."

"At the risk of getting hot tea spilled in my lap," he said, as the waiter set down a pot of the jasmine green Wilson knows I like, "what's going on in the Li Min Jin building isn't our case."

"Yes, I know. You're not wrong." I lifted the lid and checked the color of the tea. Another minute. "We can go back to panning for Jackson Ting gold after lunch. But don't you agree?"

"Agree with what? That something's off about Tan? I never even talked to the woman. But I have faith in your razor-sharp instincts."

I only half-heard that because I'd taken out my phone and was searching for a number. "Remember Mark Quan?" I said. "In Hong Kong?"

"How could I forget? He saved my life. And made a major pass at you, but I forgave him for that, because, you know, he saved my life. You've kept in touch with him?"

"We talk every few months."

"Is he still hitting on you? That forgiveness thing, it's not going to last forever."

I coyly didn't answer, and poured Bill tea.

He asked, "Is Mark still a cop?"

"No. He stayed on for a while—and by the way he

made lieutenant in spite of us—but finally he quit and moved to Cheung Chau. He teaches kung fu and runs a noodle shop. With his wife. He got married."

Funny how that last fact made Bill smile. I tapped Mark's number and was going to say something to Bill about not getting comfortable, but the phone came alive in my ear.

"Lydia Chin! As I live and breathe! How are things halfway around the world?"

Mark Quan had been born in Hong Kong but largely raised in North Carolina, so his English was unaccented unless you counted the Southern drawl. He spoke quietly, as though to avoid waking someone.

"Good, things are good," I said. "How about you? How's Sondra, how are the kids?"

When I said "kids," Bill's smile widened.

Mark said, "Everyone's good." His voice went back to normal and I guessed he'd gone into another room. "Sondra's well, Dani's learning soccer in school, and Pete's learning to make trouble at home. I'd tell you all about the school and the shop and all the mouthwatering meals you're missing, but I bet this isn't just a catch-up call, right?"

"How'd you know?"

"It's four a.m. here."

"Do you mind? I know it's obnoxious of me, but you're a night owl."

"Not so much anymore, with the kids, but I'm intrigued. Must be important so go ahead."

I told Mark the situation and what I wanted to know.

"Tan Lu-Lien, huh?" he said when I was finished. "Doesn't ring a bell. I didn't know there'd ever been a woman Black Shadow."

"She'd have been long before your time. She must have come here thirty-five years ago. I was just hoping you'd know someone who might remember her."

"I don't have access anymore, or I'd run the file for you. If she was a Black Shadow, she's sure to have one. Most of the guys I used to know are gone, either left the Job or left Hong Kong altogether, but let me see what I can do. I'll call you back as soon as I turn something up."

"That's what I call positive thinking. Thanks, Mark."

"My pleasure. Give my regards to Bill, and Mr. Gao."

Grandfather Gao had been the conduit to Mark when Bill and I went to Hong Kong. Having Mark on our side had made our work there possible. And also, as Bill had mentioned, at one point had kept him alive.

"I'll do that," I said. "Love to the family. Good night."

Bill and I settled into plates of shrimp and snow pea leaf dumplings, chicken siu mai, and sauteed water spinach. We tossed around a couple of ideas about Jackson Ting and about the Li Min Jin building, and about who might have taken a shot at Ironman Ma, and what the note might have said, but we didn't come up with anything brilliant.

As we were finishing our second pot of tea my phone played "Won't You Come Home Bill Bailey."

"It's my mother," I told Bill, tapping the phone on. "Hi, Ma. What's up?"

"Hello, Ling Wan-Ju. I'm calling to tell you I will be going out to your brother's for dinner."

I translated the brother code. Tim wouldn't invite her for dinner; he'd come to the apartment so she could do the cooking. Andrew lives in Tribeca; when she goes to see him, it's "over." Elliott's on the Upper East Side, so he gets "up." If she was going "out," she meant to Queens, to Ted's.

"On a weeknight? I mean, that's great, but why?"

"I decided to. I'll probably stay overnight, as it will be late to come home. I'll call you tomorrow."

She clicked off and I lowered the phone.

"You look puzzled," Bill said.

"Mystified. My mother's going to spend the night at Ted's. Not a holiday, no one's birthday…"

I called Ted.

"Hey, Lyd."

That "Lyd" was legit, so my skin didn't crawl. "Hey. Listen, I just got a call from Ma. She's coming out to your place? Spending the night?"

"Yeah, she called and said she had frozen wor tip and she'd be out on the van."

Unofficial vans run routes from Chinatown Manhattan to all New York's other Chinatowns: Sunset Park, Elmhurst, Homecrest, Bensonhurst, Little Neck, and, of course, the granddaddy of the outer-borough ones, Flushing, where Ted lives. My mother won't take the subway two stops by herself, but she has no issues traveling out to Queens in some guy's van, as long as she can back-seat drive in strident Chinese. She and all the other ladies. I've ridden out with her once or twice, and I feel for the drivers.

"Did you invite her?" I asked Ted.

"You mean, was it my idea? No, but of course we're glad she's coming. It'll be a treat for the kids."

"She's up to something."

Ted laughed. "Yeah, probably. If I find out what I'll let you know."

Bill left cash on the table, including a nice but not

grandstander tip, and we stepped out into the sunshine on Doyers. Immediately, my phone rang again. This time it was playing "Bad Boys."

"Ah," I said to Bill. "Linus." I slid the phone out and said, "Hey, Linus. You have something?"

He belted out, "I have nothing, nothing, *nothing*, if I don't have yoooooooou! I do, though. Want to hear it?"

"Why would I not?"

"Oh, like if you're in the middle of a shoot-out or an undercover sting or something."

"I see. Very thoughtful. But I'm not, so go ahead."

"Well." I heard the echo again, and pictured him with his phone on speaker in a phone stand on his equipment-cluttered desk. "So your boy Jackson Ting, he's all legit and all, as far as we can see, me and Trella, but we did find a couple of interesting things."

"Hold on a sec. Let me put you on speaker too, so Bill can get in on this." I pulled Bill's sleeve and we retreated into a doorway. I tapped the speaker button and held the phone so we could both hear. "Okay, Linus."

"Hi, Bill. You there?"

"I'm here."

"And Trella's here, so we can all have a party."

"What about Woof?" Bill asked.

"Woof? You here?"

Our doorway echoed with the baritone barking of a large dog.

"Okay, that's attendance. Now here's the thing," said Linus. "Ting's dad was in real estate, too, but not on the scale Jackson's been since he took over. Jackson started getting investors, loans, whatever, every time he decided to do a new big project. He was also pretty smart about buying up buildings and sites. Seemed to have a nose for undervalued properties, got them for a song. Want to hear it?"

"Hear what?"

"The song."

"No."

"Okay. So the first project, it was kind of a gamble for the investors, I guess, because it was such a jump from what his dad had been doing. But someone decided to risk it, it worked, and the ones since then, it seems to be the same early investors—something called the Star Group—plus now other people want to get in on the Ting bandwagon, so he never has trouble raising cash. You with me?"

I said, "Since you're talking about real estate and not tech, I'm just about following you, yes."

"Okay. But for Phoenix Towers, the Star Group didn't show up. I don't know why."

"Maybe because of the holdout building?" Bill said. "This project's a longer shot than the others, and they don't want to tie up their cash in something that might not happen?"

"There's a holdout building?" Linus asked.

"The Li Min Jin tong headquarters," I said.

Linus whistled. "A tong? Wow. Cool."

"Not cool, Linus," I said. "Stay back."

"That's who owns the building right in the middle of the site?" said Trella. "The one Ting hasn't been able to buy?"

"I didn't even know there was a building on that site he couldn't buy," Linus said. "You always know stuff." He spoke with obvious admiration. "How lucky am I, to have a partner who always knows stuff?"

"About as lucky as I am," Bill said.

"That's enough, you guys." I cut them off. "Much as Trella and I love to hear this, let the record show you're lucky to have us, and let's get on with it."

"Woof, put that in the minutes," Linus said. "Do you think the Star Group people maybe didn't want to get mixed up with a tong?"

"You asking Woof?" I said. "Sorry, I had to. Who are these first investors, this Star Group, do you know?"

"That would take a lot more research. They're shell companies that own shell companies."

"That's normal in real estate," Trella put in. "It's a tax thing."

"Would the research to find out who they are be legal?"

"Umm…" said Linus. "Up to a point, probably."

"All right, go up to that point and then stop. By which I mean *stop*. But so tell me—whoever they are, they still haven't come in on Phoenix Towers?"

"Nope. Phoenix Towers had trouble raising money at first. Then someone jumped in, and after that some of the others came back, and now it's fine. The Star Group never showed, though."

"Who's the someone who jumped in?"

"Something called Advance Capital Limited."

"Limited?"

"Yeah. It's a new corporation, working through a Hong Kong bank. We couldn't find any other projects. Looks like they were formed just to invest in this one."

"That's normal, too," Trella said. "Investors form new entities for a project, to isolate it from their other projects. Especially if the new one is risky." Before I could ask, she said, "My cousin Zino. He's with an investment bank." Trella's from an Italian family as large as any Chinese family I know. Some of her relations are, as Linus puts it, "sorta shifty," but you don't pick your family.

"And they're in Hong Kong?"

"The bank is," Linus said. "Doesn't mean the investors are. Like, remember those Trumps, they worked through Deutsche Bank? The investors could be from anywhere, but this is the bank that gave them the best deal. Or the only deal because the investment's risky. Or maybe they are in Hong Kong, but with American partners. I don't know. I might be able to find out, except this business of only doing legal stuff, it's kinda limiting—"

"Linus."

"Whoops."

I said, "But since we don't know who they are, and the Star Group is shell companies that own shell companies, then based on Trella's Real Estate 101 course, they could actually be the same people."

"You get an A," said Trella. "And you're right, it's possible, but then why hide? They never have before."

I had to admit she had a point.

"Anyway, we'll keep looking. Legally," Linus hastened to add. "But I do have one more interesting fact." He waited.

"Are you taking a dramatic pause?"

"I am. You want me to go on?"

"You want to live?"

"Guess who the lawyers are who handle all Ting's business? Including Phoenix Towers?"

I had a bad feeling. "Oh no."

"Oh yes. Uncle Tim's firm. Harriman McGill."

TWENTY-TWO

"CAN WE ASSUME your brother doesn't know that?" Bill asked after I'd thanked Linus, warned him once more about which side of the law and the Li Min Jin to stay on, and hung up. "That Harriman McGill's so huge that one hand doesn't know what the other is doing?"

"Oh, I'm sure we can. Tim never would have asked me to find him dirt the Heritage Society can use against Ting if he knew Ting was a client of his firm. But I think I'd better talk to him about it. Warn him."

"Very familial of you. Want me to come along?"

"That's a joke, right?" I lifted my phone again and tapped the number for Harriman McGill. One electronic menu and two secretaries later—that was an added secretary from former times—my brother came on the line.

"Tim Chin."

"Lydia Chin."

"Not now, Lyd. I'm working."

"So am I."

"Then why are you—oh! You found something on Jackson Ting?"

"You're going to want to hear this."

"So tell me."

"Not on the phone."

"Oh, stick that cloak-and-dagger stuff. Just tell me."

"I'm coming to your office."

"No, you're not."

"Half an hour."

"No. Don't. If you insist on this hush-hush silliness, I'll come to you. I'll have dinner with you guys."

"Ma's not here. She went out to Ted's. And it's not like I'm about to cook for you. I'm coming up. Don't worry, bro, I'm decently dressed."

I clicked off to avoid hearing the objections I was sure he was making, if only to the air in his office. "Walk me to the subway," I said to Bill. "I'll call you later. Maybe we can have dinner?"

He grinned. "I think," he said, "in light of your mother having gone out to your brother's, maybe we can."

THE OFFICES OF Harriman McGill were as stuffy as my brother. A silent elevator carried me up to the lower of the two full floors the firm occupied in a bland steel-and-glass midtown skyscraper. The firm's name announced itself in foot-high bronze letters set flush with the dark wood paneling of the elevator lobby. The reception area was hushed and serious, like a library. Each of the heavy dark coffee tables held only a philodendron, nothing as frivolous as magazines to leaf through while you waited. I gazed at paintings of the firm's founders instead, as I'm sure I was meant to, so I'd be properly impressed with my own importance that I had such an imposing law firm covering my back.

Harriman and McGill, each a dignified White man in a fifties suit and tie, gazed straight out from their portraits with the kind of frank and direct eyes that follow you all over the room. Harriman held a pipe, McGill a thick book he'd obviously been absorbed in when the painter came to call. Ornate gilt frames surrounded the portraits, and brass plaques identified them. Among the current senior partners were three grandsons: a Harriman and two McGills. The leather-bound weight of history was so heavy in this place, I was surprised any of the lawyers could stand up straight.

I didn't have a long time to sit and admire the gents. Tim appeared through a large heavy door about a minute after the receptionist buzzed him to let him know, reading my business card, that a private investigator was here to see him.

"For Pete's sake, Lyd," he said low, "did you have to give her your PI card?" He ushered me rapidly through twisty corridors to his office. You'd almost think he didn't want anyone to see me.

"Don't lawyers have PIs come visit them all the time? Half my clients are lawyers."

"That's not the kind of law we do." He held the door open for me and shut it firmly behind us.

This wasn't the same office I'd been in the last couple of times I was here, I realized, and Tim wasn't fully installed in it yet. This office was a little bit bigger than his previous one, and it had two windows, looking straight into the building next door though they did. Papers, pens, a wireless keyboard, and a flat-screen computer monitor sat on the sleek wood desk, and books filled the bookshelves, but the walls were still bare. Tim's framed law degree and a couple of other plaques and photos leaned against each other in a cardboard box.

"Hey, you get a better office when you make partner?"

"There are perks." He sat in an ergonomic chair behind his desk, as though I were a client dropping by for some mergers and acquisitions chitchat.

"Like what else?"

"Profit-sharing. Different levels of input into decision-making. Expected attendance at certain meetings.

New responsibilities in terms of firm management and mentoring the new hires. Look, Lyd, why are you here?"

"It's about Jackson Ting."

"I know that."

I kept myself from heaving a giant sigh. "I asked Linus to look into Ting's finances."

"You didn't. That pest?"

"He's running a business. I'm his cousin. The least I can do is help him out."

"He's a hacker. He got thrown out of high school."

"He's older and wiser now. And good at his work."

"Not that much older, and everything he does is probably illegal."

"Not this time. I told him to keep his nose clean."

"Oh, and that means he will?"

Tim's sarcasm reminded me of Ironman Ma, and not in a good way.

"Whatever it means, you'll want to know what he found."

"I'm not sure I do, if he found it illegally."

"He found it," I said, "by a little due-diligence background research. Jackson Ting's real estate attorneys are Harriman McGill."

Tim opened his mouth, closed it, and opened it again to slowly say, "Oh, no."

"No shit, oh no."

"Are you sure? Maybe that punk Linus doesn't know what he's talking about. Wait, just be quiet." I kept myself from snapping at him and sat there while he tapped his fingers along his keyboard. He peered at his monitor, then flopped back in his chair. "Goddammit. He's Harriman's client. Harriman himself, Leo. You're right."

"I'm sorry."

"You're fired."

"What?"

"Jackson Ting. Whatever you were doing, stop now."

"Tim." I leaned forward. "If Phoenix Towers gets built, it'll destroy our neighborhood."

"I know."

"The Heritage Society—"

"I know!" He whacked his hand flat on the desk. "I want it stopped. It'll be a disaster if it gets built. You don't have to tell me that. But I can't be involved in stopping it, now that I know this. You can't either."

"*I* can't?"

"Don't you get it? They'd fire me before I finish unpacking." He spread his hands to show me his rung-up-the-ladder office. "Being a team player's important here. If Ting's a client of one of the senior partners, then he's a client of mine."

"Not of mine."

"And I'm not either! You're *fired*."

"You're not even in the real estate department."

"Doesn't matter."

"Ting has other projects. If this one's stopped, he'll go on to something else. The firm will still have his business."

"Lydia, it doesn't matter!" Tim practically shouted. He collected himself. "It's not the outcome. It's the process. I'm a new junior partner. I have different responsibilities now, and the partners are watching to see how I handle them. There's no way I can stab one of our clients in the back and not end up out on the street." He blew out a slow breath and looked down at his hands. "Hey. Does Mel Wu know this? Did you tell her?"

"I didn't tell her, but she might know. It's not exactly top secret stuff. Why?"

"I don't know. I don't know why I asked that." A slow flush crept into his chunky cheeks.

Holy cow. He didn't know, uh-huh. Under other circumstances I'd have flown directly into merciless teasing mode, but he was too upset. With saintly forbearance, I kept my mouth shut.

Tim looked up. "Do me a favor, Lyd? Leave. I have to think about this. By myself." He stood.

I stood, too. "Don't bother. I can find my way out."

"No," he said, coming around his desk. "I'll take you. It's how we do things here."

TWENTY-THREE

"I CAN'T BELIEVE IT," I said to Bill over linguine Bolognese at Piccolo Angolo, a little family place in the West Village. "He's ready to sell the neighborhood up the river to keep his job at that pompous place."

"Down the river."

"What?"

"You sell things down the river. When you get arrested you get sent up the river."

"What if the river's like the Hudson and flows both ways?"

"Hmm. Good question." Bill poured me more red wine.

"Stop," I told him. "Don't waste that. I'm going home with you anyway."

"Just trying to ease the pain of your day." He moved the bottle to his own glass.

"I don't think a bottle of wine will do it. Unless I could break it over Tim's head. Or maybe Ironman's." I speared some linguine. "And Mel Wu! Who'd have thought it? My brother's got a crush on a tall Chinese American social justice attorney."

"Why not? She's pretty, smart, self-possessed, classy—"

I stopped the pasta on its way to my mouth. "That's why not! Tim hasn't dated anyone except vacuous giggly little blondes since he asked Sophia Wong out in third grade and she turned him down."

"Mel Wu speaks his language. Law book."

"True." I ate that pasta forkful and another, then sighed. "I actually feel sorry for him. Not even counting Mel, here are two things he really cares about, Chinatown and Harriman McGill, on opposing sides with him in the middle."

"Kind of like you, with me and your mother."

"You're giving yourself a lot of credit there."

"I'd be happy to come over to her side, you know."

"Don't take it up with me. I'm just the net." I gave him a sharp glance. "Don't take it up with her, either."

He shrugged and drank some wine. Our ground rules are established. I know he doesn't love the situation, but it's the best I can offer right now. He knows *that*, and he changed the subject.

"Well, at least about your brother firing you, I wouldn't worry too much. We still have three clients."

I looked at him. "Mel, Nat, and Ironman. The same case, and they all want different things."

"Or three different cases, all centering on the same building."

"Does it matter which?"

"I'm not sure. It's an issue of perspective, I guess." I sipped my wine. "I wonder if Mel knows."

"About your brother's crush?"

"Now that you mention it, I do wonder that, but no. I wonder if she—or Nat—know about the buried treasure."

"Know where it is?"

"Or short of that, know whether it exists. Or short of *that*, know about the rumors that it exists."

He put his glass down and said, "Go ahead. Ask her."

"You mean call her? When we're having a romantic candlelit dinner?"

"I'd rather you call her now than for her to still be on your mind later." He gave me a melodramatically significant leer.

I rolled my eyes and took out my phone.

"Hi, Lydia. What's up?"

"Hi, Mel. How're you doing?"

"I'm fine. Is this a check-up call? Thanks, but I'm really okay. Though I was going to call you anyway. To set up a time to go see Mr. Loo in the morning."

"Any time's good for me. Whatever works for you. But no, I'm glad to hear you're doing all right, but I wasn't calling to check up. I have a question."

"Shoot."

Given what had happened when I was with Ironman Ma, that wasn't the best expression to use, but she probably wasn't thinking about that. "I've been hearing from a couple of sources there might be something valuable buried in the Li Min Jin building. Do you know anything about that?"

"Buried? You mean physically, like pirate treasure?"

"Probably not that, but yes."

"I never heard that. What's it supposed to be? Who's supposed to have buried it? My uncle?"

"It's not clear. Apparently it's a rumor going back years. But you don't know about it?"

"No. I wonder... Could that be what Mr. Chang's message was about?"

"I thought about that, too. Maybe Mr. Loo can shed some light."

She laughed. "Shedding light isn't Mr. Loo's specialty. If it's something he can say with a scowl, he'll be more likely to tell us. How about eight thirty? We can meet at Fay Da and have coffee first."

"Perfect. See you then."

Bill waited expectantly, then frowned when, instead of pocketing the phone, I tapped another number.

"Hey," he said. "I didn't suggest you hold office hours."

"One more. Hi, Nat," I said when Nat's voice arrived in my ear. I asked her the same question I'd asked Mel. Her answer was similar.

"Buried treasure? Come on, you're kidding."

"No. It's just a rumor but a well-established one. Going back years."

"What's it supposed to be?"

"Maybe cash, maybe diamonds. You never heard this?"

"Never. Do you think it's true?"

"I have no idea. Do you?"

Silence. Then, "No. It's ridiculous. Who'd bury things in the walls of a building these days? You know what I think? I think it's probably just some of the tong members trying to account for Uncle Meng's attachment to the place. He could've moved to some glam penthouse whenever, or at least taken Jackson's offer now, but he never did. Some of those lamebrains are so unsentimental and greedy themselves they think everything's about money, for everybody."

I didn't point out that Jackson Ting's offer was much newer than the rumors. "Okay. I just wanted to be sure that now that we've heard this, you don't want me to do anything differently."

"You mean, about getting Mel to sell Jackson the building? Because it might have buried treasure? Oh, for God's sake, are you kidding me? If Jackson knocks the building down and finds Aladdin's lamp, good for him. As long as he leaves me alone!"

Bill waited for me to slide the phone back into my pocket. "You done?"

"I'm all yours."

"I fear that will never be true, but I'll take what I can get." He signaled for the check. "You didn't mention to either of them that Tan Lu-Lien might have a hand in the buried treasure."

"No. I wanted to know what they knew about it, not tell them things."

"They're your clients."

"So's Ironman. You don't find me telling him the time of day. And so," I said as I gave the waiter my credit card, "is my brother."

"He fired you."

"He didn't ask for his dollar back. That contract's still valid."

"That's legally debatable. But is that why you're such a big spender, buying me dinner?"

"It's my case. You're my partner. It's the least I can do."

"I don't know," he said. "I can think of a couple of other things you can do, too."

TWENTY-FOUR

MORNING DAWNED BRIGHT and early, and so did I. Bill rolled over and sighed.

"Quiet," I said. "Stay asleep, see if I care. I'll call you later."

He opened one eye. "You want me to come along?"

"When you're so adorable lounging here in bed? Actually, I think Mr. Loo would be more on guard with you there than with just me and Mel."

"You're going to play the we're-just-girls card, aren't you?"

"We sure are. See you later."

I raced home, showered, and dressed in respectable black slacks, a pearl gray sweater, and a black wool jacket. I'd considered a red blouse—a power combination, and red's a lucky color for Chinese people—but you can't power dress and play I'm-just-a-girl at the same time. I let my bi on its delicate gold chain hang outside the sweater, pulled on ankle books with small heels, took a shoulder bag instead of a backpack, and headed out to Fay Da to meet Mel.

She'd beaten me there and managed to score a table, not the easiest thing to do at what, for my money, is Chinatown's best bakery. Plus it was the table in the window.

"Hi," I said. "Let me just get breakfast." At the counter I picked up a sesame ball and a cup of milk tea. I slid into the chair opposite her. She wore a navy pantsuit with a pale blue blouse, and she was a couple of bites into a taro mini—vanilla sponge cake wrapped around sweetened taro paste.

"I love these things," she said. "Mom used to bring us here to pick up treats for Uncle Meng. I thought it was funny because he lived around the corner. Why didn't we bring him cookies from the bakery in Scarsdale, that he couldn't get every day? She said no, he liked Chinese sweets, and we couldn't go empty-handed. To this day I can't visit anyone without a bakery box." She lifted a Fay Da box from the chair beside her. "For Mr. Loo."

I grinned and sipped my tea. "In my family it's oranges. Or pomelos, or tangerines. You don't have citrus, you don't go."

She smiled as she drank her coffee. "Tell me about your family. I realize I hardly know you."

"And yet we've shared so much. Dead bodies, gangsters, tattooed ladies…"

"All the more reason."

"Okay." I took a bite of my sesame ball, leaning over the plate to avoid getting errant seeds on my sweater. "I was born here in Chinatown, youngest of five and the only girl." I gave her a quick Chin family history: immigrant parents, Ma's work as a seamstress, Ba's restaurant, his death. My brothers and their families. My career, my partnership with Bill.

"He seems like a great guy," she said.

"He is, a real prize. Don't ever let on I said that."

"My lips are sealed. But isn't your mother after you to get married and have children?"

"To Bill? It's taken her years to stop chasing him with a broom every time he comes near me. Besides"—I drank some tea—"she already has four grandchildren, two of Ted's and two of Elliott's. And a wedding to plan, Andrew's. He's marrying his boyfriend in the spring."

"And your mom's good with that? She's an open-minded woman."

"She really likes Tony. The boyfriend. He can cook."

Mel laughed. "But she still has two unmarried children to worry about. You and Tim." She sipped her coffee, smiling a little, not looking at me.

Oh my God. Was she fishing?

"I don't know what bothers Ma more right now," I said exploratorily. "That I'm seeing Bill, or that Tim's not seeing anyone."

"Probably that one," she said in an offhanded way. "Nothing for her to look forward to."

"She keeps trying to set him up with sweet young women. Chinese, of course. But I think they're a little too sweet, because it never takes."

"Really," Mel said, more a pensive comment than a question. "Well." She brightened. "Shall we go?"

We went. Beefy was manning his station at the Li Min Jin building door. When I asked, in Chinese, for Mr. Loo, he spoke into a cell phone. He clicked off, said—also in Chinese—"He'll be right down," and stepped aside to let us in.

I translated sotto voce for Mel. True to Beefy's word, a moment later a door opened on the second floor, and Mr. Loo made his way down the stairs. His pace was unhurried, but I got the feeling he was holding himself back so he'd seem not particularly interested in us. This was a guy in the running for tong leader. He must have been torn between not wanting to appear to be at Mel's

beck and call just because she was the landlady now
and demonstrating he could expeditiously take care of
whatever business we outsiders had and get us out of
the building fast.

"Wu Mao-Li," he said. "Chin Ling Wan-Ju." Going
on in English, he said, "I'm happy to see you." His
scowl contradicted that, unless what I was looking at
actually was Mr. Loo's happy face. "I understand you
were looking for me yesterday? I apologize. I was out
on business."

And what business might that be, I didn't ask.

"Thank you for taking time today, Loo Hu-Li," Mel
said, handing him the bakery box. He nodded, took it
from her, and gestured us to follow him. He didn't take
us upstairs but went to the back of the building and
opened a door behind the elevator. It led into a dark
room furnished with heavy upholstered chairs and low
tables, arranged into two sitting areas. Mr. Loo flicked
a switch, and fluorescent lights flooded the room with
their unflattering glow. Waving us to chairs, he crossed
to a sink counter against the wall that held a plug-in kettle and various canisters of teas and boxes of teabags,
plus the usual trimmings—a carton of milk, a diner-
type sugar container, a few spoons, and sugar substi-
tutes in a rainbow of little packages.

Mr. Loo plugged the kettle in and reached into a cabinet, extracting three mismatched mugs. He didn't ask
us what we wanted—or if—but unwrapped green teabags from New Kam Man. He opened the bakery box
and put it on the low table, revealing a variety of pastries. A step down, I thought as the water boiled, from
Tan Lu-Lien's formal hospitality in the same location

a few floors above. Or from Big Brother Choi's elegant private quarters at the top.

This must be where the tong brought visitors to whom they wanted to give an unspoken but emphatic sense of their own unimportance. The opposite of what you got—equally unspoken, equally emphatic—in Harriman McGill's reception room.

Mel and I waited in silence for the brief time the kettle took to boil, which Mr. Loo allowed to happen though the tea was green. He poured water in the mugs and handed us each one. Mine was from the Canal Street branch of Citibank.

Mr. Loo sat, and only then did he ask, "How can I help you, Wu Mao-Li?" He turned with exaggerated courtesy. "Or you, Chin Ling Wan-Ju?" Translation: What the hell is this PI doing here?

"I've asked Chin Ling Wan-Ju to accompany me when I come to this building," Mel said. "So I won't be alone."

"I hope you know you'd be perfectly safe here."

"I'm sure I would." Mel smiled, looking not quite sure of anything, probably a look she'd worked on in a mirror because it was unnatural to her. "But Chin Ling Wan-Ju is my friend's sister, and I'm grateful she's willing to come along."

"My friend's sister," not "Mr. Gao's semi-granddaughter." Smart move.

Though, I reflected, Tim was the only one of my brothers Mel had met. He'd be interested to know he'd been promoted to friend. If I decided to tell him.

"Whatever makes you feel comfortable, of course," Mr. Loo said. "Now please tell me, why did you want to see me?" Translation: Let's get on with it.

"First, I wanted to offer my condolences on Chang Yao-Zu's death. You two knew each other for so many years."

"Yes, we did." A sorrowful cast softened Mr. Loo's resident scowl. "I was here when Yao-Zu joined the Li Min Jin. In fact, I was here when your uncle came from Hong Kong, as well." Another two or three seconds; then the edges of Mr. Loo's features hardened once more. The sorrow might have been genuine, but I was willing to bet the softness was about as real as Mel's diffidence. "Thank you for your sympathy. Whoever broke in and committed this outrage will be found and dealt with."

"By the police, I'm sure you mean."

A tight smile. "Of course."

"And that's what you think it was?" Mel asked. "A break-in? From outside?"

"The window was open, its latch damaged. No one not known to the guard came through the front door, and the building's rear exit can't be opened from the outside except by key. In addition, anyone coming in the rear would find himself in the basement. To reach Choi Meng's living quarters, he'd have to pass through the entry hall. The guard saw no strangers. Everyone in the building at the time of Chang Yao-Zu's death was a Li Min Jin member." Translation: That this crime had been committed by a Li Min Jin member, by a sworn brother, was unthinkable. "Except the two of you, of course." Loo smiled like ice cracking underfoot. "And the large man with you." Turning to me: "Your partner, I understand?"

"Yes," I said. "His name's Bill Smith, which I'm sure you know already."

"I do."

"But Mr. Loo," said Mel, maybe to head off a fencing match, "who would dare break into a tong's building? That's madness."

"Under most circumstances, yes. But we may erroneously be seen as weak in this brief period, between the death of Choi Meng and the election of a new leader. Looking back—though it was done out of respect for your uncle—it may have been a mistake not to station a security man in his living quarters."

"Mr. Chang was there."

"He wouldn't have been expected to be. Those quarters were entirely private during Choi Meng's lifetime. We were attempting to keep them that way."

Mel might have been thinking, as I was, that the fact that the apartment was empty was more likely to have been known to Li Min Jin members than to Chinatown's cat burglars, but she didn't say so. "So you think," she asked, "that whomever we're talking about, he wasn't after Mr. Chang, per se? He was there to burglarize my uncle's apartment?"

"Whomever" and "per se" in one sentence, in conversation with a gangster. *Oh, Tim, this is the woman for you.*

"I can't be expected to know what would be in such a person's mind," said Loo.

Give yourself some credit; you're such a person yourself, I thought, while Loo sipped his tea and then went on.

"But this can't be why you've come," he said to Mel. "To ask me my ideas about the crime?" He sounded as though if it were why we were here, he'd be both annoyed and relieved.

"No, Mr. Loo, of course you're quite right. In addition to offering my condolences on Mr. Chang's death, I'm very much hoping you can answer a question for me. Mr. Chang had been planning to give me a message from my uncle. Something, he said, Uncle Meng had wanted me to know but hadn't wanted to write down. Mr. Chang never had the chance to tell me what it was. I'm so hoping that you know." She looked at him with innocent eyes.

He looked back at her with guarded ones. "A message from Choi Meng? No, I don't know what it would be. Do you know what it concerned?"

"I don't have any idea. He'd never mentioned anything like this to you? Or Mr. Chang hadn't?"

"No, Wu Mao-Li, I'm sorry."

"Oh. That's disappointing."

"I'm sure it must be. I regret I can't be of more help."

"If you don't know, you don't know. It's not your fault." Mel wrapped both hands around her mug. "But I do have another question, if that's all right."

"Of course."

She glanced from me back to him. "I've heard rumors about this building, that something very valuable is buried here."

Loo didn't blink. "I've heard those rumors also."

"Do you believe them?"

"No."

Mel's face stayed innocently expectant and she said nothing. I smiled inside. It was a lawyer's trick, and a PI one I'd learned from Bill. If you just keep waiting, most people will assume they haven't made themselves clear and need to go on.

Loo did go on. "Choi Meng's greatest tragedy was

the death of his wife and child. He always regretted that he had no family of his own."

"He had us. My parents, my sister, me."

"He viewed your mother's marriage in the traditional way. She had married into her husband's family. So his role in your lives was naturally limited. He was a doting uncle—I remember your visits, you and your sister chasing each other up and down the stairs—but you weren't his.

"But he was head of this tong. The Li Min Jin became his family. Through all his years as leader, in his heart he truly was Big Brother. Whenever this so-called treasure is mentioned, it's always said to be money stolen from the Li Min Jin." Loo looked hard at Mel. "The allegation that your uncle stole from his tong family is absurd. And offensive."

We drank tea in silence. I had another question for Mr. Loo, but I had a sense it wasn't my turn yet. After a minute or two, Mel said, "All right. I'm glad to hear you say that. But what if the thief were Tan Lu-Lien?"

"Choi Meng loved Tan Lu-Lien like a daughter," Loo said. "She hadn't been here three months from Hong Kong when he invited her to accompany us to the cemetery on Qing Ming to sweep his wife's grave."

"Quite an honor."

"He loved her like a daughter," Loo repeated, "and if he found she'd stolen from the Li Min Jin, he'd have had her killed."

Mel's eyes widened. She recovered quickly and said, "What if he didn't know?"

"Wu Mao-Li," Loo said severely, "Choi Meng would have known." He took a brief pause. "But Tan Lu-Lien also loves this tong. It gave her a family, too, after she arrived from Hong Kong. She has never married, and women, perhaps, need family even more than men." He smiled with cold sympathy at the two single women drinking tea with him. "I don't think she would steal from this tong any more than your uncle would have."

Mel nodded, but didn't respond.

My turn. "Ironman Ma thinks she did," I said.

"He's a fool," Loo snapped. "That kind of thinking is one reason he's not fit to lead this tong."

I smiled, trying to look as innocent as Mel. "Of course I wouldn't have an opinion on internal tong business," I said. "Though it does seem odd that some people would think there's even a choice to be made between experience"—I nodded at him—"and inexperience. But Mr. Loo, I'm very curious about a point of tong history. May I presume on you?"

I could tell he wasn't convinced by my flattery, but he was pleased I'd tried it, which was the polite way.

"If I can help," he said gruffly.

"This situation where the two tongs united—or rather, where the Li Min Jin absorbed the Ma Tou. I grew up in Chinatown, and I've never heard of any other case where that happened. Can you explain what was behind it?"

Loo leaned back in his chair and steepled his fingers. "For the Li Min Jin, the consolidation had practical motivations. More territory, less conflict." He peered at me, his sour face taking on a shadow of something like benevolence. "As a smart young woman, you can see that for yourself, and so I think that's not the question you're asking. You're wondering why Long Lo was willing to give up his authority."

"Yes," I admitted. "It's just so unusual."

"Choi Meng and Long Lo shared a sorrow," Loo said. "Long Lo had also lost his only child, a three-year-old daughter. When Choi Meng's son died, Choi Meng turned all his effort to the care of his wife and after her death, to the strength of the Li Min Jin. Long Lo, it was said, never recovered from his own loss. He seemed almost grateful for Choi Meng's overture. At the time of their discussions, the Li Min Jin was strong and the Ma Tou weak. If I had been negotiating, I might have helped Long Lo weigh the hazards of a tong war against the lure of a peaceable retirement."

"Do you think that's what Choi Meng did?"

Loo gave me a steady look. "It's what I would have done."

Mel appeared to catch the same vibe I did: that it was time for us to go. She picked up her shoulder bag.

"Before you leave," Loo said, "may I ask you something?"

"Of course." Mel smiled. "That's only fair."

"What are your plans for this building?"

Mel shook her head. "Mr. Loo, I haven't decided yet. I'm weighing many factors. I was hoping I could learn the contents of my uncle's message and that it would help me." She paused. "Can you tell me, what would be your ideal disposition of it? Assuming I was prepared to split the profits of any sale with the tong?"

Which I was not ready to assume, but I understood why she asked the question.

"I would prefer," he said without hesitation, "that you sell the building." He looked straight at her. "I'd like the Li Min Jin to…reconstitute. The world has changed. It's full of new opportunities. We need new thinking, but we've gotten complacent. This building encourages us to go on today the way we did yesterday, the same way as the day before that. Your uncle and I talked about this many times. He seemed to agree with my thinking. I saw Jackson Ting's offer as an opportunity, and I was disappointed when Choi Meng refused to sell. The Li Min Jin needs a fresh start."

And, I thought, the fresh infusion of cash you think you'll get from the sale. Plus, Ironman might be right: Without owning the building, he'd have far less chance of being seen as the legitimate new leader. Loo was canny enough to know that.

And I was just barely canny enough not to point it out.

"Thank you, Mr. Loo," Mel said. "That's a very direct answer."

"As you've done since you were a child," Loo said, with a trace of a smile, "you asked a very direct question."

TWENTY-FIVE

MR. LOO ESCORTED us to the front door. Before we actually got there I managed to catch Mel's eye. I flicked a glance upstairs.

She stopped and turned to Loo. "Thank you so much for your time, Mr. Loo. I'm going to go up to my uncle's apartment before we leave. I'd like to take some of his personal effects to my sister's little boy. Paintbrushes and so forth." She smiled. "Lydia, will you come with me?"

"Of course. Thank you, Mr. Loo."

Loo looked more pained than usual, but said, "I'll accompany you."

"Oh, no, please don't trouble yourself," Mel told him. "As you said, I'm sure we'll be fine."

We turned together and trotted off up the stairs.

"Well done," I said. "Paintbrushes."

"I guess you want to take another look around? I should have thought of that myself."

"I'm the professional gumshoe here."

We climbed the stairs in silence, glancing in the open doors of the lounges where men sat, smoked, talked, and played cards. We got stink eye in return.

"Don't take it personally," I said. "No one likes the landlady."

"I wonder how many of these guys even know I own the building yet."

"You're right. They could be giving us those looks just because they're evil bad guys." At the next landing I asked, "Loo wants you to sell the building. Do you think he really doesn't believe there's anything buried here, or he's just trying to keep you from being interested in finding it so you won't delay selling?"

"Oh," Mel said. "I hadn't thought of that. I guess it could be that, but his reasoning sounds very him. Both for why Uncle Meng and Tan Lu-Lien aren't likely to have stolen the tong's money, and for selling the building."

At the top Mel took out her keys and unlocked the apartment door. We entered and stood for a moment in the middle room. Little had changed. Chang Yao-Zu's blood had dried to brown on the low painting table and the floor. Mel looked at it and shook her head.

"Do you want to leave?" I asked.

"No, no. It's fine." She walked forward. "Is there anything special you wanted to check out?"

"I thought we might try the altar again. To see if it's clearer to you what's changed. We could also go through your uncle's desk, his painting table, things like that, though I don't think it's likely we'll find anything important. The police already searched them."

"Let's try the altar first. Then if I can't figure it out, maybe it'll come to me while we're raiding the paperwork."

As it turned out, we never did get to the paperwork.

We walked into the red-walled bedroom and over to the altar. The Buddha statue, the ancestor tablets, the candles, the oranges—now shriveled—and the incense sticks were sitting patiently on the red-and-gold silk cloth. Mel stood and moved her gaze slowly from side to side.

I saw her eyes widen.

"Oh," she said. "Oh my God, Mel Wu, you're such an idiot. Lydia, look! It's not that something's missing. Something's been added." She pointed to a cinnabar box on the altar.

The size of a carton of kitchen matches, it was delicately carved in dragons, bats, and tortoises. It sat not in the altar's center, but to the right side, directly in front of a small wooden tablet. "This was never there," she said.

"The tablet? Or the box?"

"The box. I don't know about the tablet." She peered at the black wooden board with its gold Chinese characters. Grinning, she said, "They all look alike to me."

"Very funny. Allow me. The rest of these"—I gestured at the forest of character-carved boards on the altar—"are for your uncle's parents and grandparents, and this one's for his wife. That small one where the box is, is for the baby."

"Uncle Meng's son? That baby? Do you put that on an ancestor altar?"

"Not traditionally, no. It would be on the baby's grave for the first year, until his name is carved into the stone. It also wouldn't be this fancy, just a plain plank, like the one on Choi Meng's grave now. I wonder why it's here?"

Mel shook her head.

"Mel?" I said after a moment. "Don't you think we should find out what's in the box?"

"Um, sure."

She didn't reach for it.

"You want me to?"

"No. I'm being superstitious. I don't know why. I

feel like someone's watching." She picked up the box, gazed at it for a moment, then lifted off the lid. Nestled on red silk was a silver key.

We looked at each other.

"To what?" I asked.

"I don't know," she said.

"Sure you do," said a voice behind us. "Think harder."

We both whipped around to see Ironman Ma, muscles bulging from his white T-shirt, smiling in the bedroom doorway.

Someone *had* been watching.

"What are you doing here?" I demanded, in a voice a few notes higher than usual because it was riding an adrenaline flood.

"I heard you tell Old Loo you were coming up here. It sounded like a really good idea. Hi." He strode into the room, hand out to Mel. "I'm Ironman. We met at Choi Meng's funeral."

I could tell by Mel's pallor that her heart had jolted the way mine had, but when she spoke her voice was completely under control. She sounded like an irritated teacher scolding a disruptive student. "I remember you. I just don't remember inviting you here to join us." She stared at his hand until he let it drop.

"My bad. I forgot to ask. Hey, can I join you girls? Great. So what's the key to?"

Tight-jawed, Mel said, "I don't know."

"Sure you do," he repeated. "Choi Meng left it for you. You must know what it opens."

"I have no idea, and it's none of your business either way."

"Oh, you're wrong there. It's absolutely my business. See, I think whatever it's a key to—and I think it's to some door in this building, since you ask—it will eventually get you to the fortune Choi Meng hid. Choi Meng and that bitch Tan. Maybe it's like a treasure hunt, but you have to start somewhere, huh? It's our fortune, the tong's money. They hid it, I want it, you can find it, so let's stop this game, okay?"

"Ironman," I said, stepping up to him, "get lost."

"You know you don't mean that."

"You know I do."

"My uncle," said Mel, fire shooting from her eyes, "would never have stolen from the Li Min Jin. Any more than he would have stolen from my mother or my sister or me. This tong was his family. Most tong members, even the worst of the bottom-feeders, understand what that means, but obviously, not you. You're a second-rate bodybuilder playing the role of tong member, and if the tong chooses you as leader, they'll be making a huge mistake. Now get out of my way."

That speech froze Ironman in wide-eyed disbelief just long enough for Mel to push past him, but before she got halfway through the study he took two longs strides and clutched her arm.

"Let go of me!" she barked.

He didn't, but to grab her he'd turned his back on me. I snapped a roundhouse kick into his blue-jeaned butt.

He yelped and his grip must have loosened, because Mel wrenched her arm away. I kicked him again, mostly to make him mad so he'd focus on me. He still seemed torn, so I plowed in and socked him in the ribs. Twice. That got his attention. He'd better take care of me, because I wasn't giving up.

Ironman spun and crouched into a fighting stance, topped by a fierce face—a caricature of one, really. It was the fact that he was loony enough to think balling up his features like that would scare me that made him actually scary. He stood low and showy, but his fists were too tight and his feet were too wide apart and his center of gravity was too far forward.

I feinted at him.

He gave an ear-splitting yell and threw a palm-heel strike. Dumb move; I wasn't close enough for that. I slammed his arm aside and danced back, grinning to keep him mad. I came in again, and when he kicked, I leaned to the left, grabbed his leg and yanked. His momentum and lack of balance threw him stumbling forward.

I yelled, "Come on!" Mel and I took off as Ironman crashed into Choi Meng's brush cabinet.

We dashed down the stairs. We were fast—we'd made the second floor before we heard Ironman Ma shout over the railing in Chinese not to let us leave.

TWENTY-SIX

As we careened down to the first floor Beefy jumped from his stool at the door. He faced us, arms crossed, barring our way.

"Move!" Mel commanded.

I didn't know if Beefy spoke English but Mel's tone could've split rocks. I could see that she startled him for a second, but he recovered.

I spun and yelled up the stairs in English, "You can't keep us here."

"Who wants you?" Ironman answered, also switching to English. He made his way down leaning on the handrail and favoring his left leg. Look at that. Even hurt, people around here avoided the elevator. "I just want that box. Not even the box. Just the key."

"What's going on?" That loud demand came from Tan Lu-Lien, standing at the top of the third-floor stairs. She glanced up at Ironman and down at Beefy and us. By now half a dozen other men had emerged and were milling around the small entryway looking unpleasant. Tan started down. "What's happening?"

"They stole something from Choi Meng's quarters," Ironman called. "And attacked me when I tried to stop them."

I was about to bellow my dispute of these charges, but I realized Mel was not moving, just watching Tan's progress and radiating such coiled anger you could almost see the cartoon wavy lines. Okay, not my usual shoot-from-the-hip strategy, but I could do it. We waited until Tan hit the entry floor and stalked across it to us. The crowd of men, which had grown, parted uneasily to let her pass.

"What's wrong?" she snapped.

Mel said, "My uncle's possessions are mine."

"She stole that box!" Ironman shouted, as he made it to the ground floor, too. He shoved a T-shirted guy aside and limped up to us. "It belongs to the Li Min Jin."

"What box?" said Tan.

Mel locked on Tan's eyes. After a moment she reached into her shoulder bag and took out the cinnabar box.

Ironman lunged for it. Without taking her eyes off Mel, Tan slammed her arm out like a sledgehammer. She caught him in the chest.

"Screw that—" he started, but now her head snapped to him.

"I'm the head of this tong until a permanent selection is made." Her voice was iron. "Do you want to challenge me here and now?"

I wished he would. He had ten inches, forty pounds, and twenty years on her, and I had no doubt she'd beat him bloody.

Self-preservation warred with machismo on Ironman's face. Finally he just growled, "That box is ours."

Tan turned her gaze back to Mel. She made no effort to reach for the box. "What's in it?"

Mel lifted the lid.

Tan regarded the key for a long moment. Looking up again, she said, "What does it open?"

"I don't know."

"She does," Ironman snarled. "And so do you, Tan

Lu-Lien." He raised his voice to address the milling crowd, which, I saw, now included Mr. Loo standing apart at the back. "A lot of money belonging to us, to the Li Min Jin, is somewhere in this building. Choi Meng left this key for his niece. She knows what it opens, and the money is there!"

"That's a hell of a lot of assumptions," I said. "Starting with, there's money at all. And that this key leads to it. And that Mel knows where it is."

"Old Chang had a message for her from Choi Meng. That's what it was about, this key and the money."

"I never got that message," said Mel evenly. "Mr. Chang was killed first."

"How do we know that? You found his body. You could have killed him right after he told you the secret."

"So could you," I said. I didn't like the way the crowd was beginning to stir. "So could any of you, more easily than we could."

"Why would we?"

"Why would I?" Mel said. "If he'd told me a secret that was going to make me rich? Now tell this gentleman to move. We're leaving." She turned to the door.

"No." Tan spoke in a voice that silenced the rumbling men and made Mel spin back to face her. "You can go. But the box will stay."

"The box," Mel said after a brief pause, "is mine."

"I agree. And there's no fortune hidden in this building. But it seems the only way to prove that is to open every door, closet, and cabinet here. I suppose we'll have to knock holes in every wall, too." She turned to glare at Ironman, and her voice got louder. "I'm well aware of the rumors that Choi Meng and I stole money from the Li Min Jin and hid it here. That sort of disrespect directed at me is not surprising, despite my lifetime of service to this tong. But I won't have Choi Meng's name dishonored in this way. Chang Yao-Zu's funeral is tomorrow. This is still a house of mourning. The day after that, we'll open anything in this building anyone wants opened. We'll knock holes in any wall someone thinks something might be buried in. If that leaves the Li Min Jin in a pile of rubble, so be it. It seems to be what some people want."

Then she repeated the entire speech in Cantonese, for the benefit of the monolingual gangsters in the crowd.

Mel waited until Tan had finished. "This pile of rubble," she said slowly and deliberately, "belongs to me."

Tan held out her hand.

I ran a couple of escape scenarios in my head. None of them ended in any way other than me and Mel getting clobbered and thrown out of the building without the box. But she was the client. And I was almost as furious with these hoods as she clearly was. If she wanted to make a stand on principle, I was willing to get battered and bruised along with her.

I was wondering whether gymnastics training would give her the ability to leap to the staircase railing and mow a bunch of these guys down with scissors kicks when she handed Tan the box, saying, "I expect to get it back."

"You will."

Without replying Mel turned again to the door. At a command from Tan, Beefy opened it for us. I threw Ironman a scowl as we left.

TWENTY-SEVEN

"You all right?" I asked Mel when the Li Min Jin door thunked shut behind us. Out on Bayard Street shoppers and tourists were bustling around in the sunshine as though rebellion weren't brewing inside the tong walls and Mel and I hadn't just barely escaped intact.

"Me?" she said. "You're the one who had a fistfight with that creep. Are *you* all right?"

"He's a marshmallow."

"He's a weightlifter."

"A muscle-bound marshmallow. My mother would say, that candle's all wax, no wick."

"Honestly," Mel said, straightening her jacket, "I'm sorry about that. I hired you to be a bodyguard-by-inference. I didn't think you'd have to get in actual fights."

"We're a full-service PI agency. Though it's a good thing Bill wasn't here."

"Why? I was just thinking he should have been. Nothing personal—I mean, you scare *me*—but Ironman might have been intimidated by him and not started anything."

"Thanks for the compliment. You scare me too. Bill has a short fuse and a knight-in-shining-armor complex. Kicking Ironman in the butt is one thing. Breaking his neck would have been another."

"Ah. And you're the princess the knight wants to rescue?"

"He's working to get past it."

She smiled. When she turned back to the building the smile faded. "I'll tell you this, though. They are so dead."

"Meaning what?"

"I'm going back to my office to start eviction proceedings. Whether or not I sell the building, that tong is out in the street."

"Too bad for the street. But are you sure that's a good idea?"

She took a breath. "Well, it has to be done anyway. I'm leaning toward keeping the building. If I do, they have to go. I was going to give them time, but now I'm mad." Looking back to me, she said, "If all Uncle Meng wanted was for the tong to be able to stay, why didn't he leave the building to them? To the nonprofit? He must have known he'd be putting me in an untenable position. But there was a reason he wanted me to have it. I think Mr. Chang was supposed to tell me why."

I said, "Maybe it's all about saving Chinatown, even if it means sacrificing the tong? The greater good and all that?"

"I don't know. I might be able to figure it out once I go through Uncle Meng's papers and things." Mel turned again to look at the building with narrowed eyes. "I'll do that as soon as I can get to it. But first things first. Right now, those gangsters' days are numbered."

"Okay, I get it. Before you go start the paperwork, though, do you have a few minutes to stop by the Fifth Precinct?"

"Sure, but why?"

"Mary—Detective Kee—might want to know what just went down. It could turn into civil war the day after tomorrow when they start tearing the building apart."

"My building. Maybe I'll get an injunction to prevent them from doing that."

"You think that'll work?"

"No way. It would just make it easier to evict them after they violate it. But also…"

"But also what?"

"For one thing, if I keep the building, it'll need a gut renovation anyway, so who cares how many holes they make? And if there is anything, any stolen tong money there, diamonds, whatever, I don't want it. Let them fight over it."

"If it's there and your uncle knew about it, he wanted you to have it."

"If it's stolen from the tong, I promise you he didn't know about it. Okay, let's go. Where's the Fifth Precinct?"

"Elizabeth Street."

I called as we walked to make sure Mary was in. The result of that was she was waiting for us at the sergeant's desk inside.

"Hey," I said to Mel. "You must rate. She never meets me down here."

Mary said, "You're not an innocent civilian caught up in a tong situation. Hello, Ms. Wu."

"Mel."

"Mary."

"I am so," I said, but Mary ignored me.

"Come on up." We walked up the stairs and into the Squad Room. "You guys want coffee?"

Mel said, "Is precinct coffee as bad as I've heard?"

"Yes," said Chris Chiang, joining us at Mary's desk.

"Then no. Thank you, though."

"So," Mary said, eyes boring into me, "you went back to the building."

"My fault," Mel said. "I asked her to. I don't like to go there alone."

Not only wasn't that quite what happened, but the idea that Mel might be afraid to go anywhere alone was, from Mary's look, clearly not one she was buying. She knows me well enough, though, to not try to talk me out of my responsibility to my client. At least, not in front of my client.

"All right," she said, in a judgment-reserving voice. "So what happened?"

Mel ran it down for them, with annotations from me.

"I just thought you guys ought to know," I said when Mel was done. "In case they start shooting each other."

"To get the box?" Chris asked.

"It's more complicated than that. Ironman wants the Li Min Jin to stay in the building. He thinks he'll need the weight of tradition behind him once he takes over. He might feel like it would help his image if he stops holes from being whacked in the sacred walls."

"I thought he wanted the treasure found," Chris said.

"By me, surgically, for him and his faction. Not by the general public, and especially not Loo. Loo, on the other hand, thinks the building's one of the things holding them back from becoming an innovative twenty-first-century tong. He claims he doesn't think there's money at all, though I'm not sure I believe him. He'd be happy if the building got wrecked. And Tan's furious that any of them even think she and Choi Meng stole any money. Tempers are flaring over there. Also, don't forget someone already took a shot at Ironman. Are you any closer to figuring out who?"

Mary shook her head. "There were prints on the

rock, but we can't match them. We have no useful witnesses."

Since I was the main witness, that statement didn't bear examination. I said, "Tan told us the succession isn't decided by assassination anymore, but I'm not convinced. If things get really heated in that building and someone gets oops, accidentally bumped off, bullets could be ricocheting up and down the staircase."

"If I could be sure all they'd do was massacre each other, I'd be tempted to let it go," Mary said. "Okay." She sighed. "We'll put someone on the street to make sure none of it spills over onto the public. And I'll let Cobb and Organized Crime know. From now on, you guys both stay clear of the Li Min Jin. It sounds to me like you're not so popular over there."

"I don't know," I said. "Ironman thinks you're cute, Mel's hot, and I'm gorgeous."

"He's right on all counts." Chris grinned. "And stay clear anyhow."

BEFORE MEL AND I went our separate ways on the corner she said, "I feel like I have to go to Mr. Chang's funeral tomorrow."

"We were just told to stay clear of the Li Min Jin."

"I didn't hear us agree."

"Me either. Do you want Bill and me to come?"

"Would you mind? I'd be grateful."

"Definitely. Meet you at Wah Wing Sang at ten."

She smiled and headed uptown to start to evict the Li Min Jin. I was about to call Bill when my phone played the theme song to *Martial Law*.

"Mark!" I answered it. "And it's not even four in the morning."

"You thought I was going to wait and get back at you?" Mark Quan said from Hong Kong.

"Tell me you didn't consider it."

"I considered it. But I teach my students that the best way to win a fight is to avoid it in the first place. So, if I call you at a decent hour, I win."

"Can't argue with your logic. You have something for me?"

"Yes. Don't know if it'll help, but it's interesting. I talked to an old pal who was with the gang unit way back when. He's happily retired to a fishing village, but he remembers Tan Lu-Lien. Kind of indelible, he says."

"I would agree."

"Not many of the gangs had women as full members, and she was the only one at her level. Controlled the Black Shadows' finances, went at whoever needed a beatdown, and was sleeping with the gang leader, a punk named Johnny Gee. Trifecta, right? Then one day she up and left."

"Up and left?"

"Blammo, gone. She left detailed instructions for Gee about how to handle the money, but apparently even he didn't know she'd be leaving, and no one knew where she was. My old pal looked around for an unsolved homicide, someone important that maybe she'd done that the gang wouldn't have been able to cover up. He came up empty. His second theory was that she'd pissed the wrong people off and been dumped in the harbor, though the detailed instructions made that unlikely. His third theory was that she'd been skimming the cream off the gang's milk for a long time and ran off with it, though again, if you stole someone's money, why leave instructions on how to handle what's left?

Anyway, they never found out, because by the time she turned up in New York, she was with the Li Min Jin."

"Could she have been sent by the Li Min Jin Hong Kong? She seems to have straightened out the New York tong's finances the same way she did the Black Shadows'."

"Why the sudden departure and the secrecy, then? Anyhow, when the Black Shadows located her, she was already close to Big Brother Choi and dealing with the money at the Li Min Jin New York. So the Li Min Jin Hong Kong head basically told the Black Shadows to back off."

"Would the Black Shadows have been inclined to hunt her down, do you think, if it hadn't been for that?"

"Hard to say. You don't just up and leave, but for a gang member from here to go all the way to New York to enforce that rule, that's iffy. Except if she'd stolen their money, then for sure, if they knew. But if she'd been very subtle about it, they might not have known. Once she was with the tong, it would have been suicide for them to go at her. They didn't argue the call."

"Hmm. Hmm-hmm-hmm. That's what she's been accused of here, you know. Skimming from the Li Min Jin."

"By who?"

"Half the Li Min Jin." I filled him in on the situation.

"Wow," he said when I was done. "I guess a tiger doesn't change its stripes, or some other piece of age-old wisdom. I'd say be careful if you're messing with a tong, but since it's you, maybe they better be careful. I have to go make noodles now. When are you coming over?"

"I have no idea, but you'll be the first to know."

"I'd better be. Anything else you need, let me know."

"Even if it's four in the morning?"

"For you? But remember, you call me at four, you lose. Give my regards to Smith."

"I will. Thanks, Mark."

"My honor."

TWENTY-EIGHT

I HUNG UP, thought for a minute, and called Bill.

"Hey," he said, "I was going to call you anyway. What's up?"

"I just went three rounds with Ironman Ma."

"Literally or figuratively?"

"Literally, and I'm starving."

He laughed. It's a fact and he knows it, that fighting makes me hungry. Probably it comes from all those childhood years of going to the dojo between school and dinner. My body's been trained to expect food after kicks and punches.

"Tell me where and I'll hustle over. After lunch you can come with me to talk to a guy."

I was too hungry to go far, so we met at Congee Village. Not everyone who's not Chinese will eat congee, but luckily for me Bill will eat anything. I ordered the pork and preserved egg, he went for the chicken and mushroom, we got a side of scallion pancakes, and all was right with the world.

"So where did this thrilla not in Manila take place, and why didn't I have a ringside seat?" Bill asked as he poured me tea.

"In Choi Meng's apartment and because you'd have seriously damaged him and we'd all be dead."

"You didn't damage him? You're telling me you pulled your punches?"

"I responded with a level of force appropriate to the situation. I kicked his butt black and blue."

"You saw the bruises?"

"He was limping."

"Ah. In the absence of better evidence, I'll accept that."

"You want to see more, ask him yourself."

Our congee and pancakes came. Over the meal I told Bill the whole story of my morning, including the phone call with Mark.

The food was finished before I was.

"So many fascinating points to mull over," Bill said when I was done.

"Including, Mel Wu seems interested in my brother."

"I think that fact leads all the rest, at least for mysteriousness. But it's not one we can help or hinder."

"I probably could, actually, but I don't know which I want to do." I finished the dregs of my tea. "What about Tan, though? That sudden departure from Hong Kong. It really bothers me. It seems unlike her. She's so careful, so considered. You think she really was stealing from the gang?"

"It would give the accusations here more weight. Another reason comes to mind, though."

"Which would be?"

"She's an informant."

"Say what?"

"Or, she was. She was tipping the Hong Kong authorities to the Black Shadows' activities and her handler—or she—suddenly decided she was too hot. So she was shipped, or shipped herself, out of the country."

"Wow," I said. "Okay, that's a good one. I'll call Mark and ask if his contact knows anything about that. But if she was…"

"Then the question becomes, is she still?"

"Has she been, this whole time? A mole in the Li Min Jin?"

"That's a dangerous game."

"But look. Half the guys don't trust her. I say it's because she's a woman, Ironman says it's because she's stealing from them. But what if what they're reacting to is a sense something's wrong, something they can't put their fingers on, but they feel it? What if she *is* betraying them, just not the way they think?"

"But what about Big Brother Choi? They say he loved her like a daughter. Could they have been that close and he didn't know?"

"Take it from me," I said. "You can be very surprised by what your family gets up to. Although…"

"Although, whatever Tan Lu-Lien was or is up to, it's peripheral to what we're supposed to be doing."

"Looking after Mel when she's at the building, which we might be done with for the day, and finding dirt on Jackson Ting."

"And in the service of that," Bill said, "want to come across town and talk to Mike DiMaio?"

"Of course I do. Who's Mike DiMaio?" I handed the waiter my credit card. "Oh, wait. Do I remember him? He was that bricklayer on the construction site job? You stayed in touch?"

"Right as usual. We have a beer every now and then. He and his father have their own masonry contracting firm now, and he doesn't mind talking about Jackson Ting, but he doesn't want to do it over the phone."

"Really?" I said, as the waiter returned. "That sounds promising."

We strolled west to Fulton Street, where a crew from

DiMaio and Son were doing the brickwork on a restoration project. Bill ID'd us to the guard at the gate, who walkie-talkied, and a minute later Mike DiMaio came out to meet us. He was a short bowlegged guy, and his blond mustache spread over his grin when he saw me. "Lydia! Hi! Boy, you look great! Not like this mook here. He falls apart more every time I see him."

"Not as fast as you do," Bill said.

"Yeah, well, I got further to fall, you being older than dirt already. Hey, Luis, these guys are gonna buy me some coffee. Anyone needs me, call."

"Sí, you got it," said the guard, and off we went.

"Here," said Mike, stopping at one of the food trucks that line the curb near any construction site in New York. "Smith, I know, you want black, no sugar, like a cowboy. Lydia, what'll you have?"

We got a tea, two coffees—light with three sugars for Mike—and contrary to what he'd told Luis, Mike paid for the lot. We took them across the street to a set of granite planters, which we used as benches. Bill sat across from me and Mike so he could smoke.

"So," said Mike, peeling back the tab of his coffee cup lid. "Jackson Ting, huh?"

"Have you ever done work for him?" I asked.

"Nope. We're high-quality masonry work. Complicated brickwork, smooth-as-silk concrete block. Brownstone restoration. Smith, you remember. All that stuff you couldn't do."

"Hey. I was the ace of spades."

"If that's a bricklayer joke, it stinks. Anyway, what we do takes time and money. Not Ting's cup of tea." Mike grinned at the paper cup in my hand.

"But you've heard of him."

"Everyone in the business has heard of him. But I wouldn't get you guys over here just to say I've heard of him." He sipped his coffee. "What's your interest?"

"We have a client who needs dirt on him," I said.

"Needs?"

I shrugged.

"Does he know?"

"Ting? That we're digging? I don't know."

"Well, all I'm saying, you might want to watch your backs." Mike drank more coffee. "Two, three years ago, guy I know was working on one of Ting's projects. Doing the fixed glazing. Not the window work, but they had to coordinate, you know? Bids came in for the windows. Ting thought even the low bid was high. Low bidder came to see him." Mike looked at us. "Smith, you probably know this, Lydia, I don't know if you do, but the steel and aluminum window trade on the East Coast is totally mobbed up."

"Mobbed up," I said. "The Mafia?"

"Come on." Mike DiMaio grinned. "There's no such thing as the Mafia."

"Right, I forgot."

"So according to my buddy, this window guy suggested to Ting that his price was good and Ting should take it. Ting said he could get a better product cheaper from overseas. The guy said that would be a mistake. On and on, you know? Finally Ting threw the guy out of his office. He emailed the documents to some firm in Taiwan and asked for a bid. Told my buddy he should go ahead and coordinate with the Taiwanese.

"Couple days later someone lobbed a few Molotov cocktails into the jobsite. Destroyed some equipment, damaged some steel, collapsed an excavation. Sent two steelworkers to the hospital. Set the job back a few weeks. Cost a pile to replace the equipment, repair the work. Insurance covered all that, but Ting's premiums went up, and he paid out a lot of overtime to catch up."

"Seems like the guy to watch out for is the window guy," I said.

"Story's not over yet. A week after that happened, the window guy was shot dead in his office. One bullet to the back of the head."

"That sounds as much like the nonexistent Mafia's style as anything else," Bill said.

"Yeah, maybe. Except someone had carved the number four into both the guy's hands. That's bad luck in Chinese, right?" Mike looked at me.

"Yes," I said. "Because it's pronounced like 'death.'"

TWENTY-NINE

MIKE DIMAIO DIDN'T have much more for us.

"What happened after the window guy was shot?" Bill asked. "That's the kind of thing that could start a real war."

DiMaio shook his head. He drained his coffee and crushed the cup. "Ting told the GC that when the windows came—from Taiwan—he should get a union crew to install them. It wasn't a union site. None of Ting's projects are, and he's always getting picket lines, the giant rat, you know. The GC told him he hadn't bid it for a union shop and it would cost more. Ting said he'd cover it. The GC got the word out to the union that the job was going to be theirs. The window installers' union is as mobbed up as the window manufacturers are. That was the peace treaty."

"Did they ever find the killer?" I asked.

"Nope." Mike jumped down off the granite planter. "Look, you guys, I gotta get back to work, but seriously, if you're messing with Ting, I just wanted to tell you, take care of yourselves. Things don't go his way a hundred percent of the time. But they do more than they do for a lot of guys, and around him, people get hurt."

We thanked him, walked with him back to his site, and continued on east.

"I don't know," I said to Bill as we neared Chinatown. "What do you think? Jackson Ting called in a hit on a Mafia guy?"

"Well, we know he's a blackmailer."

"He threatened to out a secret. Not kill somebody. And"—I stopped myself in my own tracks—"we don't actually know that."

Bill looked at me. "No, we don't. You think Natalie Wu was lying? She has some other reason for wanting the building sold?"

"I think at the very least there was more going on than she told me. You want to come see Jackson Ting?"

"We're going to ask him whether he's a blackmailer?"

"Probably not. Natalie would have a cow, and I'd hate to lose a client."

"Why? By my count you have four on this case already. It's a good thing your license doesn't require you to avoid conflicts of interest."

"Our licenses. You're not in on this? Besides, there's no conflict. They all have the same interests. They just don't know it."

I called the office of Ting Ventures.

There's an interesting thing about being a private investigator. Some people won't talk to you at all. You have to find some sneaky pretext to get in. Others, it's like they're fascinated with the idea. I think maybe they see themselves in a forties movie, matching wits with Sam Spade. I'd never met Jackson Ting, but I'd seen him around, and instinct told me he was the second type. I'm not always right, but this time I was: After as many different voices on the phone as it took me to get to my brother, I was told that Mr. Ting had a break in his afternoon schedule, and if I could get to the office in the next twenty minutes, he could see me. That, of course, was ludicrous. No one has a break in his schedule at the exact moment you call, unless he makes one because he's intrigued by the idea of talking to you.

Twenty-five minutes after I'd thanked the voice and hung up, Bill and I walked into Ting Ventures, in a Turtle Bay building the firm managed but hadn't built. The building was thirty stories tall, but it was there on sixteen that it stepped back to give the full-floor office a wraparound terrace. I was prepared to argue a sub-way-delay case—every New Yorker's go-to excuse—but Mr. Ting, it seemed, was in a magnanimous mood. The receptionist handed us off to Ting's assistant, and we were shown in.

Ting, in a gray suit—Armani, I thought—with jacket unbuttoned, stood from behind his glass-slab desk. His smile and his boyish good looks suggested ready wel-come, but his eyes said something else. Their look was what I saw in the eyes of the gin-playing ladies in the park: Nice to see you, it's just a game, doesn't matter a bit, and I will destroy you.

Ting stuck his hand out. In the window behind him the sun polished the East River. "Jackson Ting. You're Lydia Chin? Good to meet you."

I introduced Bill while I shook Ting's hand.

"Your partner? I get the whole brain trust? Must be important," he said in a tone that indicated we all knew it wasn't. "Can I offer you something? Coffee, tea, water?"

Having just been the beneficiaries of Mike Di-Maio's actual, as opposed to feigned, hospitality, Bill and I both turned him down. Waving us to an oxblood leather sofa, Ting sat in a matching armchair across a low glass table. On the walls hung awards and certificates, photos of buildings and photos of Ting: in a hard-hat on construction sites, at receptions with important people, at ceremonial dinners beside a beautiful Asian woman I recognized from my research as his wife. The same woman and two little kids smiled from a photo on his desk.

Ting crossed an ankle onto his knee and slid his hands along the chair arms. "So. What can I do for you? Are you investigating me?" He grinned, to show either that the question was absurd or that the answer, either way, wouldn't worry him.

"Not precisely," I said, though, precisely, we were. "It's just, every time I turn around these days, there you are."

Still smiling, he cocked his head. "I'm not sure what you mean. Have we met?"

He looked from me to Bill. I saw his problem. Who better to elucidate: a fellow man, but White, or a fellow Chinese, but female? His gaze came back to rest on me. I had the feeling that was in answer to a sense of careful political correctness but against instinct.

Bill caught my eye for an instant and then jumped in. Keeping the interview subject off-balance is PI 101.

"I think what Lydia means," he mansplained, "is that you keep cropping up in this case we're working. Specifically your interest in the Li Min Jin headquarters building on Bayard and Mott."

Ting didn't lose his smile, but it seemed to harden. He glanced at me and then spoke to Bill. "What case?"

I took that one, just so he could exercise his neck muscles. "We've been hired by Mel Wu. To protect her interests. And her, if she needs it. You know her, right? You went to school together?"

"Sure. I know her, and I know her uncle left her the building. I've made her a nice offer, and I hope she takes it. Is there a case in that?"

"Maybe not per se"—there, I could talk lawyer, too—"but there's been a murder in the building, an attempted one a few blocks away, fistfights, blackmail, buried treasure, all kinds of things, and it all seems to come back to the fact that you want that building."

He paused. "It may come back to that," he said. "But none of it comes back to me. Is that what you think? That I'm behind it all? I don't even know anything about most of what you just said." He shook his head in amusement at our silliness. "Now, the murder, that was a man named Chang, right? I heard about that one. It was a botched robbery."

"Maybe."

He waited, but I didn't go on, so he said, "And what was the so-called attempted murder?"

"Chang was Choi Meng's chosen successor as head of the tong. Yesterday someone took a shot at one of the men who's in contention now that he's gone. A fellow called Ironman Ma."

Ting nodded the way you would when a child tells you about the unicorn she saw on the way to school. "I know who he is. You're not thinking that was me?"

"Not really," I said. "It's just, there was that other murder. The window guy with the fours carved into his hands?"

Ting flushed in anger. "For God's sake! That had nothing to do with me! There was an investigation. They didn't find anything because there was nothing to find. That bastard was a small-time shakedown artist. You run into them all the time in this business. He must have crossed some other Chinese guy. Maybe he didn't tip for his food delivery." Ting paused and pulled himself under control. "Really, that's why you're here? Because of that? That's a level of racial profiling I wouldn't have expected from you." He pointed at Bill and smirked. "Maybe from him, but not from you."

"You can't deny it's interesting that it happened. And that you wanting the Bayard Street building seems to be causing a lot of destabilization in the Li Min Jin tong."

"Oh, come on. I'm a developer. I'm trying to put together a site. It's not my fault if that brings out the worst in people."

"So murders and buried treasure and blackmail are par for the course in your work?"

"Is that supposed to get a rise out of me? A hysterical denial or a confession or something? Give me a break. Look, where a lot of money's involved, people sometimes behave badly. I can't help that. Stop for a minute, though. You've said 'buried treasure' twice. What does that mean?"

Bill and I exchanged glances. Bill asked, "You're not aware of the rumors?"

"What rumors?"

"They say there's a fortune buried behind the walls of the Bayard Street building."

For a moment Ting just stared. Then he laughed. "You really do mean buried treasure. Oh my God. No, I never heard that. Who's supposed to have put it there? When? Why?"

I said, "None of that is clear, and we're also missing 'exactly where.'"

"In other words, you know nothing, but there's buried treasure. Yeah, uh-huh." A pause. "Hey, wait. Is that why Mel won't sell me the building? She's waiting until she finds the fortune first?"

"Oh, I don't know," I said. "Maybe. Or that could be more about following her uncle's wishes. Or not evicting people from their homes. Or preserving the historic nature of Chinatown."

"Oh, for God's sake. Do you have any idea how many times I've heard that crap from people like her over the years?" Ting blew out an exasperated breath. "Mel's from Scarsdale. She lives on the Upper East Side. She wears Eileen Fisher and meets her girlfriends after barre class for brunch. But she's got a glowing halo because she protects squatters and junkies and welfare cheats from anything that'll upgrade property values and increase the city's tax base. You can't tell me she gives a shit about Chinatown. For God's sake, if she sells me the building, I'll evict the goddamn tong. Wouldn't that be a good thing for Chinatown? But screwing with my site makes all her self-righteous friends think she's on the side of the angels."

"Wow," I said. "You don't like her much, do you?" I guessed I'd gotten my rise out of him.

"I never did," he said. "Even back in school she was a sanctimonious bitch."

"Not like her sister, Natalie."

"No, you're right," he said, standing. "Not like her sister, Natalie. Well, it's been nice chatting with you, but I have a meeting. Thanks for coming."

He crossed the room to open his office door.

THIRTY

"I DON'T THINK I like that guy," I told Bill as we rode down in the elevator from Jackson Ting's office.

"Not going to take him on as a client?"

"He didn't ask. You know what else he didn't ask?"

"What you meant by 'blackmail.'"

"Bingo. He wanted to know about the attempted murder and the buried treasure, but he just let the blackmail slide on by. And then when I mentioned Natalie, he threw us out."

"Which means Natalie was probably telling the truth."

"Which doesn't mean she's not hiding something else."

"Bingo to you too. What now?"

The elevator door slid open to let us into the lobby. Waiting to change places with us was the tall man I'd seen twice before, the first time at Big Brother Choi's funeral and then again staring at the Li Min Jin building from a bench in Columbus Park.

"Oh, no," I said to Bill. "I forgot the file. Wait a sec, I'll go get it." I jumped back in the elevator as the door closed. I pressed the button for twenty-three and started scrolling through my phone, ignoring the tall man and the other three people who'd gotten in with us. At fifteen I raised my phone and stared intently, baring my teeth as though I had it in selfie mode and was checking for spinach. I didn't have it in selfie mode, though, and I snapped a photo of the tall man in three-quarter profile as he got off. At sixteen.

Bill was waiting when I got to the lobby for the second time.

"You still forgot the file," he said.

"No, I have it, it's just invisible."

"You know that guy?"

"Who, the tall one? Just because he's Asian you think he's the one I was after? That's a level of racial profiling I wouldn't have expected from you."

"I didn't say which guy. That's a level—"

"Oh, stop. I don't know him, but he went to sixteen. Hold on, I'm calling Mary."

Which I did, and sent her the photo, but she wasn't much help.

"Yes, we noticed him at the funeral. Organized Crime doesn't know him. He might just be a businessman who was paying his respects."

"Not a Chinatown businessman. You, or I, or Chris would have seen him around. And I bet you didn't check out everyone at the funeral with Organized Crime. You focused on this guy because he's got that gangster look, right?"

"He does," she admitted. "We thought he might be from some out-of-town tong trying to muscle in. He still might be, or he might be a businessman from one of the outer boroughs. We'll have to wait until he makes a move. If he does."

"He might be making one right now. He just went up to Jackson Ting's office."

"Did he really? And you know that how?"

"I'm in the neighborhood doing some work for a client. Listen, I have to go. I'll talk to you later."

As I put the phone away Bill asked, "Did she yell at you?"

"She was revving up, but I didn't give her the chance. They don't know him."

We left the building. I was pondering Bill's question—"What now?"—when my phone erupted into "Won't You Come Home Bill Bailey." I raised my eyebrows and put the phone to my ear. "Hi, Ma," I said in Chinese. "How're things in Queens?"

"I'm having a lovely time," my mother said. "I would like you to come out here."

"I'm glad you're happy. I'd love to visit with Ted's family, but I'm working."

"You're working on the case about Developer Ting, I know. I am also. That's why I want you to come here."

"Um, what?"

"I've found someone who knows something about him. A retired nurse from a hospital. After your brother's family all left this morning I shopped, then I went to play mah-jongg at the senior center. I investigated there, telling the ladies my daughter was dating Developer Jackson Ting, so I was hoping to learn things about him. They were eager to help, though most of them had nothing to say that was useful. One of the ladies, named Fan Mei, thought that her friend, Nurse Dolores Reyes, had a very interesting story about Developer Ting. Fan Mei couldn't remember what it was, as her memory has faded. Although she's still quite a good mah-jongg player. I called Nurse Reyes, but I could not learn the story. She was reluctant to tell it to me, also she comes from the Philippines. Her English is not very good. I had trouble understanding her."

Luckily my mother couldn't see me roll my eyes. A

US hospital nurse, no matter what her first language is, can be counted on to speak fine English. My mother, on the other hand, is a little more impressed with her own language skills than maybe they deserve.

"Here is her address," my mother said, rattling off a set of numbers.

"Ma? What does that mean, a very interesting story?"

"Ling Wan-Ju, please pay attention. If I knew what it meant, why would I be sending you to see her? You must ask her yourself. She's at home making dinner for her husband. He won't return until seven o'clock, so you'll have time to talk to her alone if you hurry."

"Is she expecting me?"

"Of course not. Come to your brother's house for dinner after you've spoken to her. Goodbye."

I lowered the phone and typed in the numbers before they faded from my memory.

"What?" said Bill.

"My mother," I told him, "has found a witness. I knew when she went out to Flushing she was up to something."

"A witness to what?"

"I have no idea. She told the mah-jongg ladies that I was dating Ting and she was checking up on him. I gather they jumped at the chance to help her snoop. She wants me to go out there and talk to someone who, and I quote, 'knows something' about Jackson Ting."

Bill broke into a wide grin. "So she really has been working the case."

"Hey. This is not a good thing."

"Oh, I don't know. With so many clients, maybe you ought to consider taking on another partner."

I stared. "Maybe so, since the one I have seems to have lost his mind."

"Seriously, since she's gotten this far, don't you suppose we ought to go?"

"You don't mean that. It's likely to be a big giant wild goose chase."

"I give her instincts more credit than that."

"You didn't grow up with her."

"You wrote down the address."

"Automatic reaction to hearing a bunch of numbers."

"I notice we're walking toward the subway."

"We have to walk in some direction. Okay, okay, we'll go. If we can go to my brother's afterwards. My mother invited us for dinner."

"Us?"

"If she's going to insist on being part of this firm," I said, "she's going to have to get used to the management."

THIRTY-ONE

THE SUBWAY RIDE to Flushing involved a change of trains, but it was still quick. Coming up out of the station onto Flushing Main Street is always one of my favorite moments, and this afternoon of swirling cacophony was no different.

The street was lined with signs large and small in Chinese and English, with the occasional Sanskrit or Korean. Made of blinking neon, lit plastic, painted metal, or characters scrawled in black or red Magic Marker on paper, they hung on the faces of buildings, stuck out over the sidewalk, or clung to window glass. The aromas from restaurants and bakeries competed for space in my nose with the smells from street vendors' stalls. Honking horns, growling traffic, conversation in various languages were all overlaid now and then by the roar of a plane going to or from La Guardia. The sidewalks, crowded with shoppers, sellers, high-spirited high schoolers, and mothers with strollers, couldn't be navigated in a straight line. The late-afternoon sun shone over it all, and I just stood for a moment, enjoying it.

Then I took out my phone, put Dolores Reyes's address into my GPS, and Bill and I started threading our way along Main Street. We'd had lunch, of course, but still the aroma of turnip cakes frying at a street vendor's stall drew us right in. We bought one each, squirted them with oyster sauce, and went on our way.

Once we passed the Flushing Library the neighborhood's exuberance began to calm. We made our lefts and rights until we stood in front of a group of six-story 1930s brick buildings surrounding a central garden. We'd reached tree-lined tranquil residential Flushing, a world, but only a half a mile, from Main Street. A wrought-iron archway led into the complex. Reyes's building was the third one in. I pressed her buzzer.

I introduced myself to the inquiring voice that came out of the speaker. "I'd very much like to speak with you," I said. "About something you once told Fan Mei? It won't take long." I got no answer, so I added, "I'm not selling anything, I promise. I'd just appreciate a few moments of your time for something I'm working on. It would really be a help."

Most people, if given a chance, actually like to help. Nurses, besides, are trained to. After a moment of silence, Dolores Reyes suggested we come in, and the buzzer buzzed. We rode the elevator to the third floor, where a quizzically smiling brown-skinned woman waited at an open door.

"Thank you for seeing us, Mrs. Reyes," I said. "I'm Lydia Chin, and this is my partner, Bill Smith. We'll try not to take too much of your time."

"You're friends of Fan Mei's?"

"No. My mother knows her. She called you earlier, my mother?"

"Oh, yes. The Chinese lady. I wasn't sure what she wanted, though. Her English…"

"Yes, I know. I can explain."

Reyes's own English, while slightly accented, was, as I had predicted, perfect. She looked me over and said,

"Ah. You must be the young woman who's dating Jackson Ting. I understood that much from your mother. Although"—Reyes paused—"everything Jackson Ting does makes the news, and I never heard that his marriage has broken up."

"No." I smiled. "It hasn't. We're not dating. That was my mother's story."

Now, a frown. "Why did your mother tell me a story?"

"Mrs. Reyes, Bill and I are private investigators." I gave her a card. "A case we're working on involves Jackson Ting. My mother decided to…help."

Reyes's face brightened in a knowing smile. "Ah. I see. A mother helping her daughter. Although I think you didn't ask her to, am I correct?"

"I certainly didn't, and I didn't ask her to call you. I'm sorry if she bothered you. But if you really do have a story worth hearing about Jackson Ting, I'd love to listen."

In her hesitation, Bill spoke. "Mrs. Reyes, I know we're here for work, but I lived in Manila as a kid, and whatever you're cooking is bringing back my entire childhood. I'd bet a dollar you're making pork adobo."

Reyes laughed. "You'd win. All right, you'd better come in." The living room she showed us into was filled with plants and bright pillows on pudgy furniture. A rich, meaty aroma swirled in the air. "Please, sit," she said, and disappeared into the kitchen.

"You didn't have a happy childhood," I whispered to Bill as we settled on the sofa. "Even when you were in the Philippines."

"No, but the food there was great."

Reyes returned with a plate of purple cookies. Bill's eyes lit.

"Ube?"

"Yes. You know ube?"

"I love it."

Reyes passed us napkins and we each took a cookie.
I bit into mine, found a sweet, nutty taste in a crumbly
texture. Reyes, smiling, watched us both.

"Mmm," said Bill. "Better than my mother ever
made."

From everything Bill's told me, that was kind of a
low bar, but his appreciation of Reyes's cookies was
sincere, and as far as I could taste, warranted.

"I never had these before," I said. "They're terrific."

Reyes beamed. She sat in one of the chairs opposite
the sofa. Smoothing her skirt, she said, "Please understand, I don't want to get anyone in trouble."

"Of course. Neither do we," I said, which might
be true depending on your definition of "anyone." Or
"want."

"We're just trying to unravel some things. It could
be that whatever your story is, it's not relevant at all.
But my mother sent me here, and we're seeing her for
dinner." A little shameless, maybe, to use my mother
like that, but my mother started it. "I won't share the
story with her if you don't want me to. Just knowing
you told me will make her happy."

From her smile I could tell Reyes knew just what I
was doing. But she began. "I used to work at Flushing
Hospital. On the Neonatal Unit. I retired six years ago,
but I still have friends from my nursing days. Fan Mei
is one of them. I understand she met your mother at the
Chinese senior center?"

"Playing mah-jongg," I said. "My mother says she
plays well."

Reyes took a few moments before she went on. "I
told Fan Mei about this when it happened, because it

was so strange. And of course I told my husband. They both thought I should say nothing. I wasn't sure there was anything illegal about it, and no one seemed unhappy with the situation. So I didn't mention it again. As I said, I didn't want to get anyone in trouble. And though it was...irregular for the US, I'd seen this kind of thing back home."

Bill, biting into his second purple cookie, said, "God, these take me right back to Manila. Mrs. Reyes, really, we're hoping to avoid trouble, too. Anything you know about Jackson Ting might help us."

Reyes paused again, then launched into it. "Jackson Ting was born in Flushing Hospital. He was a bit early, and he was underweight and jaundiced. It wasn't dangerous, but we kept him in an incubator for a few days. His mother went home the second day after the birth and came a number of times a day while he was on the unit so she could nurse him. Sometimes the father came, too, but more often a friend came with the mother. They all seemed so happy with the baby, taking turns holding him and speaking to him. The friend sang lullabies, though the mother didn't seem to know any. The baby gained weight, and after five days, he could go home.

"A month later he was brought back for his well-baby check. I saw he was scheduled, and I wanted to see how he was doing, so I dropped into the pediatrician's office. The baby was fine, but it was the friend, not the mother, who'd brought him. That worried me, so I asked if the mother was well. The woman told me she was the baby's mother.

"I started to speak up, but I saw a question in the doctor's eyes and worry in hers. I said I must have been mistaken and that I was happy to see the baby so well.

I checked later in the hospital's records. The name and address the mother had given when she arrived in labor—Maria Ting—were the same as the woman who'd brought him in for his checkup. But it wasn't the same woman."

She paused. Neither Bill nor I spoke, giving her room to go on.

"As I said, this sort of thing happens at home. A family with too many children to feed, or a woman with children whose sister has none… I thought perhaps the actual mother was undocumented. Or running from the baby's father. Prostitutes often give up their children, too. I didn't know what these women's circumstances were. They both seemed happy when the baby was born, and he seemed well taken care of. Fan Mei and my husband both told me to leave it alone. My husband said if everyone was happy, but it wasn't an official adoption, a legal one, anything I said would only make everyone *un*happy."

"Could it have been a legal adoption?" I asked.

"I searched, but I couldn't find any record. I felt responsible, you see. He was one of my babies." She smiled. "For the same reason, I kept an eye on Jackson as he grew. He was strong and healthy. The parents seemed to adore him—in fact, they spoiled him a bit, I thought. They sent him to private school, to college. I saw the birth mother sometimes, with him and his parents, until he was about three. After that I saw her occasionally, but alone. It's been many years now since I've seen her at all."

"Mrs. Reyes, can you tell us anything about her? What she looked like, the name the friend might have called her?"

"I'm sorry, I really don't remember. It was all so long

ago." Dolores Reyes smoothed her skirt again, though it didn't need it. "I hope I haven't done anything wrong by telling you this. The parents have both passed on now, but Jackson's become a wealthy young man, partly based on what his father built. If it came out that he wasn't really the father..."

"It wouldn't matter," Bill said, with more confidence than I felt. "After all these years, and after all Jackson Ting's built for himself, I'm sure there's no damage that could be done. And," he added thoughtfully, "even if the mother wasn't the mother, the father could have been the father. Some kind of surrogate arrangement."

"Also," I said, "we won't be spreading this story. It might help us fill in some gaps, but right now I can't see that there's anyone who needs to know any of this."

"Not even your mother?" Reyes said with a twinkle in her eye.

"Especially not my mother. All I need to tell her is that we came here and you gave us some interesting background information, and she'll puff up like a rooster. Thank you so much for sharing this story with us, Mrs. Reyes. We'll let you get back to your cooking now." I stood and Bill followed my lead.

"Wait," Reyes said. She went into the kitchen again and came out a few moments later with a square plastic container, which she held out to Bill. "A box of ube cookies. To remember your childhood." She smiled and showed us to the door.

THIRTY-TWO

DINNER AT TED'S was the usual chaotic fun. My mother seemed only mildly disgruntled by Bill's presence. With her at the stove cooking, talking, and scolding the kids to behave, the kids laughing, eating, teasing my mother, and vying for Bill's and my attention, and Ted and Ling-An focused on eating my mother's cooking and talking with me and Bill, it was a lively evening.

When Ted asked, half joking, "So, Lyd, did Ma actually help with your case?" I said Mrs. Reyes had had an interesting story to tell that might fill out the picture some. That seemed to make Ma happy. She pushed a little to find out what the intel was, but Bill and I both played deflecting "Look over here!" games, and with so many people around, that pretty much worked.

When it was time to go I asked my mother if she wanted to come back to the city with us. Of course the kids besieged her with hugs and cries of "No! Stay here!" which I'd suspected would happen. She relented and told them she'd spend another night. We were gathering ourselves and starting our goodbyes at the door when my phone rang out Run-DMC doing "You Talk Too Much." That meant Tim. I'd have let him go to voicemail, except I was feeling warm and familial, so I thought I'd get nice points and invite him in on the family evening.

"Hey, bro," I answered. "I'm at Ted's. We just finished dinner. Ma's here too. Want to talk to her, or to Ted?"

"No!" he barked. "I want to talk to you! What the hell did you do?" Nothing warm about that, but recognizably familial.

"Um—what?"

"For God's sake, Lydia, someone just tried to shoot me!"

THIRTY-THREE

"ARE YOU ALL RIGHT?" I demanded of my brother Tim.

"Of course I'm all right," he snapped. "I said they *tried* to shoot me. They missed."

"Okay then, I'll call you back in a sec. I'm going to say goodbye here and talk to you outside." Luckily in the general bedlam no one seemed to have noticed who my call was from. Sticking the phone in my pocket, I kissed the kids, Ma, Ted, and Ling-An. Bill shook hands with them all, including the kids, who pumped his hand up and down with great enthusiasm. My mother, I noticed, permitted him to shake her hand but looked away while he did it. Baby steps, baby steps.

The kids wanted to wave goodbye at the door until we were out of sight so I walked, waved, and while looking over my shoulder at them I whispered to Bill what Tim had told me. When we hit the corner I swerved around it and pulled out my phone.

"Took you long enough!" was Tim's greeting. "Did you tell Ma?"

"That someone tried to shoot you? Are you crazy? Of course I didn't. For one thing, I have no idea what you're talking about."

"Good. I was afraid you'd worry her. And here's what I'm talking about. Someone tried to shoot me!"

"That doesn't really tell me much more. Where? When? Who?"

"How do I know who? You think I said, 'Excuse me, but if you're going to try to shoot me, it would be polite to introduce yourself first'?"

I didn't tell him that actually sounded just like him. "Okay, so let's move on to where and when."

"You sound like this is normal everyday life for you. 'Let's just run through this questionnaire I have for people who get shot at.'"

"Oh, knock it off. I'm trying to help. Where were you?"

"Outside the office. I'd just left."

"Did you see the shooter?"

"No, but the shot came from across the street, or maybe a car."

"Or a motorcycle?"

He stopped for a second. "Could've been. I heard one. They chipped the stone on the building!"

"Outrageous. If you were outside how do you know they were aiming at you? Come on, Tim, really, who'd want to shoot you?" As I said that I heard Ironman Ma asking me the same thing.

"Someone you got me messed up with! I don't know who they were, but I know it was me because they also threw a rock with a note on it."

"Oh! Now that's interesting." Trust Tim to get to the important part last. "What does it say?"

"Aren't you going to ask if the rock hit me?"

"No. What does the note say?"

"Well, it didn't, no thanks to you. The note says, 'Make sure Ting gets that building or next time I won't miss.'"

"Holy cow."

"Holy cow? That's it? Someone tried to kill me because of something you're working on, and all you can say is 'holy cow'? What is wrong with you?"

"Tim. Slow down. Where are you?"

"Around the corner. The police came but I managed to avoid them."

"Why?"

"You're kidding, right? That's just what I need, for the partners to think everyone's life is in danger when Tim Chin's around."

"Where's the note?"

"In my pocket."

With your fingerprints all over it. "And the rock?"

"I knew it! I knew you'd ask about the goddamn rock!" He paused. "I have that, too."

Proving that pomposity does not necessarily override good instincts.

"Okay, Tim, listen. No one's life is in danger. The note was written before the shot, which means they were planning to miss."

"What if they weren't good enough to miss? They might have killed me by accident!"

Or if they knew you and didn't have the self-control to go ahead with their intended miss once they had you in their sights.

"Lydia, I told you, whatever you're doing on that case, you have to drop it!"

"Dammit!" I said. "Your firm represents Jackson Ting. You're the treasurer of the Chinatown Heritage Society. You don't suppose you're a worthwhile target all on your own?"

"I—Those things—No one's ever shot at me before!"

I knew he meant, logically, "Those things have been true for years, and they're not likely to be involved because no one's ever shot at me before." Emotionally, though, he meant, *"No one's ever shot at me before!"*

"Okay, Tim, okay. Go home or go to the gym or go to the bar, wherever you go to calm down. I'm at the subway. I'll head in and meet you wherever you want in an hour."

We clicked off. I didn't mention Bill was going to be with me. After all, I'd told him to calm down.

THIRTY-FOUR

BEFORE WE WENT down the subway steps I called Mel. "I want you to be extra careful," I said.

"Why? What happened?"

"Someone took a shot at my brother."

"What? Your brother Tim? Is he all right?"

"He's fine. I don't think they intended to hit him, just to scare him. The shot came with a note telling him to make sure Ting gets the building."

"Telling *him* that? What does that mean? That the Heritage Society should back off?"

"I think so. But also, Harriman McGill are Jackson Ting's real estate attorneys."

A pause. "Oh. I didn't know that. What a position to be in."

"Yes, it doesn't make him happy. But Mel, watch out, will you?"

"I will," she said. "Thank you. And you'll be careful, too?"

"I always am."

Drily, Mel said, "I'm sure."

TIM LIVED, NATCH, in a tall glass tower on the Upper East Side. I announced us to the doorman behind the high-tech desk in the hushed, double-height lobby. The doorman spoke to my brother and then pressed a button to open silent glass doors to the stainless-steel elevators, which lifted us noiselessly to the fifteenth floor.

That was the end of the calm.

Tim being Tim, he wasn't waiting in his open apartment door the way most angry, impatient people would be. That would imply he could spare a minute or two from his important work. Nor did he answer the bell right away. Predictability, thy name is Tim.

When he did open the door, he did it with a yank. "Oh, shit," he said, seeing Bill.

"Hi," Bill said mildly.

Tim glared at us both and said, "Yeah, come in." He'd probably have slammed the door behind us except it had one of those silent closers and you can't fight the pressure.

I'd been up here before and seen the fabulous view across the East River—a view not so different from the one at Jackson Ting's office—but Bill hadn't. He nodded appreciatively at the dark water and the twinkling lights of Queens.

"Here," Tim snapped, leading us to the kitchen area of his sleek open-plan digs. He'd been having a cup of tea, which is what the Chin family does when tension strikes. He lifted his cup and pointed to two objects on the marble counter. "There's your rock and your note."

Mine. I didn't argue, though, just inspected them without touching. The rock was a normal-looking gray stone, just like Ironman's, and the note had come off a printer. "Can I take these? We might be able to lift prints."

"Lift prints." Amazing the way some people can make sarcastic air quotes with their voices. "Yeah, sure, get them out of here."

"Do you have plastic bags?"

"In the drawer."

"I'll do it," Bill said. "Why don't you guys go sit down?"

"Come on," I said to Tim. I left the kitchen to walk over and sit on the angular sofa at the other end of the room, facing the giant wide-screen TV. What did my brother watch on that? Baseball, soccer? Forties movies? Nature documentaries? I realized I had no idea. He plunked himself onto a matching sharp-edged chair, sipping his tea and scowling.

"Listen," I said, "I'm sorry. I know how scary it is to be shot at—"

"This isn't about something being scary! That's not the point!"

It was exactly the point, but okay. "No, I know. But I really think this was just intended to frighten you. And you have to at least consider that it had more to do with the Heritage Society's opposition to Phoenix Towers than with me."

"We've been against that project since it was announced. Then you got involved and now people are shooting at me."

"You don't think the relevant fact isn't that I'm 'involved'"—I made my air quotes the old-fashioned way—"but that Big Brother Choi died?"

"No."

Oh. Well, I'd asked. "Tim, for Pete's sake," I said. "I'm not any more *involved* than you are."

"You're looking for dirt on Jackson Ting. I told you to stop."

"And my client told me to keep going. I don't work for you. I did, but you fired me. Much as I'm sure you'd like to, you can't fire me twice."

"I'm your brother!"

I knew that didn't mean "Therefore I *can* fire you twice," but in some garbled way, "Protect me." Though I was the baby of the family, Tim was the most sheltered. The life's route he'd chosen for himself involved hard work but no surprises. Days of such uniformity would have driven me—and, I suspected, our other brothers—nuts, but I guessed Tim had a right to it.

And getting shot at certainly would upset that apple cart.

Though his getting shot at was not my fault.

Was it?

I was hoping Bill would come over and interrupt this downward spiral, but he seemed to have found endless fascination in Tim's Ziploc collection. I sighed and tried another road. "My clients," I said. "I don't take them on unless I think I can help them. I can't just quit in the middle of something."

"What are you trying to say? That you have professional ethics?"

I could have popped him one. But he looked so miserable. There was no question he'd been scared, but as I watched him sip his tea, it occurred to me more was going on than that.

"Bro," I said, "I was raised in the same family you were. We all five went in different directions, but in terms of right and wrong—personally and professionally—the same stuff was pounded into all our heads."

He nodded, not looking at me. After a moment he muttered, "You want some tea?"

What miracle was this? "Sure. Sit, I'll make it. But Bill can't stay, he has someplace he has to be." I went to the kitchen, clicked on the OXO kettle, and whispered to Bill, "Scram. Tim wants me to stay and commiserate."

"He wants you to stay? Has he flipped his wig?"

"I'll meet you at Shorty's later."

Bill pocketed the bagged rock and note. He popped his head into the living area and said, "'Night, Tim." Tim nodded. Bill grinned and left.

Tim had left the Junshan Yellow tea out on the counter, so that's what I used. I brought a mug of it back to the sofa. Setting the tea on the glass-topped coffee table to cool, I said, "Professional ethics is the issue, isn't it?"

Tim shot me a sharp glance, but then looked away again and said, "I guess you could call it that. Dammit."

"The conflict between your firm's interest and the Heritage Society's?"

"It's more than that, Lyd," he said in his lecturing-to-idiots voice. I didn't respond, basically by willing every muscle I had to immobilize itself. He gulped some tea, and when he spoke again, it was without the disdain. "If it were only that, I could resign from the Society. But the Society's only an...an expression of something else. The neighborhood. Chinatown. A place where Chinese people came, where Ma and Ba came. I know, I know, New York has half a dozen Chinatowns," he said as though I were arguing with him. "But not in Manhattan. Why should we be forced out of, face it, the main borough, so rich people can live where we live?"

"I agree with you," I said.

"If Phoenix Towers gets built," he went on, as though I hadn't spoken, "it's the beginning of the end. Other developers will grab up other buildings. Put together parcels. It's not landmarked, you know, Chinatown. Not as a district and almost no individual buildings. One rezoning application from the right people and wham! Another third-rate Battery Park City. That's what this is about."

"And your firm—"

"Yes, and my firm! Dammit. Damn the whole thing."

I drank some tea while Tim stared out over the expansive view.

"I have a suggestion," I said. "Listen, but don't answer me right away. Then think about it."

He turned back to me. "Yeah, what is it?"

"Why don't you call Mel Wu?"

"Why don't I *what*?"

"Shhh. Listen, don't answer. Mel's in a similar position. She's about to evict the Li Min Jin from the building her uncle bought so they'd never have to leave. She has to because she's a lawyer and they're a tong—professional ethics, you know—but she's conflicted about it."

"Oh, and you think just because we're both conflicted lawyers we have something to talk about? This may come as news to you, but not every conflicted lawyer is the same."

With a heroic effort *I* went on as if *he* hadn't spoken. "Then she has to decide what to do with the building. If she sells it to Jackson Ting, whatever dirt I do dig up might not be enough to stop him."

He looked into his mug. "What good do you think it'll do if I talk to her?"

"At worst you'll each have someone to talk to who understands your problem. And maybe you could help each other find answers."

"Like what?"

"Come on, Tim! I don't know like what. This might not be the best idea I ever had, but right now it's the only one."

THIRTY-FIVE

I PICKED UP a seltzer with orange juice from Shorty at the bar and slipped into a booth opposite Bill.

"Holy cow," I said. "Is it still today?"

"You sure you don't want some vodka in that?" He was halfway through a bottle of beer.

"I almost wish I did."

"How's Tim?"

"Unhappy." I recounted my brother's dilemma. Sipping my soda, I finished, "Before I left I suggested he call Mel Wu."

"You didn't."

"In fact I did. They have similar real estate–based conundrums. Why shouldn't they comfort each other?"

"I'm not sure she has that much of a conundrum. She's clearer on what she wants than he is."

"Which is to keep the building and stop Phoenix Towers, which is what her uncle also wanted. Which Tim, in his heart of hearts, wants, too."

Bill grinned.

"I know, I know," I said. "I'm the manipulative baby sister." I drank my spritzer. "I also called Mary to tell her what happened. I said we'd bring the note and the rock in tomorrow morning. I also told her not to mention to Tim that I called unless she had to."

"Something tells me I should be glad I'm not one of your brothers."

"Many things," I said, "should tell you that."

Bill went to the bar for another round of drinks. When he came back he said, "Speaking of Mel Wu, I wonder why no one's shot at her yet."

"Bite your tongue."

"No, I'm serious. Why not go right to the decision-maker?"

"Well, she's famous for digging in. Trying to intimidate her would mostly make her angry. It might get you the opposite result."

"You think all the players know that?"

"She went to school with Jackson Ting. And the Li Min Jin guys watched her grow up. I bet they do. Now come on, let's go upstairs. We have to get up early. We have a funeral in the morning."

ON OUR WAY to Wah Wing Sang the next day we dropped the rock and note with the desk sergeant at the Fifth Precinct. There was no point in asking if we could take them up to Mary; she wouldn't be in. She'd be where we were going.

Chang Yao-Zu's funeral was a replay, on a smaller scale, of Big Brother Choi's. An open coffin in a flower-filled room—the funeral home's second-largest, this time—the offerings urn and the urn for sticks of incense, chanting monks and black-suited gangsters. Tan Lu-Lien stood at the head of the coffin, with Mr. Loo and Ironman Ma scowling from the foot. The space between Loo and Ironman seemed to contain the repelling force of same-charge magnets.

Grandfather Gao wasn't there, and I didn't see any of the other men I'd pegged as tong representatives at Big Brother Choi's funeral. Chang had been temporary leader, but apparently that "temporary" made a big protocol difference. Mary, Chris Chiang, and Jon Cobb from NYPD Organized Crime once again stood in the back. I wondered if they were disappointed that the gangster turnout was so small.

Neither Adele Fong nor my brother came, and Natalie Wu and her family were also not in attendance. Mel, however, was. She had no place at the altar this time but was here as a private citizen, paying respects to a man she'd known all her life.

Bill and I went with Mel to place our incense and express our condolences to Tan. Tan's face remained impassive as she thanked us. Ironman's scowl got even more fierce when he saw me.

"I wonder if he still thinks I'm gorgeous," I whispered to Bill as we all sat.

"I wonder if he's still limping."

At the end of the ceremony Tan was the one handing out red envelopes. We'd parked Bill's Audi a few cars behind the photo-bedecked hearse because this time neither we nor Mel had funeral home cars. Mel got in with two bouquets of white chrysanthemums. The funeral band escorted Mr. Chang around the neighborhood and then the procession headed over the bridge to Cypress Hills.

On the way out we talked about nothing in particular. I asked Mel where her folks were buried.

"Ferncliff. In Westchester. 'Where Memories Live Forever.'"

"That's their slogan?"

"Kind of creepy they even have a slogan, right? Uncle Meng offered them plots at Cypress Hills, but Dad said he hadn't joined the tong when he was alive and he wasn't going to join it when he died. Mom would have liked for the whole family to be together, and at one point she suggested Uncle Meng take a plot in Fern-cliff and bring Aunt Mei-Mei's remains up there, but he was a little horrified at the thought of disturbing her." Mel gave a small laugh. "People respond to death so irrationally, don't they? We're talking about bones in a jar. What would he disturb? I say that, and I mean it, but I'd still feel bad if I didn't sweep my parents' graves on Qing Ming."

We entered the gates at the cemetery. It wasn't a full week since Big Brother Choi's funeral, but yellow leaves now lay atop wine-colored ones on the grass covering the sloping rows of graves. Mr. Chang's final resting place was just down the hill from Big Brother Choi's. The same rites were performed, under a grayer sky, to a smaller audience.

A good deal of emotion swirled in the air. From the assembled gangsters, a certain amount of sadness and a lot of anxious uncertainty. Genuine grief, but also vigilance, from Mr. Loo. Ironman radiated anger and impatience, and also pride at the heroic (though unsuc-cessful) effort he was making to hide them. Tan Lu-Lien performed the necessary rituals without expression, but it seemed to me the solid set of her shoulders was, today, an attempt to hide something else, something softer than the determination she always bristled with. Regret? Well, why not? The death of Big Brother Choi would have been a hard blow for her. Now, if she was right, the death of Chang, someone she'd known for so many years, was not just another personal loss. It also meant the loss of the tong, her home for so much of her life.

When the ceremony ended Mel retrieved her flowers

from Bill's car. She laid one bouquet on Chang's grave and walked with the other around the hill. We went with her and again stood back as she, this time alone, bowed to Long Lo and his wife and placed the flowers in the vase on their headstone. The faded flowers she removed to do that were the ones she'd put there last week.

"This is so sad," she said, turning away. "Who'll visit him now? As long as Li Min Jin members get buried over there, there'll be people to greet Uncle Meng, but Mr. Chang was the only person besides Uncle Meng I ever saw come over here. I suppose I can sweep the grave at Qing Ming when I come to do Uncle Meng's, but I'm not family."

"Does Nat come with you on Qing Ming?"

"When we were kids we all used to come for Aunt Mei-Mei—Uncle Meng, Mom, Dad, Nat, and me. These days Nat brings her kids to do our parents' graves, but she doesn't come all the way down here afterwards. The last couple of years I came alone with Uncle Meng."

I thought of something and looked around. "Mel," I said, "where are the children?"

"What?"

"Your aunt and uncle had a baby son who died. Long Lo had a three-year-old daughter. Where are their graves?"

"You know," she said, "I never thought to ask."

"With the parents?" Bill asked. "Just not marked?"

"But why not mark them?" I said. "In older cemeteries children are mostly buried in a separate area. But I don't see one here."

"Oh God," Mel said. "That's even sadder. I never asked, and now we'll never know." After another few moments, she smiled. "Who's irrational now? I'm certainly being morbid, aren't I?"

Bill said, "Well, it's a cemetery."

"Yes." Mel looked around silently for a while, then said, "Whenever you're ready, we can go. I need to get back to the office anyway."

I asked, "You're not going to the funeral meal?"

"I have a feeling I wouldn't be welcome. Though I'd like to be a fly on the wall. Maybe they'll all try to poison each other."

"You're not serious."

"No. What I'd *really* like is to be there tomorrow when they start opening doors and knocking holes." She looked from me to Bill. "If I decide to actually go, will you come with me?"

"You know it," I said.

We headed down the hill to where Bill's car was parked. As we walked through the fallen leaves, Mel's phone rang. She stepped away from us and took the call. It was brief and she returned with a bemused smile. "That was your brother."

"Tim?"

"He wants to meet me for coffee."

"Better you than me."

"Don't be mean."

"I'm serious. He'll be nice to you."

"I wonder why."

"Because he likes you?"

"Not why he'll be nice. Why he wants to meet."

"Same," I said. "Because he likes you."

Just as we reached Bill's car my phone sang "Bad Boys."

Mel laughed. "Oddly appropriate, here." She gestured toward the tong's hillside.

"Totally appropriate," I said. "It's my cousin." I answered the phone. "Hey, Linus."

"Hey. You on the street? I hear a subway."

"Life in the midst of death. I'm at the entrance to Cypress Hills Cemetery. The elevated runs right by here."

"Convenient. Anyone I know?"

"The deceased? No, a professional acquaintance."

"You know they bury gangsters there?"

"No kidding. Did you call to tell me that?"

"No, I have intel. Since you're so close by, want to come up here when you're done? We also have coffee."

"Of course you do." Coffee was what fueled Wong Security. After the trestle tables that held up the tech, the second item installed in the converted garage—before the tech itself—had been the De'Longhi espresso machine.

"As it happens," I told Linus, "we're already done. Twenty minutes?"

Mel ordered herself an Uber. Bill and I waited with her until it arrived to whisk her off to coffee with my brother. Then we got in Bill's car to whisk ourselves off to coffee with my cousin.

THIRTY-SIX

A CHAIN-LINK FENCE ran around my aunt and uncle's lot in Flushing, on Magnolia between Ash and Beech. A hundred years ago this area of Flushing used to have a couple of big plant nurseries; there's not much left except the street names, but they go alphabetically all the way to Rose. The fence enclosed the brick-and-siding house, the lawn, the driveway, and the garage. After I'd opened the gate for Bill, I went to ring the bell at the garage's side door, but before I got there the door swung open. Woof came charging out, tail wagging furiously, almost knocking me down in an effort to lick my face. He abandoned me immediately, though, when he saw Bill getting out of the car. They'd gotten to be best buds on a case that still gave me nightmares. While Bill wrestled with Woof, Trella appeared in the doorway.

"Hey." She grinned. At five foot eight, she's taller than I am, and taller than Linus by a couple of inches also. She wore a short tartan skirt, a black sweater, black tights, and heavy black boots. Her blond hair spiked in all directions.

"Hey." I hugged her and proceeded inside.

The cluttered, cable-draped, computer-crowded garage seemed to not have changed since the last time I was here, though I was sure it had. Linus kept not just the software but also all the hardware on the bleeding technological edge, so some of these machines with their red or blue diode lights were bound to be new. The room was chilly as usual, the AC always on except in the depths of winter to keep the equipment cool, the windows covered to keep out prying eyes. If it weren't for Woof needing walks and games of Frisbee, my cousin might never see the light of day.

"Hi, cuz!" Linus spun around in his ergonomic chair. "Saw you coming!" He launched his stocky self out of the chair and hugged me.

"What do you mean?"

"Couple of weeks ago I stuck cameras on half a dozen light poles."

"City light poles?"

"Tiny little cameras. Not bothering anybody. I told the program to look for a gray Audi. The system beeped when it picked you up."

"It didn't say, 'Yo, Linus, your peeps are here'?"

"I didn't put in a speech protocol. You think I should?"

"Hey," Bill said to Linus and Trella. He came inside with Woof, who was still bounding with joy at having us for guests. Bill reached into the biscuit jar and got him a treat. I walked over to the counter where the espresso machine stood and found a plate for the polvorones we'd picked up at a Dominican bakery on our way over. What I'd told Mel Wu about citrus notwithstanding, I knew pastry would go over better here. Trella went to the espresso machine itself, her particular charge. "The usual?" she asked, and on our nods she hissed up a double espresso for Bill and a latte macchiato for me. She made Americanos for Linus and herself, his black, hers with cream and about a quarter cup of sugar.

"So," I said to Linus, who'd plonked back down in his chair. "What's the good word?"

"Don't know how good it is. I can tell you it's not complete. We could find out more if—"

"No." I rolled another chair over. Bill opened a folding chair, and Trella brought us all our coffees and sat cross-legged on the rug next to Woof.

"Okay then. Here's what we have." Linus looked to Trella.

"First, your boy Ting," Trella said. "We already told you his financials look in order. But bad things seem to happen around him. Including one murder. You know about that?"

I nodded and tried my latte. Excellent, as always.

"They happen around him, these things, but no one's been able to tie any of them directly to him. Either he's really good, or he's just unlucky."

"Or," Bill said, "lucky. These bad things are good for business, am I right?"

"Totally. The homicide, I guess you know, was a window supplier. Ting had trouble with the guy, the guy sent a mug to blow up stuff, and then the guy was dead. A couple of other things like that, nobody else dead, but suppliers suddenly lowering prices after their truck tires were all slashed, subcontractors putting on the extra crews Ting wanted after someone ended up in a hospital from a mugging. None of this"—she grinned—"is all that unusual in the construction world. It *is* unusual to get away with it for as long as Ting has without anything sticking to you."

"But he has?" I asked.

"Teflon."

"But," said Linus, "there's something else kind of interesting about these bad things."

"If you look backward," Trella picked it up again,

"you can find them all in the industry press. Before they happen, I mean. There'll be an article about a strike at one of Ting's projects, for example. Then a week later the union rep's wife breaks her arm and the strike gets settled. But he's had other problems that don't make the newsletters or the blogs, and that stuff doesn't always get fixed as fast, or necessarily in Ting's favor."

"How did you find out about all this?"

"I have a couple of cousins in the construction business."

"Of course you do."

"You know," Bill said, "Mike DiMaio told us something similar. That Ting doesn't always come out on top, just more often than other developers."

"That's interesting," I said. "And that difference seems to depend on whether or not the problem made the industry news?"

"Seems to," Trella agreed.

"Hmm."

"But wait!" Linus intoned, in the voice of a late-night commercial. "There's more!"

"I thought there might be. Fascinating as all that is— and it is—I didn't think you'd ask us to come all the way here just to tell us that."

"Sure I would," said Linus. "Because I knew you'd bring cookies."

"Seriously?"

"No. The cookies are good, though. We do have something else. Not about Ting. About Wu Mao-Li and Wu Na-Li. A.k.a. Melanie Wu and Natalie Wu Harris." He slugged back some coffee.

"Their financials are all normal, too, as far as we can tell," Trella said. "Including the husband. No huge debts, no big infusions or outflows of cash. Good credit reports, all that. Natalie seems to have married well, as they say. She also seems to have been in and out of trouble when she was younger, including a fairly spectacular motorcycle accident on a stolen bike when she was fifteen."

"Ha," I said. "She told me it was a bike accident. I thought bicycle."

"The motorcycle was a friend's, so no charges, et cetera. Doesn't seem to have slowed her down. Looks like she kept living la vida loca until she met her husband. Then she settled down."

"You sound like you feel bad for her. For settling down."

"Me?" Trella's innocent wide eyes, wrapped in her punk look and given her choice of boyfriend/employer, were downright ridiculous.

"Is there more?"

"I wanna have more more more more more and more!" Linus warbled. "Don't wanna stop more more more and more!"

"Excuse me?"

"Twice. They're a K-pop girl group. Of course there's more. Not actually dirt, but interesting. Five years ago, and again two years ago, they went to a place in Woodbury called Gold Coast IVF."

"IVF? Well, Natalie said they had trouble getting pregnant. It's not surprising they'd try—oh. Oh!"

Everyone turned to me. Even Woof raised his head.

"Ting's threat," I said. "What if those kids aren't Ting's, but they're not Paul's, either? What if they used donated sperm?"

"You mean hubby was shooting blanks?"

Trella said, "Linus! Ew."

"Sorry."

I said, "That would explain why Natalie's so desperate to keep her son from taking a DNA test. According to her, her in-laws would cry tears of joy to find out those kids weren't actually their son's. They'd file his divorce papers themselves."

"Wow," said Trella. "Stinkers."

"No kidding. And—"

My phone chirped out the client ring. I hadn't given Mel her own tone, but the readout told me that's who it was.

"Excuse me a minute," I said to the coffee klatch. "Hi, Mel. What's up?"

"Something really bad. I'm sending you a video. Call me back after you watch it." Mel's voice sounded barely under control. She clicked off.

"That was Mel," I told the room. "Trouble."

A few seconds later a video arrived by text. I tapped it on and we all watched.

Natalie, looking into the camera, fear in her eyes. "Mel?" she said. "Please. Sell Jackson the building." Her gaze shifted, maybe to the person behind the camera. She said nothing else and the camera slowly pulled back to reveal a shadowed, overhead-lit room with nothing visible in it except Natalie, tied to a chair.

"You heard her," growled a male voice off-screen. "You heard her, so do it." I didn't recognize the voice, its accent heavily Chinese. "No cops, no one else, no trouble. No trouble, Ting gets the building, she goes home. Trouble, she's dead."

The screen went blank.

THIRTY-SEVEN

"WHAT THE HELL?" said Trella, while Linus sat wide-eyed. I looked at Bill and pressed "call back" on my phone. Mel answered immediately.

"When did it come?" I asked.

"Just now. A blocked number."

"Do you know the male voice?"

"No."

"Or the place? Anything familiar about it?"

"No. Where are you? You have me on speaker? You're not on the street or something, are you? So everyone in the world could see that?"

"No, no, I'm with Bill. I wanted him to hear." I held up a warning finger to Linus and Trella and didn't go further. Mel was already disobeying the "no one else" demand by calling me, and boy, did she sound right on the edge.

"Mel," I said, wondering exactly how to put this, "is there any chance this is…staged?"

"Staged? You mean, by Nat? Are you crazy? Did you see how scared she looked? I know her. That's real fear. And besides, she's not a good liar. That's why I had to back up all her stupid stories when we were kids. And why? What does she care whether I sell the building? Uncle Meng left her and her kids plenty of money. If she does care, why not just tell me? Dammit, I called you for help, and that's it, you think Nat's doing this?"

In a more muffled voice, as though she'd turned away: "You were wrong."

"Wrong? About what?"

"I wasn't talking to you."

A familiar voice said, "Give me that." A second later my brother Tim came on the line. "She was talking to me. I told her to call you because I thought you could help. She was telling me I was wrong about that. I better not have been."

"Tim?" Of course. He and Mel were having coffee. "No. No, you weren't wrong. Tell her to trust me. I'm on it."

"And you're not going to the police, right?"

"No," I said. "That's not where I'm going." Which was very lawyerly of me. That wasn't where I was going. But he hadn't asked me who I was going to call.

I hung up, but I didn't call Mary right away. I kept my right to do that in reserve, but we might not have to. "You guys," I said to Linus and Trella. "Can you learn anything from that video?"

"Maybe," Linus said, all business now. "Send it to me."

I forwarded the video. "Call me if you find anything. Come on," I said to Bill.

"Sure. Where?"

"To see Jackson Ting. I've had it with that guy."

From Flushing to Turtle Bay took us twenty minutes. I had a feeling it was usually a longer trip, but Bill's the surest, least-likely-to-get-caught fast driver I know. I googled parking lots near Ting's building, so when we got there we'd know right where to go.

"You really think Ting's behind this?" Bill asked as we drove.

"Who else? Someone just doing the guy a favor? Who benefits if Mel sells the building to him? He does, and Nat does because he leaves her alone. If Mel's right and this is real, not Nat's idea of a good idea, then it's got to be him."

"Or maybe, old man Loo?"

"What?" I looked over at him.

"Loo wants the building sold, isn't that what you said? Both he and Ironman want to trim the deadwood from the tong and start again, even though they have different ideas about who that is. Loo thinks the building's holding them back."

"Oh," I said.

"And Loo's actually a gangster. I might put money on him for a kidnapping before Ting."

"Damn." I thought for a minute, then, "No. They're going to lose the building either way. Whether Mel sells, or keeps it and evicts them. All Loo has to do is wait. Ting's the one who has a deadline and can't wait. This is about him."

"Okay, you're probably right. I just…"

I glanced over sharply. "You just what?"

Bill said nothing.

"You just don't want me to screw up because I'm so blown away that my brother told Mel to call me that I may not be thinking straight?"

He kept his eyes on the road as he said, "Something like that."

I blew out a breath. "Yeah," I said. "Me too."

I DIDN'T WANT Ting to know we were coming, but I did want to make sure he was there. "If he's not?" said Bill.

"Then we'll just track him down. From the developer-smell."

But he was. As soon as we emerged from the tunnel I called his office.

"Good ay-eff-ternoon," I said to the receptionist in my best Southern drawl. "This is Lucinda St. Clair from the Junior League? Mr. Ting made such a lovely donation and I'd just like to thank him personally. I won't take up much of his valuable time."

"Just a minute, I'll see if he's in."

As soon as she put me on hold I hung up. "He's there," I told Bill. Receptionists know whether the boss is in or out. "If he's in" is code for "will take your call."

We pulled into the lot I'd found. Bill gave the attendant a twenty to put the car right up front, nose-out. The guy didn't even blink. We quick-walked to Ting's building.

"Wait!" called the receptionist when we stalked through the outer office, and Ting's assistant said something similar as we strode past her and I threw open his office door. Ting, in shirtsleeves at his computer, looked up.

"I'm sorry, Mr. Ting, they—"

"It's all right, Delia. Go back to work." He stood, waited for his assistant to leave, and came around the desk, saying calmly, "I'm sure you know this is *not* all right. What do you think you're doing?"

"What do *you* think you're doing?" I thrust the phone at him with the video cued up and hit play.

Ting went pale. "What the hell is that?"

"Stop it! Where is she?"

"I have no idea." He looked at me. "You think I did that?"

"Oh, no, why would we? Just because you're going to lose a fortune if you don't get a commitment on that building by the end of the month, and just because you already tried to blackmail Natalie, but I guess that wasn't moving fast enough for you—"

"Wait. Who told you that?"

"Who do you think? Where is she, Ting?"

"I don't know." He looked at me cautiously. "I leaned on her, yeah, okay. So she'd persuade that pretentious bitch sister of hers. But this—I had nothing to do with this. I don't do this kind of shit!"

"Just like you had nothing to do with the dead window supplier?" said Bill. "Or the union rep's wife with the broken arm, or the slashed truck tires? You don't do that shit either?"

"I didn't! None of it!"

"Really? Lucky you, then, that all these things happen around you. What is it, Ting, you have a fairy godmother?"

Ting clenched his jaw and glared at Bill, Bill stared back, and I stood rooted to the spot.

"Oh my God," I said. "Oh my God. He doesn't have a fairy godmother. He has a tiger mom."

THIRTY-EIGHT

TING SWITCHED HIS glare to me. "What the hell does that mean?"

"It means," I said, "that I'm an idiot. Tan." I turned to Bill. "I told you her suddenly picking up and leaving Hong Kong bothered me. You thought she might be an informant. But I—"

"What are you talking about?" Ting snapped.

I ignored him. "She said she left there—and arrived here—during the Dragon Boat Festival. That's in June. Loo told me that within three months of her starting at the Li Min Jin, Big Brother Choi invited her to go to the cemetery on Qing Ming to sweep his wife's grave."

"Her, *who*?" Ting said.

Bill ignored him, too. "Which tells you… ?"

"The Dragon Boat Festival is in June. Qing Ming is in March. If she came to the Li Min Jin three months before Qing Ming, that would have been January. So where was she between June and January?"

"In a safe house, until whatever storm it was blew over?"

"No! For God's sake, she's not an informant. She left Hong Kong because she was pregnant."

Bill let out a slow "Ohhhh."

At the same time, Ting exploded. "*Who*? What are you talking about? What does this have to do with me?"

"Tan Lu-Lien," I told him. "Your mother."

"Are—" He threw up his hands. "You've completely lost me. My mother was Maria Ting, and my father was Ke Ting, and who the hell are you talking about?"

I stared. Could it be possible he didn't know? "Tan Lu-Lien," I said, "came here from Hong Kong in June 1984 and, if I'm right, gave birth in Flushing Hospital on November 28. The name she gave the hospital"— I held up my hand to stop him from speaking—"was Maria Ting. She claimed she was undocumented."

"Undocumented, that's bullshit. My mother was an American citizen!"

"Maria Ting was. Tan Lu-Lien, Maria Ting's cousin, probably came here on a tourist visa. We've met someone who remembers your birth, and your mother. It wasn't Maria Ting. It was Maria's friend. Your mother gave her baby—you—to Maria and her husband as soon as she brought you home from the hospital. They were your mother and father from that moment, but they're not your biological parents."

"You're crazy. I have a birth certificate with their names on it. Not adoption papers! I'm…" He trailed off. He might be a smug, scheming operator, but he wasn't stupid.

"Nothing I'm saying contradicts any of that. A woman told the hospital she was Maria Ting, married to Ke Ting. She had her baby and gave him to the Tings and they took him. No one needed to know and no one knew. The baby was you, and I think the woman was Tan Lu-Lien."

He went back behind his desk and sat heavily, staring at the glass surface, or the floor below it. He didn't look up as he said, "Get out."

I was tempted to do it, but I had a sudden flashback

to my brother in his office, telling me the same thing. For the same reason: He'd needed to mull over what I'd said. My brother, who'd told Mel he thought I could help.

"Listen," I said, trying for the place where gentle meets firm. "I know this is a lot to take in. If I'm right— and I am, Jackson, I know I am—this explains the violent incidents. And why they only happened around events that got made public, that Tan Lu-Lien could read about. She kept her eye on you, Jackson. She stayed in touch with her cousin. She even visited for a while. I'd bet it was her money that sent you to private school."

Ting shook his head. "Dad said—he said he'd inherited money from a distant cousin and wanted to spend it on my education. But why?" Now he did look up. "What the hell? Give a baby away and disappear from its life like that? But still come around? And what do you mean, it explains—oh, shit..." After a long moment he said again, "Oh, shit. The Li Min Jin?" He wasn't stupid, no, but it had taken him time to catch on.

"You'd have seen her at Choi Meng's funeral," said Bill. "At the foot of the coffin. Short hair, hard face—"

"That woman? You're trying to tell me that's my *mother*? Oh my God."

"I think she disappeared," I said, "because she didn't want you to have any connection with the tong. And to give you a chance to grow up respectable. A success. I think she watched and helped out where she could."

He nodded, though I wasn't sure he was convinced. "And—my father? Was Ke Ting my father?"

"Possible but unlikely, unless he'd been in Hong Kong the winter before you were born."

"He came here at the age of four. After that he never left the country. If it's not him, who is it?"

"I don't know. Tan will have to tell you."

Ting drew a long breath. "You said she 'helped out.' You didn't just mean money, did you? You meant, the window guy. The union rep's wife. All that."

I nodded. "And," I said, "Natalie Wu's kidnapping. What you just saw." I added, "Your mother's known Nat since she was a baby, too."

"Don't call her my mother! Oh, God." He stood and walked to the window. After a long moment, he seemed to gather himself. "Is this true?" he turned and asked me, straight on.

"I'm sure it is. It took me too long to figure it out, but I'm sure it's true."

He didn't ask for proof. That would come later, I thought: Mrs. Reyes, DNA tests. Right now we were in the middle of a crisis, and Jackson Ting, to his eternal credit, realized his role.

"Okay," he said. He drew a few long, steady breaths. "Okay. I'll call Mel. I'll tell her to say we came to an agreement. My—that woman—will let Nat go, and then I can negotiate for real with Mel."

I was pretty sure that at this point Mel would never sell Jackson Ting the building, so this was a short-term solution. But at least it would get Nat untied from that chair and out of wherever that was. Which I was also pretty sure was somewhere in the building.

Ting made his call to Mel. "Those investigators are here. They showed me the video. I had nothing to do with it, Mel. Dammit, no, nothing. Just listen. Just listen! I'm going to say we made a deal. That you're selling me the building and it's all good. They'll let Nat go, and you and I can talk about the next step."

Don't say it, I silently ordered Mel, while Ting listened to whatever it was she *was* saying. *Pretend there's a next step to talk about.*

Apparently she got my ESP instructions, because Ting said, "Good. All right. I'll get in touch with—" He looked over at me. "What did you say my—that woman's name is?"

I told him, and he told Mel. "Tan Lu-Lien. What? No, I can't. This isn't the time, Mel. It's very complicated. I'll tell you later. I—"

"Jackson," I said. He looked at me again. "Ask Mel if she has Tan's phone number."

"Tan's phone number," he said into the phone. "Do you have it?" Back to me: "No."

"Then we'll have to go down there."

"Where? To the building?"

"Yes."

"All right," Ting said into the phone. "We're going to Chinatown. No, don't. What good will that do? No. Mel—oh, all right, do whatever you goddamn want, you always do." He clicked off.

"She's not going down there, too?" I said.

"Of course she is. Mighty Mel to save the day! God, she never changes."

So few of us do, I thought, as Ting grabbed his suit jacket off the hook on his door. We passed through his assistant's office, where he told her to cancel his appointments for the rest of the day, and the reception area, where the receptionist got to see that the boss was going out. We waited impatiently for the elevator, trotted to the garage, retrieved the nose-out car, and sped along the FDR to Chinatown.

THIRTY-NINE

ON THE WAY downtown I called Mel. "Don't come. Leave this to us."

"Are you crazy? That's my sister down there."

"It won't help."

"Forget it."

"Mel—"

"No."

"All right," I said. "At least don't go into the building before we get there. Meet us by the park."

I hung up and Bill said, "She's going to be there?"

"She's made a career out of rescuing Nat. Why would I expect her to sit out the big one?"

Before we'd gone another half block my phone rang again. Mary. I let it go to voicemail and listened as she left her message. "Hey. Call me. Something very interesting."

She didn't sound angry or harried, the way she would, for example, if she had word of a kidnapping and had word that I had word of it too. I risked the call. "Hey. What's up?"

"I'm looking for Natalie Wu."

Isn't everyone, I thought, wondering if I'd been wrong, but I just said innocently, "How come?"

"Because," said Mary. "On the note that came with the rock when your brother was shot at? Surprise, surprise. We found her prints."

Surprise was right. "Oh. Um."

"I had Forensics go over the rock from Ironman's shooting again, just in case, but no. Still just the one set, the ones we can't match."

"Wow. I wonder…"

"Yeah, me too. She's not at home, and her kids' nanny says she doesn't know where she went. Do you know where I can find her?"

"No, but if she turns up I'll call you." For more than one reason.

I relayed this intelligence to Bill. Jackson Ting, in the back seat, said, "Rock? Note? Who was shot at?"

"My brother Tim," I told him. "Long story. I'll tell you later."

"People are shooting at people?"

I turned around. "Seriously? Chang Yao-Zu is dead, Natalie's been kidnapped, you're offering a fortune for a building full of gangsters in the middle of a power struggle—a building some of the gangsters think there's already a fortune hidden in—and you're surprised people are firing guns around? Two people were shot at," I told him. "Neither of them was hit. I don't know if that was planning or incompetence." Actually, as I'd told Tim, I was pretty sure it was planning, at least in his case.

Because of the note.

With Natalie Wu's fingerprints on it.

I turned to face forward again.

Bill said quietly, "You know that makes it more likely she's actually in on this?"

"I know," I said. "But you saw her face. Mel says Nat's not a good actor. I don't think she is, either. I think that fear we saw was real. But," I added, "if I find out she shot at my brother, I'll give her something to fear."

We exited at the Manhattan Bridge and swung onto Canal Street. Where we were going was a few blocks south, but it's nuts to actually try to drive into Chinatown in the afternoon, especially if you need to park. On Canal, Bill made a swift and illegal U-turn, pulled up to a yellow curb, and propped the delivery sign from his glove box in the windshield. I jumped out and, taking a page from Bill's book, handed Old Shu the fish seller twenty dollars to tell any inquisitive traffic cop that the car was waiting for the shop guys to pack up boxes of fish.

"Forty," Old Shu said in Chinese, with a grin. "I might have to pay the cop."

I was going to tartly suggest he give the cop a fish, but instead I slapped a second bill onto his outstretched palm.

A block later we were on the corner by the park, and a minute after we arrived Mel came striding down the sidewalk. I guessed she was experienced in Chinatown's impossible traffic, too.

As was the man following closely in her wake. My brother Tim.

"Tim," I said when they reached us. "What are you doing here?"

"Don't start. This whole thing's been a bad shock for Mel. You think I was really going to let her come down here alone? She needed a friend."

The idea of anyone letting—or not letting—Mel do anything was absolutely oxymoronic, and I'd have thought, given the past week, that I met the "friend" requirement. I'd grown up with Tim, though, and I could recognize a nonnegotiable decision when I saw one, even one based on a ridiculous premise. Not for nothing is his zodiac animal the ox.

The ox then noticed my traveling companions. Distaste curled his lip. It was clearly aimed at both men, but it was Jackson Ting he stepped a little too close to. "Ting. What are *you* doing here? Come to gloat?"

"Not now," Ting said. "This isn't the time. You want to fight, I'd be happy to wipe up the floor with you later, Chin, but there's more important things going on at the moment. You saw that video? Then what's your problem?"

"Wow, check it out, a line he won't cross," said Tim. "I wouldn't have believed it."

"Knock it off, Tim," I said. "Jackson's help is what we need right now."

"Jackson?" Tim glanced from me to Ting and back again, raising his eyebrows. To Ting he said, "You claim you had nothing to do with this. So what good do you think you can do here?"

"If your sister's right, I'm the one the kidnapper will listen to. What's her name again?" He turned to me.

Tim snorted. He sounded just like our mother. "You don't even know her name, but she'll listen to you? Impressed with yourself much?"

"Tim," I said, "shut up. I'm not going to tell you to get lost, though I wish you would, but this kind of thing is in my wheelhouse, not yours. Bill, Jackson, and I are going to handle this, and if I can't stop you two from coming along, all right, but you will not say or do *anything* unless I tell you to. Is that clear?" I aimed at the easier target first. "Mel?"

Mel's mouth was a taut angry line, but she nodded. "Tim?"

"I—"

"Tim?"

After a moment, my brother slowly nodded, too.

I spoke to Jackson Ting. "Her name's Tan Lu-Lien. She's temporarily—very temporarily—head of the Li Min Jin."

"Head? You didn't tell me that."

"No, I didn't. Let's go."

I started off. Bill was right with me. I didn't look back to see who else was coming, though I was pretty sure it was the entire regiment. We hadn't made it to the corner when my phone rang. I wouldn't have answered it but "Bad Boys" told me it was Linus.

"Hi," I said. "Something?"

For all his love of fooling around, Linus also knows when to get right to business. "Not earth-shaking," he said. As usual, I heard the echo of the speakerphone. "But something. The voice is definitely a man's, no distorter or anything. Trella thinks there might be a British accent overlaying the Chinese one—that is, he's a Chinese speaker whose English is British English. The phone's a burner, with a SIM card. It has GPS, but it was off."

"A SIM card. So the phone probably wasn't bought here."

"Correct. Likely it's from overseas."

"Any idea where?"

"If I had them here—"

"If you had them there, it would be because we already caught the kidnapper. But this is great, Linus. What about the video? The room?"

"Just about zilch. The light's fluorescent. The room might not have windows, but it's hard to say. Machine noise in the background, but that might not even be from the same room. Or the same building. That's it, that's all I got. What about you?"

"Struck by lightning. Tell you later. About to enter the lion's den with Bill and a whole mob of civilians."

"A mob?"

"Well, three. But one of them's Tim."

"Seriously? Uncle Tim and you doing something together? Trell, did you catch that? But what's he got to do with this? And the lion's den, what do you mean? What's going on?"

"Later. I promise. This is really helpful, your intel. Keep at it. Let me know if you find anything else."

"Will do. Whatever you're doing, good luck."

"You, too."

I relayed Linus's information sotto voce to Bill as our mob strode down the sidewalk. The others didn't need to hear it yet. I wasn't sure what it meant, though I had my suspicions. If I was right, we'd know soon enough.

Then there we were, at the building at the center of it all. I rang the bell, and as soon as Beefy pulled the door open I said in Chinese, "We're here to see Tan Lu-Lien."

"I'll see if she's in." Beefy took out the cell phone he wore clipped like a weapon to his belt. I'd expected *She's not here* right off the bat, so this was a slight improvement. I'd never tell Beefy I thought of him as a receptionist, but I was pretty sure my receptionist-language theory held: Tan was in, though I'd bet we were about to find out, not to us.

Jackson Ting, though, was also used to office games, and right now it appeared he wasn't interested in playing. He gave his name loudly and said, "Tell her I'm here."

Beefy made his phone call, and Jackson's name worked like a charm. He clicked off, let us in, shut the door behind us, and said, "Wait here."

FORTY

BEEFY HADN'T FINISHED telling us to wait before I heard a door open above and the quick trot of footsteps down the stairs. Tan Lu-Lien came into view, frowning as she descended. Reaching us, she cast a swift glance at the rest of the group and addressed Jackson Ting. "What are you doing here?" The question of the hour.

"I think you know."

"I don't know. Come with me. The rest of you, wait here."

"No," said Jackson. "They come too."

Tan's entire body stiffened. I looked for Jackson in her hard features. Now that I knew, I could see the resemblance, though he was softer, the product of an easier life. A life she'd given him.

Ting was also searching Tan's face. When she didn't speak he said quietly, as though to himself, "It's true. I can see it's true. Oh my God."

Wordlessly, Tan turned and stalked without looking back, not up to her comfortable third-floor lair but straight behind the staircase to the lower-order reception room where Mel and I had met with Mr. Loo. This time, though, I suspected it wasn't a need to make a point that brought us here, but a need to get us out of the way fast, before word got around the building that we were here.

Once we were all inside and Tan had shut the door,

she turned to Jackson again. "You shouldn't have come here."

Before he could answer Mel snapped, "You shouldn't have kidnapped my sister."

So much for keeping silent, but that instruction had been more for Tim than Mel anyway.

Tan turned slowly to face Mel. "What are you talking about?" she said in measured tones.

"Oh, for God's sake, cut the crap!" Mel took out her phone and played the video.

Tan watched, her face impassive. When the screen went blank she said, "Play it again."

Mel did.

"Let her go," said Jackson, after the second time. "You didn't need to do this. Mel and I had come to an agreement already for me to buy the building. We just weren't ready to announce it yet."

Tan gazed at Jackson, then gave a small laugh. "For a real estate developer, you lie rather badly." After a moment she smiled. "I'm pleased to know that." The smile faded. "Wait here. All of you." Striding to the far end of the room, she turned her back and sent a text on her phone. The answer came. She sent another and then slipped the phone away. Crossing the room again, she opened the door and called Beefy over.

She spoke to him quietly at the door. He unhooked his phone again, made a quick call, and half a minute later another white-T-shirted guy, a little shorter and broader—Beefy's next of kin?—came down the stairs and took up the front door post while Beefy came into the room.

"Gong-Niu will remain here with you," Tan said. "I'll be back soon."

"No!" said Mel. "I'm not staying here while you—"

"Mao-Li. You and your sister were Choi Meng's family. You grew up before my eyes. Do you really believe I would threaten her life?"

"I don't know what to believe, except what I saw on that video."

"You have nothing to fear. Please, wait. I'll come right back."

Bill looked at me, ready to take my cue, and I looked at Mel, ready for hers.

Mel stared into Tan Lu-Lien's eyes.

Tan didn't blink.

Mel stepped aside and let Tan pass.

Tan, with one more glance at Jackson Ting, left the room to go who knew where. Beefy shut the door behind her, crossed his arms, and looked around at us all.

Gong-Niu, Tan had called him.

Bull.

His name really was Beefy.

The room had plenty of chairs, but while we waited none of us sat.

Jackson Ting paced, and it seemed to me he side-stepped the rest of us, even avoided meeting our eyes. If I'd just come face-to-face with the woman I hadn't even known was my mother until an hour ago and had come to accuse her of kidnapping Natalie, not to mention killing the window guy, breaking the arm of the union rep's wife, and assorted other mayhem, I might have done the same.

Mel stood rigidly by the door, her arms hugging her sides.

My brother Tim practically hugged her sides, too.

"You think we did the right thing, letting Tan leave

like that?" I whispered to Bill. "We might never see her again. Or Nat."

Bill watched Jackson pace, and answered, "This is the first time she's met her son since he was a child, and he's thinking bad things about her. She'll be back."

"Bad things" was an understatement, but I let it go.

Ten minutes went by. I knew it was ten because I checked the clock about forty times after Tan left. I was about to join Jackson in pacing, too, when Mel burst out, "That's it! She lied and she's taken off. I should have called the police. I'm doing that now." She pulled out her phone, which made Beefy drop his arms and step toward her. That made Bill step toward him.

Tim squared up to Beefy also.

Much as I would've loved to see Tim and Bill together on a tag team, I grabbed Tim's arm. "Are you insane?" I hissed. "He'll mash you into juice."

"Let me go!"

"Bill can handle him." I actually only gave that a fifty percent chance of being true, but if I got my brother out of the way, I'd be able to pitch in, too.

Mel swung the phone behind her, out of Beefy's reach.

Bill moved between them.

Beefy shoved Bill.

Bill shoved back.

Tim balled up his fist.

I yanked him aside and stepped up next to Bill.

And then, just before the action could really start, the door opened.

Everyone froze. All eyes swung to the three people in the doorway.

Natalie Wu, disheveled but free, stepped tentatively

into the room. She saw Mel and with a small, wordless sound rushed over.

Mel grabbed her up in her arms. Still in the doorway was Tan Lu-Lien, and behind her, wearing a black leather jacket with a red stripe down the sleeve, stood the tall, thin gangster I'd seen a couple of times before, the man not from Chinatown whose identity no one knew.

FORTY-ONE

I WAS PRETTY sure I knew, though.

As Mel comforted Nat, Tan and the tall gangster walked into the room. At Tan's instruction Beefy stepped back outside and closed the door.

I faced the new man. "Well, well," I said. "Johnny Gee, am I right? Direct from Hong Kong? Once the leader of the Black Shadows, now high up in the Hong Kong branch of the Li Min Jin?"

"And also," Bill said, "an accomplished motorcycle rider and not a bad marksman. Welcome to New York."

Jackson said, "An investor. You said you were a potential investor."

"Wait," Tim erupted. "A motorcycle rider? A marksman? He's the guy who shot at me?" By the end of that he was practically squeaking.

Tan held up her hand. Radiating tightly coiled fury, Gee pushed past everyone and strode across the room. He stopped and stood staring out the window. Down here on the first floor there was nothing to see except the brick wall across the rear yards, but I didn't think he was standing there for the view.

Tan watched him, then turned to Mel and Nat. "I'm sorry," she said, "I didn't know. If I had, I would have stopped him."

Mel gave a tiny nod.

Tan walked over to Jackson. She spoke directly to

him as though the rest of us weren't in the room. "I never wanted you to learn this, and I'm sorry that you did. It can't be helped now, though. I'm your mother, as I suppose you already know. Johnny is your father."

Jackson stood as motionless as if he were rooted to the ground. He didn't say or ask anything.

My brother Tim, though, can always be counted on to demand an explanation, as though he has a God-given right to any facts he wants. "What are you talking about?" he challenged Tan. "Who is he"—pointing at Johnny Gee—"and who are you anyway? What's going on?"

He did have a point. Why would my straight-arrow brother know who anyone was in the Li Min Jin, aside from his strange bedfellow Big Brother Choi? Also, the bewilderment in Tim's voice was reflected on Mel's face, though minus the aggression. She knew who Tan was, but this was the first she'd heard about why Jackson was here. Nat, peeking out from Mel's embrace, showed the same perplexity. Well, it was better than panic, the embers of which were now fading from her eyes.

"Tan Lu-Lien is in charge of the Li Min Jin New York's finances," I explained to my brother. "She's also the temporary head, since the death—natural— of Big Brother Choi and the death—by murder—of Mr. Chang."

I held up my hand to fend off whatever else he was about to ask, and raised my voice to include the room at large. "When Tan Lu-Lien came here from Hong Kong nearly forty years ago, she was pregnant by Johnny Gee. Who didn't know, am I right?" Johnny Gee, by the window, didn't acknowledge the question. I went on. "She gave the baby away and spent her life in the Li Min Jin, taking care of the money and also, from a distance, taking care of her son."

I looked at Jackson, still motionless. I could see, from the corner of my eye, understanding start to dawn on other faces.

"Why?" Jackson finally asked Tan. "Why not…" *Stay with me*, I was sure he wanted to say, but he didn't say it.

"Because," Tan said, "she's wrong. Johnny did know."

Johnny Gee still didn't turn. His shoulders were set in an angry line.

"With a baby," Tan said, "there would have been no way I could keep my position in the Black Shadows. Nor any way I could keep you out of it. You and I would have become dependent on Johnny, and you would have been raised in the gang. In the tong, if Johnny was accepted there, which was no better. Many young people join gangs for the romance of crime or the power of violence. I joined the Black Shadows to be free. I had limited options for a future, and that's the one I chose."

She looked into Jackson's eyes for a long moment. "I wasn't going to let your options be limited, too."

Jackson looked away.

Tan's hard face didn't change, but I thought I saw something like resignation in her eyes.

"I'd managed to disappear and come to New York," she said, "but I knew he'd keep looking, and I knew he'd find me. Not because he wanted me back. But he would have come for you."

Jackson finally spoke. "For me." It wasn't a question, just the kind of repetition you use to make sure you understand.

"The only way I could safeguard you was to join the tong. Johnny was still a Black Shadow. If I could get the tong's protection, you and I would both be safe. But," she said, "not together. It was hard enough for a young woman to join the Li Min Jin. The financial skills I'd developed made it possible, but for a mother with an infant, the idea would have been ludicrous. Even if I'd been allowed in, being raised in the tong was the future I'd run away to save you from.

"Maria Ting was my cousin. Maria and Ke wanted children very badly and had been unable to have them. The solution was obvious. And," Tan added with a smile, "it's worked out well for you."

"Worked out well," Jackson repeated. "With your... help."

"Of course. I wasn't in a position to raise you, but you were still my son. It was my share of the profits from the Li Min Jin's enterprises that sent you to prep school, to college and graduate school."

"Did they know?" Jackson said. "My *parents*." He emphasized the word. "Did they know where the money was coming from?"

"They knew it was mine. They had no idea I was in the Li Min Jin. When I joined the tong, I told Ke and Maria I'd taken a position in an accounting firm. They thought I was rising through the firm. They never knew anything else.

"I watched you grow, but from a distance. I didn't want anyone to associate Ke and Maria with the tong. I went to your high school debate club finals. I attended your college graduation. Public events where my presence wouldn't be noticed. After you got your MBA, I watched you join Ke's firm and learn the business. I was very proud. You were a natural. You've inherited my ability with numbers."

At first, Jackson said nothing. Then, in a hard voice, he said, "You gave me other help, too."

Tan tilted her head in acknowledgment. "When I saw a need, I tried to meet it."

He'd been talking about the violence that had trailed his projects, but a different light bulb went off in my head. I said to Tan, "Ironman thinks you've been stealing money from the tong."

Six people were scattered around the room in addition to Tan and Jackson, but Tan spun around as though startled to find she and her son weren't alone. She searched me out, met my eyes, and said, "Ironman is wrong."

"I know. But by the time Jackson took over Ke Ting's firm and started to work on the bigger projects, Choi Meng had long since given you complete control of the tong's money for investment purposes. So you invested."

Bill was the first to catch on and his reaction was a grin. "I'll be damned. Shell companies on top of shell companies. The Star Group. You're Ting's secret investor."

FORTY-TWO

"You?" Jackson said to Tan. "You're the Star Group?"

"The Star Ferry," I said. "An indelible piece of Hong Kong."

Tan looked at me, amused. "Very good. I didn't want to risk a more Chinese-sounding name, but I wanted something that would bring the venture luck." Back to Jackson: "You've made a good deal of money for the Li Min Jin over the years."

"Not just you? The tong? The tong's been investing in my buildings?"

"When you started to do projects bigger than your—bigger than Ke's, you had trouble raising cash. It looked like you might not succeed."

"And then the Star Group came out of nowhere. I thought it was because someone saw the potential in what I was trying to do. Someone believing in my vision, my ability."

"I did."

"No. No. You were just propping me up because you're my..." He couldn't say it.

"It's part of my job to invest the Li Min Jin's assets in conventional enterprises. I wasn't 'propping you up.' I had a responsibility, which I took seriously, to grow our resources. I wouldn't have invested in your projects if I hadn't thought the investment would be profitable for the Li Min Jin."

"'Invest in conventional enterprises.'" Jackson pronounced the words as if they were made of lemons. "You mean, to turn dirty money legit. The tong paid for my education, and I've been returning the favor, haven't I? You've been laundering tong money through my projects for years."

"My job was to invest our assets," Tan repeated. "If I hadn't chosen your projects, that money would have gone elsewhere. Perhaps to your competitors. Tell me, has what I've done turned out badly for you?"

"It could!" he snapped. "My God, it could ruin me if anyone found out."

"All these years, no one has."

Because no one's looked, I thought.

Jackson didn't seem to know what to say.

I did. "But the Star Group didn't invest in Phoenix Towers."

"No," said Tan. "How could I? Choi Meng was opposed to the project."

"Did you do it secretly? Are you also"—I thought back to what Linus had told us—"Advance Capital Limited?"

"No." That loud answer came from the man at the window. "I am." Johnny Gee turned to face us, anger still burning in his eyes. "Lu-Lien, his *mother*," he said, as though he'd eaten Jackson's lemons, too, "successfully kept my son out of my reach all his life."

"You have three sons and two fine daughters," Tan said mildly.

"But he was my first child. My eldest son."

Jackson looked sick.

"She kept him out of my reach, but not out of my sight." Johnny Gee walked over to stand a few feet from Tan. They both kept their eyes on the rest of us and didn't look at each other. "I got reports from America."

"I knew that was happening, that Johnny had forces here," said Tan. "As long as I was under Choi Meng's protection, there was no danger."

"What changed?" I looked at Johnny Gee. "Why did you come here?"

Gee said nothing. Tan was the one who answered me. "The Phoenix Towers project is ambitious. It's on as different a scale from what Jackson's done before as his early projects were from Ke's. It could be Jackson's step into a major real estate empire."

"Real estate empire?" my brother burst out. "It'll destroy the neighborhood!"

Tan shrugged. "Neighborhoods change."

I shot Tim a glare. Mel laid a hand on his arm. One of those things worked because he turned purple but clamped his mouth shut.

"But," Tan said, "because of the need to assemble a complicated site, many investors were doubtful. They held back, waiting. When even the Star Group didn't invest, neither did anyone else. The project's financing was endangered."

"So when I couldn't raise the money..." Jackson trailed off.

"I called Johnny."

"Finally," said Johnny Gee. He was gloating. "Finally, she needed me."

"The phone calls you made to a high-up Li Min Jin Hong Kong member," I said. "They were to him. About this."

Tan's forehead furrowed. "How—"

"Ironman. You used cell phones so he couldn't tap the line, but he knew you were making the calls. He thinks you were discussing the Hong Kong leader's plan to cut the Li Min Jin New York loose."

Johnny Gee said, "What plan? Why would we do that? The Li Min Jin New York is a valuable asset."

"I'm sure it is," I said, while Tan hissed something under her breath. People curse in their native languages, so her expletives were Chinese, and yet I heard "Ironman."

"Especially with Tan Lu-Lien in charge of the finances," I went on. "That's probably why you haven't interfered before, even though she ran off with your son. She was rising, becoming more and more valuable in the New York organization faster than you were in Hong Kong. By the time you were big enough to challenge her, everyone was making too much money. No." I shook my head. "Ironman's way off base on that. What you were talking about was Phoenix Towers. And how Jackson needed funding for it. Tan saw getting in touch with you after all this time as a risk worth taking. And you saw an opening. A way to get closer to your son."

Johnny Gee sneered. "Closer to my son. *Closer* to a grown American man I'd never met. What sentimental shit. Just what I'd expect from a woman. One woman, I used to think, just one I'd ever known, wasn't like that, but I learned years ago I was wrong. She's as soft as the rest of you." His eyes flicked contemptuously from me, to Mel, to Nat. He didn't look at Tan, who still hadn't looked at him.

"My son is a grown man," he repeated. "Closer means nothing. But Tan Lu-Lien called me. She'd kept him away from me his whole life, but now she came to me. To *me*, his father. Because she had to. Because when it really mattered, she wasn't enough." His smile was thin and bitter. "I was happy to help."

"Happy" was clearly not the word he meant. "Vindicated," maybe. Or "triumphant."

"She said my son," he went on, "*my son*, was going to change New York. And from there, he was going to build an empire! If that was true, why would it matter if we'd never met? If we never did? He was my son, and the victory would be our family's victory."

I glanced at Jackson. He looked shell-shocked.

Keep it going, Lydia, I thought. *Give everyone a chance to breathe and absorb this.* "But Choi Meng didn't want to sell," I said. "Wasn't that a problem for you, for the Li Min Jin Hong Kong, that the Li Min Jin New York was holding out and could stop the project?"

"Yes," Johnny Gee said, his voice flinty. "I'd have stayed out if I'd known that, stayed out as Lu-Lien did. But she didn't tell me, did she?" Finally, he looked at Tan. His gaze was poisonous. "She was willing to endanger me and the tong to help her son."

"Our son." Tan kept her eyes forward.

"A son you'd never let me meet," Johnny Gee said.

"Because I wanted better for him. Not this." Tan swept her arm to encompass the room, the building, the criminal life of the Li Min Jin.

"So you forced me to into a corner with Hong Kong but refused to take a stand here."

"You weren't forced to do anything."

"Forced a woman's way! Forced with sweet words of family and sons that twist a man's heart. You knew what you were doing."

"I couldn't directly oppose Choi Meng. He'd been like a father to me."

"While I was kept from my son, and a stranger was a father to him."

"I've been helping our son all his life," Tan finally snapped, spinning to face Johnny Gee. "You knew where we were. You made no offer, no overture. You just spied on us. You did nothing that would lead me to believe you understood why I did what I did."

"What you did," he said, "was to keep my son from me."

They stared forty years' worth of daggers at each other.

"And then"—Johnny Gee smiled—"Choi Meng died. Hong Kong wanted to end the stalemate and get the project started, or withdraw our investment. So I came to New York. To see the project for myself. To see my son for myself. To see the man whose empire I was going to make possible."

"And kidnapping Nat?" I said. "Shooting at Ironman?"

"Things were moving too slowly. The stalemate wasn't changing. I needed to make a point. My son needed my help." Johnny Gee smiled again.

Now Jackson came to life for the first time since Johnny Gee had started speaking. He shook his head and laughed. "Unbelievable. Unbelievable. Phoenix Towers would be doing Chinatown a favor. Bright, modern apartments to replace run-down rat holes. A school. Community facilities. And I'd get rid of the tong! Sounds great, right? Except it was tong money that was going to make all that happen. And two gangsters—my gangster *parents*—helping me out. My God."

While the glow of Jackson's halo was distracting his gangster parents, I caught Bill's eye. Johnny Gee had just admitted to assault with a deadly weapon and kidnapping. We needed to get the civilians out of here and turn the rest of this over to Mary. Too much info flooding around. If anything else came out, something

Tan Lu-Lien or Johnny Gee suddenly realized shouldn't have gotten through the sluice gates, we could all be in trouble.

But my ever-dependable brother Tim wasn't finished. He yelped to Johnny Gee, "But why did you shoot at me? What point were you making with that?"

"Shoot at you?" Johnny Gee glanced at him impatiently. "I don't even know who the hell you are."

"That's crap! You took a shot just like the one you took at Ironman. From a motorcycle, with a note and everything. Why?"

Johnny Gee balled up his fists. "Listen, Junior—"

"What did you call me?"

Great. Johnny Gee was looking for something to pound, and Tim was painting a bull's-eye on himself.

"Okay," I said. "Let's all—"

But okay it was not.

FORTY-THREE

SHOUTING ERUPTED BEYOND the door. More than one voice. Some in English, some in Chinese. All men. All demanding to be let in. Beefy and another voice warning the others to back off.

Tan set her hard jaw, stalked to the door, and threw it open. Beefy and Neo-Beefy stood like a seawall holding back a small flood of men. Tong members, I assumed, and the younger ones, not the veterans. All were angry, and some were armed. At the front of the wave as it threatened to break over the Beefys was Ironman Ma.

"What's this?" Tan demanded loudly in Chinese. "What's going on?"

Sudden quiet. A few of the men shifted uneasily. Others muttered or spoke aloud words like "thief" and "bandit." One yelled "Traitor!"

"Who said it?" Tan waded out into the crowd, pushing past Ironman like a swimmer shoving flotsam aside. "Who called me traitor? I've given my life to this tong. Step forward. Say it to my face."

No one did.

"As I thought. Ironman, your friends are cowards. Fine company you keep." She ran her gaze up and down Ironman, turned to the men, and gave a cold smile. "Fine company you all keep. Now go."

She turned her back on them to reenter the room. Even Ironman could read the insult in her lack of fear.

"Tan Lu-Lien!" he shouted. "Everyone knows your loyalty was to Choi Meng, not to us." He was also speaking Chinese, probably to make sure his audience stayed with him. "Choi's gone. Now's your chance to prove your loyalty to the Li Min Jin."

Tan stopped. Without turning, in words that were each heavily emphasized and each dripping with acid, she said, *"Prove my loyalty?"*

Ironman said, "You have the key. Show us the door it opens. Show us the hidden fortune. Return it to us. The rightful owners."

Now Tan slowly turned and surveyed the crowd again. "How far and how fast this tong has fallen." Another long moment, then, "We buried Choi Meng a week ago. Chang Yao-Zu, only this morning. Is your greed so great you can't give them peace until tomorrow? I said we'd go through the building then, opening whatever you want until you're satisfied there's no fortune."

"We'd give them peace if you would," Ironman said loudly. "But you're betraying them. If we go through the building tomorrow, no, there'll be no fortune. You'll be gone with it. All of you. I can see who's in that room, Tan." He half-turned, to address the crowd of men. "Jackson Ting's in there! Wu Mao-Li. Her sister. Johnny Gee from the Li Min Jin Hong Kong. And two private bodyguards. Why would they be meeting secretly here except to make deals for the stolen money? The building? Things that belong to *us*?"

I'd heard my brother whispering translations for Mel and Nat, and for Bill, who'd moved over to get in on it. That last, apparently, was too much for Mel. With a curse, she strode out of the room to stand beside Tan Lu-Lien.

"This building is mine," she declared. "Everything in it is mine. If there's something you think belongs to you, sue me for it. I've gotten an injunction against any damage to or removals from this building effective immediately and going forward indefinitely until such time as you vacate and I'm in sole possession." She lifted her phone, implying she'd just found out the injunction had come through. "A courier will be here with the papers any minute."

That was a total lie. When we'd discussed an injunction, she told me she wouldn't be getting one. *If there's anything there,* she'd said, *let them fight over it.* But she was the owner and she was a real estate attorney, and she sounded convincing as hell.

"We're leaving now," Mel said. "My sister, me, and whoever else wants to go. I'll have the papers served on you, but I don't want to spend another minute in this place. Move."

Clearly, Mel was trying what I'd been about to—getting the civilians out of the way and leaving the tong members to their own battle.

"No," said Ironman, with the weight of the crowd behind him. "First we see what's locked up in the walls. Then you can leave. Without it."

Mel took another stride and stood face-to-face with Ironman. I thought their glares might ignite where they met, but suddenly the front door flew open and a new voice shouted, "What is wrong with you all?"

Ironman spun around. Loo Hu-Li was stomping into the entryway, followed by what could only have been the older members of the Li Min Jin. Like Ironman's faction, these men carried guns, or knives, or, in two cases, baseball bats.

Stopping a few steps in, his crowd behind him, Loo shouted, "Ironman Ma, is this how you demonstrate your capability to lead this tong? By turning the members into a mob about to set on Choi Meng's niece for a fortune that doesn't exist?"

"Old Loo, your time has passed," Ironman yelled back. His men parted like the Red Sea to allow him a clear path to Loo Hu-Li. He walked halfway along it. "You want this building gone so that the members, turned out in the street, will follow what you think is your *superior experience* to a new home. Superior experience! Tired old thinking from a tired old man." He cocked his head. "Or are you sharing in the fortune? Is that why you're so anxious to let Jackson Ting destroy the building Choi Meng loved?"

Ironman invoking Choi Meng and his love for the building seemed to me a landmark in hypocrisy, but this wasn't the time to mention it.

"That's enough!" Jackson Ting stepped forward. He'd clearly been following the verbal Chinese brawl, but when he spoke it was in English, as though claiming something that was still his. All eyes turned to him. "I don't care who loved this shithole, but you can all keep it. I'm pulling the plug on the project. I only hope my PR people can do enough damage control to get me out of this with some kind of reputation going forward." He turned to Tan Lu-Lien and Johnny Gee, behind him. "Thanks a lot, *Mom* and *Dad*." Vitriol soaked those words. "You abandoned me, and then you thought you could use me. Screw you. Screw you all."

A heavy silence filled the entry hall. I nodded at Bill. He rounded up Tim and Nat. I caught Mel's eye and we all started walking slowly to the front door. I hoped

Jackson was joining us, but I didn't want to look back to see. All we had to do was get out of here and leave these guys—and Tan—on their own. The unanswered questions, mine and everyone else's, could wait.

Loo stepped aside to let us pass.

But Ironman wasn't having any.

"I said no!" he shouted. "No one leaves until I see what the goddamn key opens."

He was behind me, so I didn't see him raise his gun. The first I knew about it was when I heard the bullet whine and felt plaster pelting my head. Ironman had shot a hole in the ceiling.

I whipped around, yelling, "Are you nuts?" but in the general uproar no one heard me. Another gunshot from the other direction broke a light, sending down a rain of glass. Men waded into groups of other men, swinging fists and bats.

Tan shouted, "Stop!" and no one did.

Loo's mob swarmed into the lobby to attack Ironman's, leaving a gap in the entryway. Bill wrapped his arm around Nat and they ran. From behind, Tim came rushing up, grabbed Mel with one hand and me with the other, and kept going. My brother, propelling me through violence to safety.

Relative safety. On the front step we all screeched to a halt and stuck our hands high in the air, in the face of a phalanx of riot-shielded cops.

FORTY-FOUR

"JESUS CHRIST!" shouted Mary, though not through the bullhorn in her hand. "Get away from there!"

The street was blocked by NYPD cruisers and two Emergency Services trucks, plus the Bomb Squad van. Ambulances idled farther up the block. A helicopter's rotors thudded overhead.

Behind us, the Li Min Jin door slammed shut. We dashed forward. The phalanx parted to let us through. Chris Chiang and Mary, both in helmets and body armor, stood behind the shield-wielding cops.

"They're armed," I said to Mary and Chris as Bill and I joined them. "Two Li Min Jin factions. Knives, bats, guns."

"Why do you think we're here?" Mary said. "Citizens saw them marching down the street. I'd ask why *you're* here, but I don't have time for whatever stupid excuse you'd hand me. I heard shots fired. Anyone hurt?"

"Not yet. The fight's still going on in there."

"Any civilians still inside, or only tong members?"

I looked around. I saw Mel, Nat, and Tim being decanted into a cruiser. "Jackson Ting," I said.

"*Ting's* in there?"

"That tall gangster no one knew? That's Johnny Gee from the Hong Kong Li Min Jin. He's Ting's father. And Tan Lu-Lien is his birth mother."

"What the—what?"

"Ting only just found out."

"Is that what this is about?"

"No. It's about the treasure in the walls. Ironman thinks Tan's about to run off with it. Loo's trying to make the case that that's nuts and prove Ironman's not fit to take over the tong."

A new, male voice: "Treasure? What are you talking about?"

I turned to see a handsome thin-faced White man in uniform. Tony Eprile, the Fifth Precinct's captain. With him was a young Asian guy with a shirt and tie under his body armor. Mary handed the Asian guy the bullhorn.

"Ren Hsieh," the guy said. "Hostage negotiator. Fill me in so I can get to work."

"How many hostages?" Capt. Eprile asked.

I said, "If you mean non–tong members, only one, and I'm not sure he's a hostage. I don't know why he didn't leave with us."

"Fill me in," the negotiator said again. So I did, with the occasional interpolation from Bill. Hsieh made quick notes as we spoke.

"They really think there's treasure in the walls?" Hsieh asked when I was through.

"I'm not sure," I said. "Ironman says he does, but he may be just strutting, showing off to his guys. Tan and Loo both say they don't, but Loo doesn't want it to be there because he wants the building gone."

"All right," Capt. Eprile said. "Get in the car and don't come out. Ren, take it away."

Hsieh raised the bullhorn. He kept his voice calm.

"Loo Hu-Li! Ironman Ma! I'm Ren Hsieh. This is my phone number." He rattled it off. "Whatever your quarrel, you're endangering people, and we can't allow that." He said it again in Cantonese, and again in Mandarin.

No more guns sounded, but the doors didn't open. I didn't get in the car and neither did Bill. What were the cops going to do, shoot us? In fact, no one even seemed to notice.

Hsieh spoke again. "Let Jackson Ting come out, and anyone else who wants to. We'll hold our fire." Again, he repeated himself twice.

Nothing.

I whispered to Bill, "Do you suppose the NYPD has done the impossible and united the tong?"

"That would be an unfortunate example of the law of unintended consequences."

"For Pete's sake," I said. "You sound like Mel. And Tim."

"Loo! Ma!" the negotiator said. "The Li Min Jin's been respected in Chinatown for a century. You just buried two leaders with honor. Is this how you want to end?" Nothing. "Someone talk to me. The street's shut down and the neighborhood's panicking. People here need to be able to go on with their lives. Isn't that what the Li Min Jin is about? Your sports teams, your scholarships? Are you going to let all that go up in smoke? Talk to me. We'll work with you, but this can't go on. Call me."

Nothing.

At least, not on his phone.

But on mine.

I grabbed it out of my pocket and checked the read-out. "Ironman," I said to the people around me, and again into the phone. Eprile, Hsieh, Bill, Mary, and Chris all snapped around to me.

"Get rid of them," Ironman said.

"The police? Me? Are you high? Not one of these

cops would listen if I said go sit in a bucket because your pants are on fire."

"This is an internal Li Min Jin matter."

"Sure it is. What are you doing in there, having an indoor gang war? Like an escape room but with real guns? I'm sure the NYPD would love it if you all butchered each other, but the whole 'serve and protect' thing gets in the way." Mary gestured impatiently for me to give the phone to Hsieh, but Ironman was talking in my ear.

"Loo and his senile old men can do what they want, but I'm not leaving here without the treasure."

"What if it's not there?"

"It's here! Goddammit, it's here!"

"I think you're wrong, and I think you're crazy, and I'm giving this phone to the hostage negotiator because I'm about to tell you where to shove it, and I think that's not how this goes." I handed my phone to Hsieh.

"Hi," he said calmly into it. "Ironman? I'm Ren. Tell me what's going on in there and what you want." He listened, nodding, and finally said, "If no one's hurt we can discuss safe passage. The first thing you need to do is open that door and let everyone who wants to leave, leave. Yes. No. No, not until everyone's out. They come out without weapons and with their hands up. No. Then? We'll make sure they're unarmed and unhurt. Then I'll talk to you about what comes next. No. No. Ironman, look outside. We could storm the building, or we could trap you all in there until you starve. The only reason we haven't broken down the door yet is because we understand there's at least one civilian inside. But if we feel he's in danger, then what's to keep us from coming in? Some of these guys"—Hsieh's voice relaxed into a comfortable, buddies-at-the-bar tone—"these SWAT guys, they'd rather I just shut up and turn everything over to them. They're chomping at the bit to use their expensive ordnance. They have big guns, two of them are Army snipers, and they like to blow stuff up. I can't keep holding them back. You have to meet me halfway, Ironman. Open the door, let people leave." He lowered the phone and whispered to me, "Do we know his faction controls the door? Did he tell you that?"

"No."

Lifting the phone again, Hsieh said, "Ironman, I'm going to say it again, this time through the bullhorn. To make sure everyone knows." He raised the bullhorn and called, "Anyone who wants to come out before we come in, open the door and come now. Unarmed, hands up, slowly. We'll hold our fire. Look around out here. Once we come in, I can't make any promises."

For about a minute, nothing.

Then the door cracked an inch or two, just enough to peer out of. A few seconds later it opened and a fat bald guy came out, hands in the air. One of Loo's crew, I guessed. A riot-shielded cop dashed forward and hustled him away. Behind him, a skinny one, and then three more, miscellaneous but all Loo's. Either Loo's guys were controlling the door, or they were the only ones who wanted out. Cops grabbed each as he emerged. Another two, and then Loo himself. Not Jackson, and not Tan or Johnny Gee, but it was a good start.

Or not. As Hsieh lifted the bullhorn to speak again, I heard the backfire bang of a gunshot.

Loo, blood spreading on his chest, fell forward.

All hell broke loose.

More shots, from inside, from out here. Cops swarmed forward. Bullets shattered glass. Voices yelled commands. Voices shouted. Voices shrieked. I dove to the pavement.

"Shit," I said, which pretty much covered it.

Also, 165 motionless pounds of Bill covered me.

"Are you still breathing?" I said, feeling like my heart had stopped.

"Yes."

My heart started again. "Thank God. Now get off."

"I don't know," he said. "I'm pretty comfy."

"You won't be if you don't move."

He shifted his weight, managing to sneak a kiss onto my neck as he slid over beside me. I didn't object.

FORTY-FIVE

THE CHAOS LASTED only about ten minutes, but it felt like days.

Jackson, Tan, Johnny Gee, even that SOB Ironman kept crowding into my head until I admitted I was worried about them; it took me a while because I *knew* I was worried about Mary and Chris, who'd gone charging in with the rest of the cops. Leading with their shields, the NYPD had managed to surge through the door before anyone—Beefy? what had become of him?—could shut it. That meant there'd be no long siege, which was good, but it also meant we out here had no idea what was going on in there, which was driving me nuts.

As soon as the bullets stopped flying around outside, an EMS tech in helmet and armored vest ran to where Loo was lying facedown on the street. He waved another guy over, and they lifted Loo onto a lowered gurney and whipped him away, which said to me he was still alive.

Ren Hsieh, crouched behind the car with us, kept trying urgently but methodically to reestablish contact with Ironman, alternating between the bullhorn and my phone. He shouted, got no response. He called, it went to voicemail. He texted, nothing happened. He shouted, got no response. Over and over. I guessed if I were in the middle of a firefight I might not answer a cop, either.

Even if I could.

Then it ended. The sound of shooting stopped abruptly. After a bit, the door opened. Pairs of cops began to bring out handcuffed men, old and young. Ironman was among the first, looking battered but walking under his own steam. Another couple of guys, then Johnny Gee, seething but apparently intact. A few more. A long pause.

"What the hell?" I whispered to Bill. "Everyone else is dead?" I tried to make a joke of it, but strangely, it wasn't funny.

"They must be sweeping the building," Bill said.

Hsieh nodded. "That's the protocol."

As we watched, a cop appeared at the door and called for the EMS guys. Three of them rushed forward; another three waited with rolling gurneys to be summoned by the triage guys if needed. They were, and they went in, and then a few more people trickled out, some walking and handcuffed, some on gurneys—and handcuffed to those. Bill, Hsieh, and I stood up behind the cruiser to watch the action. Bill said nothing, but he took my hand while we surveyed the cops leaving the building. I was sure he could feel my heart pounding. Then the unmistakable form of my best friend from babyhood came out the door and crossed the sidewalk. Her progress was slow because she was supporting Chris Chiang, who wore a white patch of bandage on his shoulder.

I rushed forward before a cop, or Bill, could stop me. Not that Bill tried; he was right beside me.

Hugging Mary, I said, "Are you okay?"

Hugging me back, she said, "Are you still here?"

"What about me?" Chris said plaintively. "Don't I get a hug? I got shot!"

"A flesh wound," Mary said. "A scratch."

"Literally," Chris admitted. He stretched his neck to see his shoulder. "I think it's stopped bleeding already."

I said, "Glad it's not worse."

"Can I get a hug anyway?"

I gave him one.

"What happened in there?" I asked. "What about Jackson Ting? And Tan? I didn't see them come out."

"We couldn't find them."

"Couldn't—But they were in there when the shooting started, and by then you guys had the building surrounded. Where could they have gone?"

"Secret escape tunnels," said Chris. "Bet they popped up on the other side of the East River."

"We'll sweep the building again," Mary said. "But the initial sweep was pretty thorough, and they didn't turn up. She's really his mother?"

I shrugged. "What can I say?"

"Whatever it is, you're going to come down to the station right now and say it."

WHICH WE DID. The Fifth Precinct was buzzing when we got there, and its two holding cells were stuffed with tong members. Cops and white-shirted brass came and went. I didn't see Johnny Gee or Ironman in either of the cells, which likely meant each was being accorded the honor of his own interview room.

Because Chris was the injured party, he dropped behind his own desk upstairs in the Squad Room. Mary perched on it. I sat in the chair in front of it, and Bill pulled another over. Chris picked up his empty NYPD mug with his good arm and eyed it pitifully.

"Seriously?" said Mary. "You're going to play that?" He looked sad. She snorted. But she got up and got him coffee. "Bill? Lydia, you want tea? All we have is Lipton, so take it or leave it."

"I'll take it with gratitude. I really was worried about you, you know," I said as she came back with two mugs in each hand, reminiscent of our high school waitress days.

"Fine. Then how about next time before you wave a red flag at a bullring full of gangsters, you think about me and Chris, since you're obviously not bright enough to think about yourself?"

"That's not fair. That's not what happened."

"Oh? Then tell me what did happen."

"Johnny Gee kidnapped Natalie Wu."

"Who's Johnny Gee?"

"The tall gangster no one—"

"Oh, right, him. Okay, go on."

I went on. As I silently praised the gods of tea, even Lipton, Bill and I together filled them in on the kidnapping and its gangster family summit aftermath. We included a side trip to the trouble trailing Jackson Ting's construction projects, and one to Johnny Gee's investment in Phoenix Towers.

When we were done Mary and Chris shared a long look, then both turned back to me. "You're telling me," Mary said, "that Tan killed that window guy? Broke that woman's arm?"

"She just about admitted it."

"Bill?" Mary raised her eyebrows, asking Bill for confirmation. Whether she really needed that or she was just trying to annoy me I didn't know, but I chose to sip my Lipton in saintly silence as he nodded.

"And by herself, I'd think," he said. "I mean, not

farmed out. She wouldn't have wanted anyone, even a hired gun, to wonder why she cared."

"In Hong Kong, in the Black Shadows," I said, "she was an enforcer. She said she liked it."

Mary drank coffee and stared darkly into space. "When you got the kidnap video," she said, "you didn't think to call us?"

"Of course I did—"

"But they said 'no cops,'" she interrupted wearily.

"It wasn't that."

"Oh? What was it?"

"First, I was sure it was Jackson. Until the light bulb went on that Tan was his mother. Then I thought it was Tan."

"You were wrong both times."

"Come on, Mary! This was no normal kidnapping with a ransom demand and all that. Would you guys going in have made things better?"

"We might have avoided a firefight."

"The firefight wasn't about the kidnapping! It was a coincidence!"

We all four stared at each other and then burst out laughing.

"'A Coincidental Firefight,'" Chris said. "When I retire, I'm totally writing that book."

"All right," Mary said. "You two can go. I'm not even going to tell you to stay out of trouble, because you won't do it, and then I'll get mad."

"Besides," Chris stuck in, "I need the material."

Mary gave him a glare and then said, "If I tell you to stay *alive*, do you think you can manage that?"

"We'll try," I said. "What about my brother? And Mel and Nat?"

"I'll check." Chris jumped up before Mary could answer me. He winced and then winked at me and left the room. We sat in silence surrounded by the police station bustle until he came back. "Mel and Tim have been questioned and released. They're downstairs waiting for Nat. Detective Vivas says she'll be done with her in another minute or two."

"Great. Thanks, Chris. Hope you heal fast. Bye, Mary." Bill said much the same, and we beat it.

At the bottom of the oak staircase, we found Tim and Mel on the deeply scratched but highly polished bench by the sergeant's desk. Tim gave me a long glower. "So this is your life?" he said. "Even worse than I thought."

"Come on, Tim," said Mel, but gently. To me and Bill, "Are you all right?"

I noticed Tim glancing at me sideways, as though he was interested in my answer though he didn't want me to know it. "Fine," I said. "You?"

"Still shaken," said Mel. "This isn't the way I usually spend my days."

"You may not believe it, but us, either."

"And I never want to again!" Tim barked.

"You may not believe it," Bill quoted me, "but us, either."

Mel jumped up, looking past me. "Nat! Are you okay?"

Bill, Tim, and I turned to see Nat coming down the stairs. She hugged Mel and said, "I'm fine. Are you?"

Another round of reassurances and then I said, "Let's get out of here before Mary comes down and arrests us all for loitering."

FORTY-SIX

I EXPECTED WE'D all split up on the sidewalk outside the station house, but because the Earth was passing through some sort of radiation cloud that caused bizarro events, Tim said, "Listen, I bet we're all exhausted. Let's go to Tai Pan for tea and sweets. What do you say?"

I wanted to say, *You're shaken up, you want company, and you're including me and Bill? Who are you and what have you done with Tim Chin?* Instead I answered, "Sure."

Mel did too. Bill and Nat fell in behind us, and we headed for Canal Street.

It was getting close to the end of the day, not a crowded time in a Chinatown bakery, so we snagged a table at Tai Pan easily. Bill went to the counter with our tea orders while Tim took a tray and a pair of tongs and hit the display cases.

"Nat," Mel said, "I'm really sorry."

"About what?"

"That that crazy guy kidnapped you! I'm sorry you got caught up in anything to do with the building. The stupid thing isn't your problem, it's mine."

Nat, bad liar that she was, shot me a look. I was tempted to give her away just for worrying that I would, but instead I kept my eyes on Bill's progress back toward us. Bill distributed the paper cups from his tray, and then Tim arrived and put down a baker's half-dozen pastries, tarts, and buns, which meant seven for the five of us. When everyone's eyebrows went up at the sugar glut he said, "I didn't know what people liked." A strange sensation: My brother was trying to be nice.

And a familiar one: I hadn't actually been in a fight, but I was ravenous anyway.

Arms crisscrossed as people cut gooey, sticky, crumbly, or powdery things in half or in quarters or in thirds and took this or that to sample as they sipped. Everyone started talking at once.

"How did Johnny Gee know where to find you?"

"Did Tan Lu-Lien really not know about the kidnapping?"

"Did Ting really not know she was his *mother*?"

"Were you saying she killed someone for him?"

"I can't believe that SOB claimed he hadn't shot at me. I mean, why bother, if he admitted shooting at Ironman?"

That last, of course, was Tim, who always has more words than anyone else.

I was enjoying the companionable chaos, especially watching my brother actually trying to be civil to Bill, when "Bad Boys" rang from the phone in my pocket. I took it out and said, "Hey, Linus."

"Where are you? Are you okay?" He sounded breathless.

"I'm in Tai Pan having mango cheesecake. Sure I'm okay."

"We just turned on the news! Big police action on Bayard Street. SWAT teams and hostage negotiators and everything. Me and Trella were worried."

"So you're saying every time there's a violent incident in Chinatown, you think I'm in the middle of it?"

"Well, no, I didn't mean—"

"Never mind. I was. Me, Bill, the clients, and Tim. But we're all fine."

"Uncle Tim? In a police action?"

"It's a world full of wonders, Linus."

"I guess. Hey, Trell, they're okay. But they were there, for real. What was it about, cuz?"

"Long story. I'll tell you guys later."

"'Woke up in a bad place / Should probably get up so I'm not late / Stared at my phone for the past eight / Minutes at nothing, my head aches!' 'Story,' great rap! And it's long. Will you bring mango cheesecake?"

"Uh, sure."

"Okay then. Trella, mango cheesecake incoming! Listen, cuz, I was going to call you anyway, just before the news came on, because we do have one more kinda interesting fact we found, but maybe you want that later, too?"

"No, go ahead." Though, I reflected, if Jackson Ting—wherever he was—was really pulling the plug on Phoenix Towers, we might be done with this whole thing any minute now.

"Well. You remember how we told you about Gold Coast? The IVF place Natalie Wu and her husband went to?"

"I hadn't, but I do now." I looked across the table at Nat, who was listening to my brother elucidate something while she finished off a red bean bun. "What about it?"

"It wasn't only them. It was the other one, too."

"The other what?"

"Sister. Mel Wu. She went there, too."

"She…what?" I stopped as a whole Christmas tree string of light bulbs lit up in my head. "Linus, thank you very much. I'll call you back."

I slipped the phone away and waited for a lull in the conversation. When it came I stood. "Nat," I said, "would you come outside with me for a minute?"

Nat gave me a confused look and glanced at Mel. Mel gave me one also, and the sisters had never looked more alike than at that moment. Tim said, "Lyd? What's up?" Bill didn't say anything and didn't look confused—though I'm sure he was—but put his hands on the table, prepared to rise and help me however I wanted.

I gave Bill a quick tiny headshake and kept my eyes on Nat.

Shrugging, Nat stood and followed me out of Tai Pan.

I walked a few steps down the sidewalk so we couldn't be seen from the table where I'd marooned Mel between Tim and Bill. Though if anyone could handle it, she could. I stopped and turned to face Nat. "I might have left it alone if it weren't my brother," I said. "But you crossed the line."

"What are you talking about?" Nat's impatient tone and puzzled brow-crease were way overdone. You'd think someone used to pulling stunts would have learned to put on a better act over the years, but if your older sister has your back all the time, I guess you don't need to. Me, I had no sisters.

Just my brothers.

"You shot at Tim. From a moving motorcycle. For God's sake! You could've killed him."

She stared.

"Don't bother," I said. "You're deciding whether to

keep bluffing. You can't. I know all about it." I didn't actually *know* anything about it, but if I left her any squirming room I never would.

Briefly, the defiant stare remained. Then Nat's face relaxed into a small smile with a hint of pride in it. "I wasn't moving when I took the shot. You think I'm crazy? And I wasn't planning to hit him."

"You could've screwed up!"

"No, I couldn't have. I'm really good. Remember, I told you about my little silver revolver?"

"Fine. It's still a felony. And you still scared the day-lights out of him. And he took it out on me."

"I'm sorry."

"No, you're not. That was actually the point. To scare me, not Tim. You must've thought I was moving too slowly trying to convince Mel to sell."

"Yeah, well, I didn't think you were moving at all. I knew you didn't want Phoenix Towers to go ahead. Maybe you decided my problem wasn't a big enough deal."

"For me to help Jackson Ting destroy my neighbor-hood? Actually, it wasn't."

"See? I thought so. So I tried to make my problem your problem. When I heard about the other shooting, Ironman's, I thought maybe if you were scared for your brother you'd get in gear."

"Just so you know," I said, "I don't just leave clients in the lurch. I told you I'd try to help. I wasn't about to talk Mel into selling, but I was working on getting Jackson off your case another way."

"What way?"

"If he's canceling the project, it doesn't matter, does it? But I think you owe me the real reason for this panic about Jackson's claim. It wasn't the publicity. It was the DNA test. It was the IVF."

She froze.

"You said you'd had trouble getting pregnant," I went on. "You didn't mention the IVF. When I found out—"

"How?"

"Oh, come on. Investigating is pretty much what I do, you know? I started looking at *you* because it was obvious you weren't telling me everything. If you're going to keep lying to people, you really should take an acting class or something."

Her cheeks reddened.

I said, "When I found out you'd used IVF, my first thought was you'd had a sperm donor and your kids weren't Paul's, and that was the real reason you didn't want the DNA test. But they are his, aren't they? It wasn't a sperm donor. It was an egg donor. Mel's their biological mother."

"Goddammit," Nat said softly. "Goddammit." Then, "You can see, can't you?"

"Not really. The test would have shown Paul was Matty's father. No one would have asked for your DNA."

"Now. But once Matty's DNA was on record, the risk would always be there."

"You're never going to tell him?"

"When he's older! When Paul's horrible parents can't try to take them away. If they ever found out I wasn't even their mother—"

"You are their mother. You carried them. You're raising them."

"Try telling that to my in-laws. That sneaky scheming Oriental dragon lady bitch—and they've called me all those things, by the way—she got her claws into their son but couldn't breed, so her sister helped so his fortune would stay in their slant-eyed family. See?"

I said nothing.

"You probably think I'm exaggerating. I'm not." Nat bit her lip and looked away. Women with vegetables and fish in shopping bags headed home to cook dinner for their families. They eddied around us like a stream around rocks.

"Does Paul know?" I asked.

"Of course he knows! What kind of a person would do something like that without telling her husband?" Nat's face softened into sadness. "You think I'm that kind of person, don't you?"

"I don't know you. Just what I've seen these last few days. Maybe you are."

"I'm not. I'm really not." She sniffled, and her eyes started to water. Even for a good actor that's a hard trick. Nat, I was sure, couldn't fake it. "They're my kids. He's my husband. I don't want to lose them. I can't! It would kill me. Please. You won't say anything, will you? Please? Promise me?"

I stayed silent.

"Please! I really wouldn't have shot your brother."

Probably I was giddy from tension, exhaustion, and too much sugar, but I suddenly burst out laughing. What she'd said struck me as the funniest way to extract a promise anyone had ever tried.

Nat smiled tentatively.

"All right," I said. "Not just my brother, though, okay? Promise me you won't shoot *anyone*."

"Done." She grinned, with something of her old spark. "And thanks."

In that aura of mutual sunniness we turned to head back up the block to Tai Pan. Just as we got there Mel pushed out the door, followed by Tim and Bill.

"What's up?" I said.

"Tan Lu-Lien called," said Mel. "There's something she wants to show me."

FORTY-SEVEN

"TAN LU-LIEN?" I said. "Where is she? Is she with Jackson? What happened to them?"

"She's a few doors down from the Li Min Jin building. She didn't give me time to ask anything. She just told me where to come and hung up. Except she said no police."

"What a surprise," I said. "Okay, let's go."

"You don't have to," Mel said.

"Are you kidding?"

She glanced at Bill. He said, "I'm in."

"I'm coming, too," said Nat.

And of course Tim said, "I'm not sure this is a good idea. It could be a trap or something."

Mel said, "She wouldn't hurt me. She's the one who made Johnny Gee let Nat go." She spoke in reassuring tones, with a small smile at Tim. I'd been about to respond with something along the lines of *If you're scared don't come then*, so I guessed he lucked out.

Tim looked entirely unconvinced, but when the rest of us started hustling along the sidewalk, he hustled right with us.

Bayard Street had been reopened, but the Li Min Jin building was still sealed off with crime scene tape. I wondered if the NYPD would take the opportunity to search for the buried treasure while they were in there.

Three buildings east, Mel pressed the buzzer at the

door beside the hair salon. The door buzzed back, and she opened it, leading us not up the rickety stairs to the apartments but to a door at the back of the perm-chemical-scented hallway. It led to a flight of stairs to the basement, lit by the lowest-watt bulb I'd ever barely seen by. Mel reached the bottom and called softly, "Tan Lu-Lien?" while the rest of us were still filing down. The basement was all shadows and columns and dust, dim arcs of hanging wires and hulking hints of boxes and building debris.

For a moment, nothing. Then a shadow stepped out from a deeper shadow. Tan gave a soft laugh. "Is it friends and family day?"

"You said no police," Mel said evenly. "You didn't say come alone."

"No, I didn't." Tan surveyed us all and then turned to the dark behind her. "Jackson?"

Jackson Ting stepped forward, too.

"Wait," I said, feeling a buzz up my spine. "Is this like the clown car at the circus? How many gangsters do you have hidden down here?"

"I'm not a gangster!" said Jackson.

"Debatable."

"It's only the two of us," Tan said. "Neither of us had a reason to be involved in a battle between Ironman's faction and Loo's. At the same time as you left through the front door, we came down here. When I leave Jackson will say I kidnapped him and forced him to come with me." She gave Jackson a long look. In the dim light her face was impossible to read.

"When you leave?" I said. "The entire Fifth Precinct is looking for you."

"They won't find me. But before I go, there's something Mao-Li needs to see." She faced Mel. "I told you I didn't know what message Chang Yao-Zu had for you from your uncle. I didn't. But I guessed. To my regret, I told Johnny." She shook her head. "Johnny hasn't changed, over all these years. Impatience and fast action are still his trademarks. I wasn't sure what you'd make of the information, but I was willing to wait and see. Johnny wasn't."

"What are you saying?" Mel asked. "He killed Mr. Chang?"

"If you never got the message, you wouldn't act on it. Jackson was under a deadline. Whatever decision you made might not come soon enough. Johnny did what he believed to be expedient."

"The message," Mel said after a brief pause. "What was the message?"

"I want you to see for yourself. Please..." Tan looked around and gave a small, ironic smile. "Please, all of you, follow me."

Although the route she led us along had twists and sharp lefts and rights, and included one more staircase down and then a little farther on another one back up, and was lit nowhere any better than the first staircase had been, I could tell we were moving basically west. I wasn't surprised that when Tan stopped, she said, "This is the basement of our building. I apologize, Mao-Li. Yours. The Li Min Jin building."

The obvious question was so obvious that the only one who thought it necessary to ask it was Tim. "Why have you brought us here?"

Tan didn't respond but strode along past stacks of boxes, mounds of broken furniture, piles of drywall and wood scraps, and other heaps of that unnamable junk dusty basements silt up with. Stopping at the hot water heater, she grasped a piece of the wall behind it, what looked like a badly applied sheet of plywood with just enough edge for a finger hold. She pushed and pulled until it was free; it had been attached, apparently, to nothing. She hefted it aside.

Behind it, practically invisible in the shadows, a rectangle outlined a low door.

Tan took the silver key from her pocket and slipped it into the door's lock.

"Are you saying," Mel asked, in a voice of astonishment, "that there really is a treasure buried in this building?"

Tan turned with a soft smile, not one I'd seen on her before. "Yes. A treasure is buried here." Unlocking the door, she opened it and stooped through. A light went on, though because of the door's height I could see nothing of the room, just the floor. I thought I saw the corner of a carpet on the rough concrete, but it wasn't until after I ducked under the doorframe—after Mel, but before the others—and straightened up that I saw what the room contained. Even so, it took me a minute to work it out.

Mel didn't work it out. She stared at the two porcelain figures, one male and one female, each about four feet high, clothed in silk outfits and seated on carved chairs on a raised platform. She took in the carpet, and the painting of a dragon and a phoenix, intertwined. Other paintings hung on the walls, too—a duck and a drake, birds on a branch in snow, cherry blossoms—and a pair of chairs sat on the carpet facing the two figures. The air, though cellar-damp, was lightly perfumed with incense, and the light in here was also dim, but not five-watt-bulb dim as on the circuitous route we'd traveled through the basements. The switch Tan had flicked as she entered had lit a hanging brass lamp that covered the room in a soft glow.

Softly, Mel said, "What *is* this?"

Nat's furrowed brow echoed Mel's bewilderment, and this time I didn't think Nat was acting. Bill wore his normal poker face, but I'd have been willing to bet he had no idea what was going on, either.

Tim did, though. We'd been raised together, after all, and though neither of us had ever seen this before, we both knew what it was. He said, "It's a ghost marriage."

FORTY-EIGHT

"A WHAT?" said Nat.

I waited for Tim to answer, but he didn't, an unusual reluctance for him when the chance to explain something came up. He seemed a little pale. Spooked out by the supernatural? My brother was full of surprises.

I took it. "When a son dies unmarried," I said, gazing at the figures, so beautifully detailed and dressed, "the tradition—I guess it still exists—used to be to find him a ghost bride. Someone's daughter who also died unmarried. So neither of them would have to spend eternity alone. Look. The female effigy in red, the male one in black. On the wall, phoenix and dragon uniting. This is a wedding chamber." I turned to Tan. "It's Choi Meng's baby son, isn't it? And Long Lo's three-year-old daughter. That was what was really behind the combining of the two tongs. The two families. A marriage."

Tan nodded. "When Choi Meng's son died, his wife wouldn't be parted from him. She insisted he be buried here, in the building, where they lived." Tan pointed to a pair of plaques in the wall behind the figures. "After the ghost marriage, Long Lo's daughter was brought here, too. To be with her husband."

"When Uncle Meng bought the building, he said it was so his family would always have a home," Mel said. "I thought he meant the tong."

"The tong, also," said Tan. "Both families. Choi Meng bought this building for both families."

"At the cemetery, Lydia," said Mel, still staring at the figures, "you asked where the babies' graves were. They're here. Behind those plaques, in burial vaults."

"Yes," Tan said. "And no."

I was reading the Chinese inscriptions. "My God," I said. "This one. This one is for both children. They're together. The other—it's Choi Meng's wife. Your aunt, Ni Mei-Mei."

"She's not buried in the cemetery? Uncle Meng's headstone says—"

"It says that's her *final* resting place," said Tan. "Choi Meng buried her here, where she'd died. So she wouldn't be alone in the cemetery."

"She died in this room?"

"She killed herself here. A year to the day from when the baby died."

Mel's hand went to her mouth.

"Choi Meng came down here often, to sit with them. Every day, sometimes more than once. You understand why this room was secret. That sort of sentiment would only be seen as weakness in a leader.

"But he told me, and he told Chang Yao-Zu, that he intended all his family to be together after his death. He wanted his wife and the children moved to the cemetery. To unite them. I believe that was Chang Yao-Zu's message to you."

"The key," I said. "To this room. It was left by the baby's plaque, the one that traditionally shouldn't be on the altar. It should be near the baby's grave. I guess, in a way, it was."

Mel looked at the figures and the plaques behind

them. "This is why Uncle Meng wouldn't sell the building. So he could come and be with them every day."

"And why he left it to family, not the tong," Nat said.

Mel nodded. "Of course I'll move them. We'll have a funeral, all the correct rites." After a moment, "But I still think"—she looked straight at Jackson—"I think I'm not selling."

Jackson appeared dazed. I supposed it had been a long day for someone who'd woken up a real estate developer with respectable deceased parents and no personal experience with firearms. "It's all right," he roused himself to say. "I told you I'm canceling the project. I wish I'd never started it. This is all too much."

"Not too much," Tan said gently. "Not too much for my son, mine and Johnny's. You'll be fine now, and you won't see us again." While we'd been absorbed in what we were seeing, she'd worked her way to the entrance. "The door's not much. Mr. Smith can probably take care of it. I just need a few minutes." She fixed a look on Mel. "Thank you, Wu Mao-Li." She ducked under the doorway and slammed the door shut.

I charged over and turned the knob, but it was locked from the outside. "Step aside," Bill said, grinning. "Let me take care of it." He drew his leg back and kicked. The door flew open.

Tan was gone.

FORTY-NINE

"ONE OF THESE DAYS," Mary said, licking her ginger ice cream cone before it could melt down her hand, "you really are going to get yourself killed. Either by criminals, or by me."

"You sure you don't want two scoops?"

"Are you trying to bribe a cop?"

"I want two scoops," Chris Chiang said. He was on medical leave ("For a scratch," Mary said with an eye roll), but he had agreed to join us at the Chinatown Ice Cream Factory for my penitential ice cream treat.

"I do, too," said Bill.

"I have to buy yours, too? Aren't you my partner?"

"What does that prove?"

"Nothing," I admitted. "Go ahead."

Chris got coffee and vanilla fudge, Bill got a double scoop of ube, and I brought up the rear with pineapple and my credit card. We walked to Columbus Park and found a bench near the folk song group.

"No sign of Tan?" I said as the accordion started up.

"That's a sore point," Mary warned me.

"Hey. My client—"

"Oh, shut up."

The bamboo flute joined the accordion.

"We're shipping Johnny Gee out, though," Chris said. "What Tan said about him killing Chang is hearsay, but grabbing him in the middle of a gun battle is enough for us to kick him back to Hong Kong."

"I bet Mark Quan has a buddy or two who'd be interested to know he's coming. I'll give him a call. And the others?"

"Loo's going to have a long recovery. Old man, bullet in his lung, blood loss, all that. Ironman we're holding on reckless endangerment. Bullets from his gun all over the lobby and three in the asphalt in the street, thank you, Jesus."

"Why the thank-you?"

"Because the bad guys were all inside. A bullet in the street means he was shooting at us." Chris finished the vanilla fudge in his cone and moved down to the coffee. "That might be the best we can do, but it's a Class D, and he could get seven years."

"So," I said tentatively, "Tan gone, Loo in the hospital, Ironman in jail—sounds like the Li Min Jin is leaderless. And about to be evicted."

Mary lifted her eyebrows. "You don't expect thanks, I hope."

"More like forgiveness?"

"Maybe."

"Hey. My client—"

"I told you—"

"No, really, my client. Hi, Mel. What are you doing here? You missed my buying spree at the Ice Cream Factory."

"That's okay. I'm actually getting ice cream later. I'm meeting your brother here, and I saw you, so I thought I'd come by to defend your honor. Honestly"—she faced Mary—"it was all my fault."

"What was?" Mary asked.

"Whatever you're mad at Lydia and Bill for."

"I'm mad at Lydia for being an idiot and at Bill for not stopping her. No way I'm blaming that on you. I've known them for too long. But some things never change, so why should I waste my energy?"

"I endorse that," said Bill.

"Me too," said Chris.

"Let's go back to the important part," I said. "You're meeting my brother?"

Mel smiled. "I think Mr. Gao was right about him."

"Grandfather Gao?" I was surprised. "About what?"

"After you two left the shop the day we met, he told me that Tim Chin was turning himself into an old man, but he still had a young man's good heart. He needed to find a reason to show it. And someone to show it to."

"Grandfather Gao said that?" I asked as Mary stifled a snort.

"Oh," Mel said. "There he is. See you later, you guys. And Mary? It really was all my fault."

She turned and walked out of the park. I saw her greet my brother with a kiss and slip her arm through his.

"Wow," said Bill. "Your mom'll love that when she hears about it."

"You think it's not all over the Chinatown grapevine already? She said last night how nice it was that Tim had met a smart, charming young woman in his own profession. Of course, she made sure to add, with a deeply meaningful look at me, that in his profession, that was the kind of person it was possible to find."

"Uh-oh," Bill said. "Does that mean she doesn't think I'm smart and charming?"

"I'm smart and charming," said Chris.

This time Mary and I both rolled our eyes. I turned

and watched Mel and Tim walk down the block, dodging pedestrians and swerving around sidewalk vendors, in the middle of the day in the middle of the week, in Chinatown.

* * * * *

ACKNOWLEDGMENTS

GREAT THANKS TO:

My agent, Josh Getzler.

Claiborne Hancock and the folks at Pegasus Books.

Henry Chang, for local knowledge.

Jill Block, for professional erudition.

Barb Shoup, for literary criticism.

Patricia Chao, for froggy encouragement.

Jonathan Santlofer, the Man of Steel.

Elisabeth Avery, Jackie Freimor, Sharyn Kolberg, Margaret Ryan, Carrie Smith, Cynthia Swain, and Jane Young, for being, among other things, damn fine writers.

Steve Blier, Hillary Brown, Susan Chin, Monty Freeman, Charles McKinney, and Jim Russell, for being, among other things, damn fine cooks.

and.

Cheryl Lu-Lien Tan and Charles Chris Chiang for all those sanity-saving walks and coffees in the park.